Best of British Fantasy
2019

Best of British Fantasy
2019

Edited by Jared Shurin

NEWCON
PRESS

NewCon Press
England

First edition, published in the UK June 2020 by NewCon Press

NCP 239 (hardback)
NCP 240 (softback)

10 9 8 7 6 5 4 3 2 1

Contents

Introduction:
"Someone Will Be Along to Dig You Out."

Jared Shurin

Welcome to the second volume of *The Best of British Fantasy*.

This year's anthology collects 23 stories (24, if you're lucky enough to be reading the limited edition hardback), from a wide range of new and established voices. As with the inaugural volume, these authors represent the glorious range of writers that are at work in Britain and Ireland today.[1] It is an honour to select these stories every year.

The best metaphor for a 'year's best' anthology is the classic parable of the blind men and the elephant. As you may remember, each of the blind men touches a different part of the elephant and immediately, if justifiably, believes they know the entire nature of the beast. The man holding the tail thinks an elephant is like a rope, the one touching the leg thinks it is a tree, the one holding the trunk assumes it is serpentine.

All, according to their experience, are correct. Yet every one is also, objectively, wrong.

It is only by collecting enough blind men that we can begin to understand the true nature of the elephant. A novel, however brilliantly written, is, at best, a single blind man with exceptionally sensitive fingers. An anthology, while not having that singular depth, gives us more hands: the collection of impressions required to feel out the edges of a vast and multi-faceted beast.

---

[1] The series has included, and will continue to include, stories by authors from, or currently resident in, both the United Kingdom and Ireland. Despite Britain's formal withdrawal from the EU, I feel the cultural and historical connections between these two neighbouring, Anglophone countries are such that I would not feel comfortable separating them.

In the introduction to last year's volume, I wrote – passionately – about the role of *The Best of British Fantasy* could play in capturing the past for the sake of the future. An anthology, I argued, can provide a snapshot of a particular point in time, capturing the feel of a moment for far distant readers. Many of the legendary anthologies – say, *Dangerous Visions* or *Nelson Algren's Own Book of Lonesome Monsters* – accomplish this: ambitious collections that use fiction to help the 21st century reader glimpse some of the themes, concerns, and cultures of mid-20th century life.

In thinking about an anthology's duty to the future, I completely neglected what it means in the present.

As I write this, we have entered the second month of mandated social distancing. My two countries – where I was born and where I live – are both facing economic and cultural ruin. Tens of thousands have died, a growing statistic that becomes more gruesome every day. I, like many of you, have friends and family risking their lives every day in hospitals, at care homes, in supermarkets and warehouses. We live in communal, collective anxiety.

Perversely, there are fewer opportunities for distraction. The cultural sector is near-universally furloughed. Sports have come grinding to a halt. Amazon, for the second time in as many months, has removed the 'buy' button from books as 'inessential'. Reality is inescapable.

Given the state of our present, fantasy stories may seem trivial or 'inessential'. But they have two, slightly contradictory, but very important, roles to play.

First, fantasy helps us escape reality.

Escapism can often be a dubious virtue, but given our current imprisonment, there's unquestionable value right now. We cannot step out to dinner, but we can still cross into Narnia. It is easier to walk into Mordor than to the office. Reality is inexorable and inescapable. What is happening is so unquestionably important, that our minds do nothing else but whir frantically, trying to make sense of it.

As a result, and unsurprisingly, a recent ONS survey reveals that almost half of Britons currently report high levels of anxiety. The simple act of escape – of turning off, of giving yourself a break – has become essential. Escapism need not be Disneyfied, cheery, or overly simplistic: it is a matter of moving from here to there; a good story that allows the reader to ponder someone else's problems for a change. In this volume you'll find many ways of escape. Some are literal escapes, such as a flying carpet or a persuasive spirit. Others take place in captivating worlds, far from our own: ancient sailing ships, forgotten kingdoms, deep under the ground or high atop impossible sculptures. They draw us in – or, more critically, out – with seductive atmosphere, high-flying adventure, good humour, haunting horror, and impossible feats of magic. Enjoy them, as they are meant to be enjoyed: without guilt. You – we – all deserve some time away. As Gareth E. Rees writes, we can use stories to seek out a 'fragile, momentary sanctuary'.

Second, fantasy helps us understand reality.

Some realities are simply too big to be understood except through stories. Stories, narratives, help us comprehend the incomprehensible. Stories are our hands on the elephant; they allow us to find the edges of the things, to capture abstractions into shapes.

Our current situation is too much for a single narrative. There's no special spell or magic cloak; there's no sword to wield or dragon to slay with it. There is no ring of power, no wizard, no prophecy or Crack of Doom. We're trapped in the worst of stories: there's too much going on, no resolution, a billion conflicts without a villain.

And that's why we need fantasy: it allows us to simplify the incomprehensible; as Douglas Adams put it, to 'eff' the ineffable. A good narrative helps us reduce the inexplicable into a form that we can understand, resolve, and even act upon. Although the stories contained within were all first published before the Covid-19 outbreak, they are good stories (the best, in fact), and address themes that are still very relevant. We have a child learning to accept loss, a man learning to love, a family learning to survive. There are stories about sacrifice, and commitment, and bravery.

There's a tale in here about how scary change can be, and another about coming to grips with the past. There are several about loneliness, some about isolation, several about loss, and many more about friendship, and all the strange and wonderful forms it may take. Perhaps most importantly, there are stories here about survival, acceptance, and love. These are fantasy stories that understand tragedy, loss and fear, but also remind us that there is much, much more in life: redemption, companionship, and hope.

Perhaps the most eerily prophetic story in this book is the first, by Helen McClory. It captures, disturbingly, a world fearing [redacted]: seemingly wracked by a generic, all-encompassing, apocalyptic event. McClory manages to give voice to formless dread, but also, and far more importantly, reminds us that this is a shared experience, and, somewhere over the horizon, this too shall pass. When reality is cruel and abstract, fantasy can provide reassurance and perspective. As McClory elegantly reminds us: the world around you is kinder than you imagine now.

I look forward to sharing a kinder future with you.

Jared Shurin
London,
May 2020

A Manual for Avoiding Further Harm from [REDACTED]

Helen McClory

If at any time during the event you hear a small blast of a horn three times, you should immediately find shelter under a tarpaulin, a door leaning up against a wall, or a farmhouse kitchen table (no other will do), or inside of a terracotta jar if the jar covers at least sixty (60) per cent of your body. Wait in your shelter until the safe signal plays (a small blast of a horn in a higher, upbeat pitch). You may leave the shelter at that time. If the safe signal does not play, do not leave the shelter. Stay in the shelter until a regional warden arrives to help you with your evacuation.

Do not worry overly; if you are trapped by fallen debris, someone will be along to dig you out. If you suffer from pains related to [redacted], then be reassured you will almost certainly survive. If you run out of food, you can survive at least two weeks with few long-lasting repercussions. If you run out of water, it is safe to drink a little of an uninfected volunteer's blood (drawing lots to determine who will volunteer is the best method). Do not attempt to drink the rainwater, or water from a leaking pipe, unless the person whose blood you drank has no more to spare.

Remember that in times of strict privation and especially if you are alone, you must have your wits about you. Be cheerful and do not show any signs of weakness, even to yourself; someone will rescue you, your loved ones and neighbours will have survived, the country will be back on track again after a short evaluation and adjustment period, the damage will very likely not be too severe. Do not lose hope, or if you do lose hope, at least do not leave the shelter if the safe signal has not played.

Do not leave the shelter even if someone calls you by name. Even if, when you are within eyesight of this person, they seem like someone you ought to follow, or would follow into any disaster. Do be careful that any people you see are acting within the guidelines and approval of the relevant authorities. In a disaster it is impossible to tell who, without the correct paperwork, passes and uniform, is the kind of man you can trust. Be especially wary if the man who calls your name seems to know you and want to help. Ask yourself three important questions: what does he want? Does he know what he wants? Can I believe in the continuity of his personality, or is his personality subject to swift and unpredictable changes? It is the opinion of the experts that no one changes at all, unless exposed to the effects of [redacted], or placed under the extreme stress of having seen others exposed to [redacted]. However, statistics show that this is a great number of people.

If you are running out of things with which to occupy yourself while in your shelter, and consider leaving it before the safe signal has played, DON'T. Find a game to play. Try counting the cracks in a nearby surface, or recalling the exact colour of your father's eyes and comparing it to something in nature. Having a good cry can also be useful, but do not cry so much that you become thirsty. Do not cry at all if severely dehydrated, as this can be detrimental to your odds of survival. Try playing back in your mind a time when you were really happy, taking in all the smallest details and not omitting moments during the happy time when you were not completely happy, some small frustration or other. But do not dwell on the frustration. Do not recall that you knew the man who called your name at this point in your life. Do not attempt to reconstruct how he was then towards you. Remember that recollections of the past can also be a source of exposure to the effects of [redacted].

For your own safety, keep the past as an ornamental object with little power of impact on the present moment. Do not remember the way his arm lightly brushed against yours on a long bus ride. Do not remember walking across a bridge over a green river with him, or looking at flowers in the trees, or swimming in the ocean at night with him. Do not recall all the ways in which he was a fascinating and tender person. Do not recall his faults either. If he calls again don't answer him, or only answer in an upbeat, careless manner. This is for your own safety. Remain in your shelter.

If you are becoming distressed by your thoughts, consider the current events around you, but only to be as strict with yourself as you need to be. Stay in your shelter, alone. Someone will come for you. A regional warden will be with you shortly. You will not run out of food. You will not run out of water. Nothing is permanently damaged. The countryside only looks destroyed. The world around you is kinder than you imagine now. You have likely been exposed to [redacted] but you will survive this. Every human being has been exposed to it and the vast majority go on to make a full recovery, or find ways to carry on. There are many other sources of destruction of your person, and if you are observant of these instructions, [redacted] is not likely to be one of them. The safe signal will play shortly. After this you will be able to return to your normal life.

Tyrannosaurs Bask in the Warmth of the Asteroid

Gareth E. Rees

The monkey knows that something is wrong. She's a metre away, behind reinforced glass, leathery lips curled back, baring her buckled teeth. At first, I think she's laughing, but this is not laughter. This is fear. She's braced for an attack. I press my nose against the glass. Perhaps it's me she fears, a forty-nine-year old man. If so, it's a justified terror. We've done our damage to the world, we white men, but I doubt she has singled me out as a particularly egregious threat. The glass is smudged with marks left by the noses, lips and fingertips of other zoo visitors who have stood in this spot to look at the crested black macaques perched on rootless trees and blocks of artificial rock. No, it's not me. There's something else. An existential threat that she can sense but which I cannot see. She stares past my shoulder, trembling. Hands tightly grip the rock on which she sits. A torrent of golden piss gushes from her vulva, splashing over her fingers. The other monkeys start to leap up and down, shrieking frantically.

This doesn't seem normal. When I arrived with my daughter this morning, I expected most of the animals to be asleep, or in hiding, which is how I remember zoos from my youth; not freaking out like this. I cannot tell if it's a manifestation of my anxiety or a real phenomenon but there's a tension in the place. When we tried to visit the lemurs, they were racing around their enclosure in a frenzy and we were quickly ushered out. The keepers cancelled the public feeding session, telling the line of parents and toddlers that the lemurs were feeling funny today and needed to let off steam before they settled down for a rest.

Maybe it's the heat. This endless summer drought, longer even than the one we had last year, and the one before that. There's not a cloud in the sky. The sun is bastard hot. I can't stand it myself and I'm not covered in black fur, nor confined behind glass, hands covered in my own piss. Perhaps that's what's wrong with the monkey. But what do I know?

I look at my daughter. She's staring at the monkey too, but with a bored expression, impatient for the next enclosure and the next incarcerated animal.

'It's a crested black macaque,' I say, pointing to the information plaque. 'Endangered.'

Almost all the plaques say *endangered*. This place isn't even a zoo, according to the promotional literature on the website. It's a wildlife refuge for rare animals, born in captivity, unable to return to their felled habitations, their scorched plains and polluted rivers. This crested black macaque is pissing for my entertainment in a glass box in the East Sussex countryside when she should be foraging in the jungles of Indonesia; jungles we have hacked down so we can have takeaway coffee cups. To make matters worse, macaque meat is prized by some indigenous peoples who like to flame roast them whole, then eat the peppery flesh. I've seen pictures on the internet of dead monkeys with rictus grins, like simian Egyptian mummies, piled high on market stall tables beside charred bats and pythons.

I don't tell Molly any of this additional information. She's almost ten, smart as a whip, but still too small, too innocent, to hear the whole truth. I brought her into this world, and I must shield her as best I can. Give her a childhood in which she can be free to wonder and dream, to hope, unburdened by guilt and the crush of information, the awful weight of knowledge. A childhood close to the one I enjoyed, when everyday actions like driving a car, drinking from a plastic bottle and eating a burger did not feel like you were hastening the apocalypse. When visiting a zoo did not feel like you were gawping at the last survivors of a catastrophe for which you were responsible. A time before the sixth great extinction, before the ice caps melted, before antibiotics began to fail and a blood infection took the life of the mother of my only child, leaving me to bring up Molly alone these past five years.

I must stop thinking like this, so I have been told, repeatedly, by my friends, my family and my therapist. I must quieten that anxious voice and focus on Molly's happiness. As my wife is no longer around, and I am too unbearable to live with, according to the women I've dated, then it's up to me, and I must become better than the father I am. I try, though, I really try. But it's hard. Other people seem to become fathers effortlessly. They build things with their kids. Take them skateboarding. Bake cakes. Picnic in the park. They look happy, too, like they were born to do it. But I feel like I'm putting on an ill-fitting costume, pretending to be a dad, here at the animal park on the sort of day out I see other people posting on Facebook.

It doesn't help that Molly's an unsociable kid who prefers to sit in her room and read or play computer games. She has a habit of dismissing my suggestions for weekend activities. It saps my motivation a little, trying to sell something to her that not even I want to do, which is why we usually end up kicking around the house, watching *Doctor Who* and eating takeaways. That said, Molly was encouragingly excited this morning as we drove across East Sussex, through the Pevensey Levels, fields baking hard in the heat. The countryside looks good in the sunshine, I admit, even when that sunshine is killing it. The road took us past the Long Man of Wilmington, a chalk outline of a figure etched into the downs, holding a staff in each of his hands.

'A giant with no face,' said Molly. 'And no pants on either, so he's naked, Dad, outside in the nude.'

'It's a hot day,' I said.

I read an alternative theory somewhere that those vertical

lines were not staffs but the outline of a door between the physical world and the spirit world. It has stuck with me, that idea, but I never interpret it as a figure entering our realm, nor a guard at the threshold. Instead all I can see is a figure making a swift exit, arms reached out to pull the door closed behind him, sealing the portal, leaving it all to hell.

Don't go there, he tells the other spirits. *Go anywhere but that fucking place.*

Shortly after the Long Man vanished into the folds of the hills, the zoo appeared, set a little way off the road, among the parched fields. My daughter laughed at the plastic giraffe peering over the hedgerow, a sign for Wellesbury Animal Park hung around its neck. The car park was already busy, so we parked in the gravel overspill area, then joined a queue of people in t-shirts, shorts, flip-flops and summer dresses, carrying rolled up towels and picnic bags, Instagramming each other with thumbs up, pouting. I gritted my teeth and held Molly's hand tight, trying to focus for once on the here-and-now, so I could treasure a moment with my daughter and inhabit it properly, see the magic of the world through a child's eyes, where the past is just a story and the future is so far away that it might as well not exist.

Molly has had enough of the macaques and their nervy antics. She leads me down the corridor and out to the open-air pens, past the beaver enclosure and the flamingos, wings clipped, amassed by a concrete pond. Next door, a giant anteater does laps of a scrubby lawn, its long snout curving into the dusty corners of the perimeter wall. Molly squeals with delight. 'Look at its funny head!'

I am surprised by the sheer heft of a beast that feasts on tiny insects, with its oversized forelegs and claws so destructive it has to curl them up and walk on its knuckles. It's moving at pace, not foraging for food but obsessively lapping its habitat, staggering slightly at times, as if drunk in the heat. There is some shade from the sun beneath a tree, but the anteater keeps on moving.

Over the back fence of the enclosure is the car park and the A27, hissing with weekend traffic. The anteater is no more aware of what is beyond the fence than I am of thriving alien planets or alternative multiverses. A supreme entity might be observing we humans right now in the same way I observe this anteater, unaware of our own prison and the limits of our perception.

There I go again. *Compulsive melancholy*, my late wife called it. A form of OCD, says my therapist, an obsessive repetition of negative thoughts that my psyche uses as a weapon against itself, like an autoimmune disease of the imagination. But I'm not so sure about that. At times I feel as if I see things closer to how they really are; rather than me wilfully looking on the dark side of life, it might be that most people are wilfully blinding themselves to the truth. After all, I'm not making things up. The ice caps really are melting. The weather really is weird. Britain really is in another crippling recession within a general decline. I really am losing clients for my graphic design business. My wife really did die of an antibiotic-resistant infection. The newspapers might have used words like 'freak' and 'virulent strain' but there have been others since. Other fathers, other mothers, other sons, other daughters.

This is not a groundless anxiety from which I suffer. I don't see problems that don't exist. These are objective truths; there are statistics and measurements to back it up. It's all actually happening. If others aren't experiencing stressful reactions to the situation, then it's a flaw in their psychological makeup, not mine.

'Dad, do you think Mr Anteater has a funny head?' says Molly.

'It's absolutely hilarious,' I reply.

Between the zoo and the theme park section of Wellesbury Animal Park, there's a miniature bandstand with a gang of animatronic animals on it: mandrill, lemur, python, vulture, alligator, tarantula. Molly hits a button and the animals jiggle from side to side, jaws flapping open, singing in vibrato voices, 'Carnivores swing, herbivores jive, the food chain keeps us alive!'

The robot animals have seen better days. Threadbare fur and rickety mechanics. There's something awry with the mandrill's jaw. It keeps falling open too far, then getting stuck, vibrating and clicking as if it's about to snap off. The audio track crackles hoarsely through clapped-out speakers as the animals sing: 'We are happy happy jungle friends, let us hope life never ends'. Even Molly looks disturbed.

'Let's go and eat lunch,' I say.

In front of the cafe, the picnic benches are heaving with people, skin red with sunburn. Some loll about on a verge of yellow grass almost turned to hay. Others line up for attractions: an inflatable slide, tin can alley, tea-cup ride. With a piercing whistle, Thomas the Tank Engine chugs to a stop at the miniature railway platform and families pile off the carriages as the tinkly piano theme song blasts from a Tannoy. I shudder at the sight of Thomas's tortured face on the front of the train, human flesh stretched and grafted onto steel, a mutant cyborg enslaved by fat controllers. Molly was banned from watching it as a toddler, not that she wanted to, thank god, innately understanding the implications of its diabolical body horror.

We find a space among sprawled families on a lawn between the entrance to the Adventure Maze and the Costa kiosk where we sit with our pre-packed sandwiches. As Molly regales me with an overly complicated argument about why we should buy a pug, I notice a black cloud behind the theme park, incongruous against the brilliant blue expanse. No, not a cloud but smoke. Smoke, fed by a line of black curling upward, a dark scar, yellowing the sky on either side of it. A farmer perhaps, burning some waste, a barbeque out of control, or merely the fracked earth of Sussex coughing up a lung. It's mesmerising, the slow, creeping stain. I lose the thread of Molly's argument completely, not that it matters, as her voice is being drowned out by the amplified flatulence of a life-size fibre glass Indian elephant on the nearby footpath. The elephant makes a trumpeting noise when people press the yellow button and a farting noise when they press the brown button. Every passing child presses the brown button. Molly sniggers each time and wafts her hand near my backside. After a while I cannot take it. I throw our remaining snacks into our backpack.

'We'll go someplace else,' I tell Molly. She shrugs and sighs deeply, like this happens all the time. Which it does, I suppose, come to think of it. But I cannot help it.

Through a corridor of soft toy shops and arcade games, we pass from the picnic area into the adventure playground zone and sit on a bench outside the GET SOAKED waterpark where artificial geysers spurt, kids shoot each other with plastic jet-guns and a red slide spirals into a paddling pool. The waterpark is packed with revellers in trunks and bikinis. Naked toddlers. Grandparents in white hats eating ice cream. Teenage girls drinking slushies from oversized plastic containers. The air fills with squeals and laughter, punctuated by the odd gruff shout as a child gets admonished. It's the sound of life going on for other people, as if they exist beyond an invisible partition, separate from me. I know this is how Molly feels too, sometimes, and I wonder if it's my fault, or her mother's fault for dying young, or the fault of society's historical abuse of antibiotics, or if that's just what we're like, me and her.

It's early afternoon and the sun is high, with a warm breeze offering little respite. The few remnants of shade are cast in hard angles against the concrete and plastic. Many people huddle beneath the slide to stop burning in the sunshine. I try to understand how the park can operate these fountains when there's a hosepipe ban on. I assume it's the same water going around and around, gathering more traces of suntan lotion, sweat and child piss with every cycle.

I cannot eat any more of this sandwich. I feel sick.

Molly seems bored, eating her crisps, gazing longingly at the wooden gangways, ropes and slides of the adventure playground, full of children running in madcap circles and screaming with faux fear.

'You can go and play if you like,' I tell her. 'Meet me back at this bench. If I'm not here, wait for me.' She nods. Smiles wanly. Then skips off to the wooden fort structure in the centre of the network and disappears inside its ramparts. Moments later, she's on the wobbly rope bridge between two towers, waving down at me. There are some other kids loitering on the bridge, but I doubt she'll make friends with them. She rarely does. It makes me sad. She's a victim of both genetics and circumstance.

The smoke is now overhead, black clumps of spiralling charcoal, emitting wisps, trailing from a column that's thickening and darkening. The sky is turning rapidly from blue to orange, casting a sepia hue over the zoo, like a smartphone camera filter turning everything into the 1970s. Nobody seems to care, and I assume it must be from a distant bonfire, perhaps a house on fire in a nearby village. But it seems a lot closer than that, only a few fields away, though I find it hard to measure distances at the best of times. It's quite worrying to look at, but worrying is what I resolutely wanted to avoid today, for my daughter's sake.

'Molly!' I yell up into the interior of the adventure playground's central fort. 'I'll be back in a minute!'

'Okay, Dad'. A distant cry from above, but she sounds happy enough.

I return through the corridor of shops looking for the toilet. On the way, I notice that there's a security guard in the soft toy emporium, talking to the woman behind the counter. I slip inside the shop, pretending to look at some fluffy lemurs, and eavesdrop on the conversation, assuming that they're discussing the smoke. But they're talking about one of their fellow staff members, who has allegedly been talking behind people's backs, something they're keen to discuss behind her back.

'Excuse me,' I say. 'What's going on with that smoke?' The security guard shrugs. 'Fire in a field.'

'Is it close?'

'Oh, it's a way away.'

A way away?

One of the quirks of my anxiety is that I constantly look to people for reassurance and yet never believe their comforting words. However, when I come across people who are utterly oblivious to any sense of a problem at all, like these two staff members, I find it disarming, making me feel silly for harbouring a concern, like my woes are entirely fictional.

They return to their conversation and I continue to the toilets near the Thomas the Tank Engine railway. When I emerge, the sky looks radically different. Gone are the black wisps. The smoke has unfolded like two great moth wings, with a dense brown thorax core that intensifies with every passing second. Next to it is what looks to be another source of smoke, a separate feeder channel pumping more noxious gasses into the swirling whole. I glance around me in panic, but people are eating ice creams, queuing for chips and sauntering between attractions. A staff member with a walkie-talkie is nattering happily with the litter-picking guy.

Clearly, there's nothing wrong.

But, clearly, there is something very wrong.

Where is the smoke coming from?

Molly will be all right for a few more minutes so I hurry across the picnic area, past the farting elephant, to the perimeter hedgerow. As I approach, the air becomes palpably hotter. Above me, the clouds of smoke seethe into each other, giving birth to a denser mass that is beginning to block out the sun, rolling like a thundercloud across the zoo enclosures, out towards the levels. Nearby, there's a skinny young security guard in a white shirt, shifting uneasily, turning his gaze between me and the smoke.

'What's happening?' I ask.

'Oh, it's a fire in the field,' he says, overly casually. 'We're keeping an eye on it. Should be fine.' He doesn't seem certain.

Bites his lip. I am sure that I can hear the crackling of flames.

'John, mate! John!' Another security guard jogs into view, clutching his walkie-talkie. When he sees me, he stops dead in his tracks. Beckons over his colleague. Whispers something in his ear. They turn and run to the office building near the turnstiles. A fire engine siren whines in the far distance.

Repressing my panic with deep, measured breaths, I return to the main complex, walking at pace towards the café area and adventure playground, back to Molly. Suddenly, she seems very far away, as if the ground is stretching beneath me, the earth pulling us further apart. The heat on my back intensifies even though I am increasing my distance from the source. I weave through folk still queuing and eating and bickering with their kids beneath a vast orange mass that is rapidly absorbing all the blue from the sky. There's a covered corner pen for people to vape in, not unlike one of the animal enclosures. Inside, three men stand docile in a haze of vanilla steam. They can definitely see the smoke canopy billowing over us, because one of them points up at it, and the others follow the line of his finger, nodding. They laugh. Clearly, they don't think it's worth worrying about, but I'm losing trust in the nonchalance of others and I'm determined to leave as soon as possible.

Shouting my daughter's name over and over, I push through the arcade game players and out into the adventure area, where giggling kids run around the base of the wooden fort.

'Molly!' I shout up into the structure. I can see a few bare legs dangling but cannot tell if it's her or not. 'Please Molly, I need you down here now.'

No answer. I climb the ladder onto the first platform. Then squeeze up through a hatch to the second, where the rigging takes me up past a couple of bewildered boys playing with action figures. They look startled momentarily then go back to their game. Eventually, I'm at the top turret, poking my head out like a tank commander. There's no sign of Molly, but I can now see all the way across the animal park, where there is a wall of fire in the adjacent field, a red tidal wave at breaking point, moments away from crashing onto the perimeter hedge.

This is what it must like after the ship hits the iceberg. That strangely serene period when it is afloat, as it should be, and yet fatally compromised, doomed to sink.

I cry out Molly's name again when I see three kids below, one of whom is her, I'm certain, heading towards the monkey enclosures. I clatter down the rigging, scuffing my knees and shins, jumping from the bottom platform onto wood-chippings. As I jog past the water park, I see that people are beginning to look up at the sky.

It's as if a wave of realisation has swept through the park. A rising hubbub of nervous voices. Outbreaks of frantic activity. Parents gather up clothes, rub their children dry, jab at their phones looking for information.

Entering the monkey enclosures, I see Molly standing with a couple of older girls by the mini-bandstand of animatronic animals, whacking the buttons and howling with laughter at the mandrill with the broken jaw, which is now dangling from a piece of wire.

I grab her hand, but she pulls away, disgusted. 'Dad!'

'We need to go now, Molly!' I tell her.

She curdles with embarrassment. 'No.'

'Look up, Molly. Look up!'

As she looks, her expression softens, as if she finally sees the smoke, or rather, comprehends what the smoke means. She takes my hand.

'Find your parents,' I tell her companions, then I lead Molly in a brisk walk through enclosures of antagonised animals, circling, leaping, screeching. We pass red pandas, meerkats, capuchin monkeys, rock hyraxes, and capybaras, all trapped behind glass, aware yet powerless, and out onto the main pathway, where a model of a Tyrannosaurus rex guards the turnstiles.

The breeze has strengthened into a wind, carrying the smoke far across the Sussex sky. There is no longer any sunshine, only the hint of a pale disc casting ochre shadows on the gravel as we hurry through the car park. There are others out here too, clambering into their cars, reversing out. I curse our luck at being parked so far away in the overspill area. I pull harder at Molly's arm, breaking into a jog, as shouts and calls rise from the zoo behind and sirens cry out in the distance.

By the time we reach our car, feathery grey snowflakes of ash have begun to fall. Molly brushes them from her hair and gets into the back seat. A shambling mass of people pours from the zoo, dragging kids and pushchairs. A queue of cars already snakes around the access road. We're going to have to move quickly if we want to leave.

Our tyres crunch on stones as I manoeuvre through a gap in the lines of parked cars, but it makes no difference. We soon come to a stop and, as more vehicles mobilise from their positions closer to the exit, we gain only a yard or two every five minutes. I flick on the wipers to keep the windscreen clear of ash but it falls thicker and thicker.

The slow pace is a torment. Fortunately, Molly doesn't yet realise the extent of the danger. She sits, bewildered, staring out, asking me when we'll get to the road, complaining that she's hungry. I turn on some classical music and talk softly about what we're going to have to eat later. Maybe pizza from the takeaway, any toppings she likes. Even ice cream. A tub each. I struggle to keep the fear from my voice as I see flames startlingly close to the zoo buildings and the steel structures of the ape houses and aviaries, the fire whipped along by rising wind and brittle vegetation.

'Are the animals going to be all right, Dad?' Molly asks, face pressed against the window.

'I don't know.' I fight back tears. 'The zoo has procedures.' It's all I can think of to say. Staff members are amassed by the emergency assembly point by the entrance, but this has taken them by surprise and the situation is escalating rapidly. They don't know what to do about the burgeoning mass of cars trying to leave through the same narrow exit onto a single lane road.

A woman in a hi-vis jacket tries to help fleeing pedestrians pass through the grumbling mass of vehicles but she's getting abuse from panicking drivers. Horns blast but nobody has any power to move faster. In order for us to leave, we must approach the zoo entrance before we can turn right, taking us closer to the inferno. It's as if we are at a demonic drive-in. The low brown buildings in front of us are crested with a backdrop of belching flame. To the left, the top of a netted enclosure is visible above the fence. I see something flit upwards like a firework, a bird maybe, or a small monkey, before it falls away.

A cacophony erupts. The bleats and howls of terrified animals in the inexorable heat of the blaze. Smoke plumes burst from shattering windows. There's a whoosh and crack as one of the fences beside the main building crashes down. Molly screams as the giant anteater staggers through the gap, flames roaring from its back, hind legs dragging. It gets only a few yards before it buckles and hits the gravel in a smouldering heap. Molly screams again.

'Fuck this.' I pull the car to the side of the road, switch off the engine and kick open the door. I lift Molly from the back seat. She's grown a lot bigger this past year, but I can still carry her. I can still hold her and tell her I love her and that I will look after her, like I did the morning her mother died. I can stop her from watching this horror, at least for today.

'It's okay, sweetheart, we're going home now.'

I turn away from the zoo and march with my daughter in my arms, through lines of cars in the snowing ash, towards the wide green fields beyond the A27, where I know we shall find a fragile, momentary sanctuary.

Burrowing Machines

Sara Saab

There was a strange agitation to London that summer from the very beginning, a hormonal moodiness, a belly heat, if cities could be said to go through such things. We had enough sunshine to roll around in, but twilight snapped to dark between one sentence and the next, like someone'd tossed a quilt over the giant lamp of the sun. They'd found all those new fossils while digging up the duck pond at Hampstead Heath and they shut the footpath the whole way round. People like me who were barely getting themselves out the door for a jog in the park in the late afternoon haze gave up on exercise entirely.

By May, I was sleeping from the end of my night shift all the way through to my final cut-the-bullshit alarm at 8pm. I'd crawl out of bed feeling like death warmed up. I'd put on my orange hi-viz and cargoes, and a stripe of lipstick, God knows who for, and walk down to Camden Town Station with my hard hat's suspensions pushing against the blood-beat of a headache at my temples.

The drilling work in the tunnel, at least, started miraculously on schedule. I lost myself for underground hours that summer, planning the reroute of London's Victorian water mains around the burrowing machines' trajectory, the construction of temporary wall struts and the boring of holes for soil samples. I spent most of my waking hours fifteen meters below ground in a dark punctuated by machine headlights, flashlight beams, and shadows, and on the rare occasions I met Adarsh at the Old Man's Arms for a fish supper and a dry cider before work, he'd give me that look that told me he thought I was in urgent need of rescue from my life.

"No one but you would be this into *burrowing*, Jo," he said when I met him in early June.

"We haven't had a new tunnel for the Northern Line in three decades," I reminded him around a tartar-sauced chunk of battered cod.

"How filthy is that dirt you're shovelling anyway? All London's millennia of shite, and bones, and bubonic plague, and *more* shite."

"It doesn't bother me. If you saw these giant tunnelling machines do what they do, I think you'd appreciate it."

Adarsh sipped his craft ale, eyebrows high enough on his forehead that they almost skimmed his turban.

"And you hear the river through some of the walls," I added.

"The Thames?"

"No, you numpty. The River Fleet."

"The underground stream." Adarsh poked a stuffed olive with a toothpick. Made me think of Fran, who'd hated all foods that didn't belong in sandwich bread.

"Proper river. High and low tides. Currents. Everything. At high tide, it vibrates in the stone."

The River Fleet – London's geologic minotaur, winding North to South, fallen out of favour, diminished and trapped underground in its labyrinth of sewers back in the eighteenth century. The tourist-friendly experience was the faint hush of it through a tiny sewer grate on Ray Street in Clerkenwell. Being separated from the Fleet by just an underground tunnel wall in the small hours of morning was an entirely different thing.

But that was just trivia. None of it would matter until later.

In late June, we started to slip behind on the tunnel expansion project.

When I looked at Annabel's Gantt charts, it all seemed minor – engineers taking unexplained sick days, a pervasive anxiety that stretched ten-minute breaks to twenty. Like that same out-of-sortsness that had been weighing on me was spreading.

The first really observably weird thing happened on a Saturday night, two hours after the last Northern Line train. We were doing a tunnel walkthrough when one of our junior engineers, Philip, noticed a hole punched in the wall of the existing southbound Tube tunnel.

Grey moon rocks of concrete and a pile of dust dampened in the maintenance crawlspace beside the train tracks. We stuck our flashlights through the hole, wide as a crockpot, to the void on the other side. Our beams spotlighted the adjoining space. Glaze and slime on old brickwork. Water babbled along well below the level of the hole.

"I didn't know the Fleet flowed right alongside here," Philip said, and ran a hand round the hole's ragged edge. "That's maybe half a meter of concrete."

"Are there burrowing machines on the other side? In the Thames Water tunnels?" I asked no one in particular. I knew there weren't. There shouldn't be.

"Nah," said Philip.

"Structural weakness," I said. But the concrete around the hole was sound. No sagging, no hairline cracks, no subsidence.

What it looked like to me? Like someone had battered through the tunnel wall – from the River Fleet's adjoining tunnel, into ours.

They filed a police report and launched the obligatory Health and Safety investigation, but by mid-July, nothing. After another week, Thames Water's guys patched up the hole. We bolted in some steel mesh to reinforce the concrete along that segment of the Northern Line.

The tunnel expansion was finding its feet again. We had a thirty-meter span of freshly excavated tunnel we could walk into upright, arms outstretched, and more importantly, we hadn't burst a single Thames Water pipe under my watch.

Privately, I tried to adjust myself out of my funk.

Adarsh talked me into a deal on twenty hot yoga passes at a studio in Chalk Farm. I stupidly showed up for the first lesson in tracksuit bottoms and a cotton sweater (Adarsh hadn't told me what hot yoga was), and left so dehydrated I barely went to the loo for two days. I gave Adarsh nineteen passes back. Then I got together with his friend Aman a few times – awkward daytime rendezvous because of my flipped schedule. I bought myself an urban spa retreat, booked a week off in autumn, signed up for a wine delivery service. Cheap screw-top bottles of Picpoul. The crates took over my tiny kitchen, but what do you do?

Did it help? I thought so. I did. I felt cared for, if only by my own self. But the world wasn't done with me, and neither was my brain.

So, I suppose, first, the dreams. About Fran. Dream-Fran. Fish-Fran.

That July she turned up night after night, carrying the blue fishing rod, our Christmas gift to our father, the one I'd been toying with when she wandered off. Glossy as a brand-new car, that rod, and I can still see the polish of it nearly three decades on. In dream-Fran's other hand was the tin bucket we used for treasure unearthed on mudlarking adventures along the bank of the Thames.

When I remember my sister, I remember her with her braids and wellies, her missing teeth. But dream-Fran wasn't like that. She was indistinct – not like she'd been rubbed out or sun-faded, but sort of like she was made of squid skin. Her eyes were black dots in jelly flesh, her nose two upward punctures you'd miss if you weren't looking. The bucket and rod were what tipped me off that it was her.

Fish-Fran didn't do anything in the dreams, just hung around me. I couldn't see where we were exactly, but it felt like we were in the tunnels, that same cosy swaddled feeling and layering of shadows.

"Where did you go?" I asked her, every night.

"I went to find the mouth of the Thames that Daddy talked about," she said.

Or, "I was hunting for rubies and sapphires in the mud."

Or, "I went to look for something important in the water."

"Are you alive?" I asked her.

But instead of assortments of answers, I got nothing, or once, the touch of her jelly skin on mine.

London is so rammed with stories it's hard to connect the dots across the width and depth of it. But now that I've pieced it all together, something else happened in July, the first clue to really hang onto. A piece of a puzzle no one wanted to see completed.

The fossils from Hampstead Heath went to the palaeontologists. They measured and prodded them and said: an ancient organism, amphibious, big, really big. We don't have a name for it yet.

Anyway. That's what there was. Dad had let us fish with the glossy blue rod, but said we couldn't eat anything we caught in the Thames: too sickly, too poisoned. Throw it back, he'd say.

London and its millennia of shite and history, like Adarsh said.

On the night of Saturday July 23rd, the red LED of the station clock showing a half hour to midnight, I was an endless up-escalator away from both the trains and engineering crew, chatting to the station supervisor in the ticket hall over a cup of Darjeeling and a pack of chocolate digestives. It was some banter about the new line, how convenient it would be to have a direct route from Camden Town to Luton Airport once our work was done.

There was a slight rumbling beneath my work boots and then a metallic scraping sound. More rumbling. A short time later a ruffled announcement rang out on the tannoy.

"Inspector Sands to Northern Line southbound platform four." *Inspector Sands*: code for an emergency at a Tube station, among Londoners an open secret.

We were already on the escalator, taking the steps as nimbly as our boots would allow, my stomach a bony fist.

Downstairs, pandemonium. It was the last southbound service on a Saturday night. Drunk passengers hammered wildly on the windows of the train from within and from the platform; its doors were still closed. The train driver had abandoned her cab, was shouting 'I don't know' at the platform supervisor, then, louder, at the station supervisor who arrived along with me.

Below the periodic shattering of glass under blows from the train's emergency escape hammers, there was a sound like a faint waterfall, and a stench like a swamp. The waterfall noise was loudest at the dark maw of the tunnel where the train had been holding at a red signal.

The rails flooded in a minute. Grey water began to rise toward platform level. We had engineering crews not far away reviewing plans and prepping the night's work, as well as passengers on board the stricken train. There weren't enough people at that time of night for a crush, but I remember a lot of panicked milling and a nervous kind of shouting that reminded me of the animal pens at my aunt Calista's dairy farm. After we got the train's doors open, we focused on the most critical thing: getting everybody the hell out of the station.

Upstairs, after every passenger had been evacuated and emergency services had arrived, it was Philip who was first to realize it.

"Jo, can I talk to you for a minute?" He pulled me aside. "Hopefully I'm all muddled up, okay? But that was a nine-car service. The last service is always nine cars. I left the excavation as soon as I heard it. Ran down to see. Counted the carriages." He counted idly on his fingers now, hesitated on the second set of five. "The eighth carriage I could see was still sort of in the tunnel, it hadn't come all the way out, and it was dark behind." Philip could barely look at me. There was an awful look in his eyes, a burden I could tell he was about to pass to me, a live grenade.

"There were only eight. Only eight cars."

"Where was the ninth?"

Philip shook his head. He was two years out of apprenticeship, a competent, honest kid from South London whose mother had forced him into the vocational program when all he wanted was to record drill albums and chase his sliver of fame from club to club.

"No ninth carriage back there, Jo," he said. "Just water and stink and fucking darkness."

Within a week there were names and pictures: fifteen souls who'd made the mistake of choosing the wrong carriage, the wrong train, the wrong bloody night. I scrolled past the news story because I couldn't look at their faces. Most were university students; there were two cousins on a stag night; a pensioner coming back from the theatre with his grandson.

There was a protracted search: divers, the Fire Brigade, daily press briefings. They'd keep looking, they said. They wouldn't give up. But they found nothing. The ninth carriage had disappeared.

The Northern Line was out of service citywide, our worksite off-limits. I made sure to take no pleasure from rejoining the world of the living. I barricaded myself in bed with the curtains drawn and experimented with sleeping pills that would stop me from dreaming of fish-Fran.

Adarsh called enough times that I switched my mobile off. I didn't have the stomach for him, for anyone. Or, not quite: I would have talked to my father if he were still alive. I would've done anything to speak to him.

Another week and an emergency dam was put into the River Fleet's tunnel. This allowed an engineering team – thankfully not mine – to drain the southbound Northern Line track.

In early August, they'd drained enough water and shifted enough rubble that they found the hole.

It was massive, a breach tall and wide as a Routemaster. It was in the same section as the last hole, an implosion of concrete that'd torn through our mockery of a reinforcement mesh like a tongue through a sheet of tissue. Measurements confirmed the hole was easily big enough to let through a train carriage, if you could get around the logistics of a twenty-five ton block of metal detaching from train and track and manoeuvring through to a parallel tunnel.

The search operation scoured as much of the underground river as it could. And found nothing. All of London turned its attention to the River Thames, especially where the Fleet let out into its postcard-perfect sibling through the embankment wall beneath Blackfriars Bridge.

"How can a whole train car of people go missing underground?" asked Adarsh, when he'd insisted on a fish supper enough times that I had to oblige or risk him attempting some kind of intervention.

"I don't know." Speech tasted wooden. I couldn't touch my dinner, nursed a double vodka soda even though the late daylight was obscenely cheerful. "It doesn't make sense."

But of course I speculated – all I did lately was speculate – trying out ideas too laced with impossibility to be anything but thoughts I had in private. I wondered how many of us had made the same leap, sensed the same wrongness about the city in spite of the smiling glare of its streets.

I wondered what we'd upset. What history we'd woken.

No brand of sleeping pills was strong enough to make Fran go away.

By the muggy middle of August I was becoming accustomed to her following me around the subterranean tunnels of my dream world.

"Where are we going, Jo?" she asked one night in her five-year-old voice, skipping ahead of me down a tunnel, the flashlit shadow of the fishing rod extending long and black and hook-ended before her.

"Anywhere. Shall we go and find you?"

She reached a grey, oozing hand toward me. "I'm right here."

"And other times?" I asked. "Where are you when I'm awake?"

"I'm nowhere there. I don't live there. It's too wet." I took my sister's hand. We walked side by side. The feel of her repulsed me, but I clung to my memory of real Fran as hard as I could.

"And I like swimming, but not *that* kind of swimming," said Fran.

"What kind of swimming?" I asked. The tunnel was tight. My shoulders scraped wet brick.

"Swimming until you can't see *London Bridge Is Falling Down*. Till you can't see Jo or Daddy. Swimming until you get hurt."

"But there's none of that bad swimming now," I said.

Fran stopped. She set down the mudlarking bucket and put steamed-dumpling fingers to the damp wall of the tunnel.

"Yes there is, Jo. I feel it. It's back. You and daddy can't make it go away."

"Can you?" I asked.

"No," said Fran in a singsong. "Nobody can."

We went back to work on the tunnel that week. It was almost too sombre to bear. Not a single joke, not a sloppy innuendo, not a crack about the weather, not even the reliable no-daylight vampire analogy. Not once. But the vibrations of the burrowing machines still soothed me, I suppose. I felt more myself than I had in a long time.

The project was two months behind, but no one mentioned it. Not even Annabel-of-the-Gantt-charts dared breathe a word about deadlines after what had happened.

And late was better than never. Our fresh thirty-meter excavation was soon double that. We were doing good work.

One night we got a little careless, detonated a badly calibrated blasting emulsion to loosen stubborn bedrock too close to the soft side wall. And we had on our hands another breach between Tube tunnel and river tunnel, this time a small one, fist-sized, likely harmless.

Philip brought me over to assess the damage.

"The Fleet must be at low tide," I said.

"How do you want to fix it?" he asked.

"I reckon cement, this time," I said. Ancient brickwork on the Fleet's side had been damaged by the blast, chunks of it missing. There was a peephole gap clear through. I put my ear against it as if it were a subterranean conch shell.

The dirge of the buried river, soft and insistently there.

"Jo?"

"Go get the drilling crew and Thames Water's engineer, please."

"Yes boss." Philip's flashlight beam bounced away toward the mouth of the excavation.

I was alone.

I knelt in front of the breach, waterlogged rock and silt cool against the padded knees of my cargoes.

I can't describe why I got so close. I felt turned around, turned upside down, like the furniture of my life was hanging from the ceiling. I wanted to sleep in the sunshine and rave all night. Wanted to compress London to a snow globe, then to a point. Wanted to swim in the Thames and take that impure brown water into my lungs.

There was dripping and burbling and my breathing overtop, a symphony.

I shone my flashlight through. On the other side, a blinding, slick, prismatic reflection, no depth. Bulk, right up close.

I took a work glove off. And I touched. Felt the give and muscle of an enormous living thing.

I suppose all stories are passed along with cheap words, tinsel and streamers. I know there's nothing I can really say. And maybe the moment you touch a monster and don't draw back is the moment you become one, moult your humanity. But I'd never felt so old and I'd never felt so buried alive. The expanses and alleys and green spaces of London were at that moment barely pockets of oxygen, barely enough for a day's survival in a very, very long life.

And then it was gone. And Philip was back.

"You probably have this under control," I said, because I didn't, and I hurried toward the industrious snake of the up-escalator, my body a bundle of broomsticks wrapped in leather.

We completed the tunnel in the autumn of the following year. I attended the ribbon cutting ceremony for the new Northern Line service – Camden Town to Luton Airport – in a pinstripe jacket and pencil skirt I'd dry-cleaned for the occasion. They stood me somewhere near the back, which was fine by me. I'd been offered a plus-one but didn't invite Adarsh. I wanted to be there by myself.

Then, around Christmas, under a frosted Blackfriars Bridge, curls of metal chassis still glossy with the livery of a Northern Line train began to let out into the Thames where the mouth of the Fleet was. They ran dragnets at the outlet for a month or more. No human remains were recovered.

Around the same time, a new species of amphibian was discovered in the shallows of the Thames. The Royal Society wanked and self-congratulated for weeks. The specimens were thought to be juveniles, or, crazy as it sounded, larvae. They were proper big babies, long as a human arm.

The tabloids published an exposé, all of them printing the same pixelated photo of an alleged specimen alongside a strip of measuring tape. It had hundreds of needle teeth and kind of sad, mopey, monochrome eyes and a keratin knob on its forehead and – most importantly – what appeared to be the yellow strap of a carriage handle embedded in its eel-like, translucent flesh. But tabloids are tabloids, and London is chock full of stories. So people forget.

Oh, and the fossils in Hampstead Heath's duck pond had a name now. They called the prehistoric beast the Dendan, after a mythical fish in the Arabian Nights. Said it was likely king of the aquatic food chain in its time, being bigger than a galleon, with a carnivore's teeth and a stomach the size of a hotel room. A good one. A penthouse suite.

You'd think more people would have made the connection. Maybe I find it easier to believe impossibilities than others do. I don't know.

I climbed out of my funk, little by little. The dreams mostly stopped. I like to think Fran had told me all I needed to know.

Now when I think about our terrible last day with Fran on the bank of the Thames, I can't help but see it differently. Less like me being distracted and losing my little sister when our father went to fetch a pail of bait from the car. Less like her being picked up by a dirty and depraved pervert. More like Fran seeing the prismatic writhe of fish in the shallows, wading out to try to catch one, or to play.

I force myself to imagine it was quick after that, the bad swimming, the hurt.

Anyway, it's all guesswork and fantasy. I don't see the harm in building a sand fortress that protects your heart a little better.

That's that. They asked me to work on the eastbound expansion of the Central Line, but I said no thanks. I enrolled in a paleozoology diploma course. Lectures at 9am every other day. I'd forgotten how frantic London is during rush hour, how many lives there are to be shuttled along its roads and its bridges and tunnels. Deaths, births, seasons. How many stories the city can absorb like a sponge.

Birds Fell From the Sky and Each One Spoke in Your Voice

Kirsty Logan

At night, the estate was a ghost town. But no one else was there except Sidney, so he guessed he was the ghost. Sidney's house was the first one to be finished; technically, he shouldn't be living there for another six months. But what with the fire in his old place, there wasn't much choice. He'd thought the developers would have argued with him more, but as they seemed to have run out of money to build the rest of the estate, maybe they were just glad to have sold at least one house. Sidney had planned to move in his own stuff, but it was all rot and soot now. Nice to get a new start, anyway, even if the empty house did echo a bit.

He drove through the estate. The roads all started paved and reassuring, but only the one leading to his house remained so; the others were deceptive, turning to dirt partway through, leading nowhere except deeper into the woods. He passed a half-built play-park, ground soil still in huge sealed bags. Streets named for trees, though only pretty evergreen ones, not the looming naked ones that spindled across the back gardens here. Everything unfinished, wrapped in plastic, thwacking. A fox shrieked. He reached for the radio button, but changed his mind.

And there was the house at last, a looming black shape against the deeper dark. He wished he'd left a light on. He parked and scooped an armful of velvet out of the backseat.

On the doorstep he fumbled with his keys, the velvet puffing dust. Just a phrase, that: there was no doorstep, just a raised UPVC door, the lip of which he always caught his Converse toe on as he stepped inside. Key in the door, handle down – catch of the toe and trip, of course, but he righted himself.

The house smelled of paint. There was a note from the decorators on the kitchen table. He'd been away for a week while they set everything up: repainted door-frames, tightened threshold bars, polished out fingerprints.

Sidney deposited his burden on the couch and wandered the rooms. It looked brand new, he thought, then laughed at himself. Of course it was new. Wasn't that the point? The night windows reflected Sidney back at himself. He stared at this new housemate for a moment, then looked away.

He lifted the velvet curtains from the couch and hung them from the plastic rail. They were too heavy; the rail sagged, leaving finger-widths of darkness at the top and sides. So flimsy, these new builds. He should have known it wouldn't work to mix old and new. Tomorrow he'd go and get something light and synthetic, something that crackled and couldn't be tumble-dried. He pulled down the curtains and folded them; they'd be good for the shop. Velvet curtains were definitely a thing in the 90s. He remembered his babysitter's house had them, though of course it was actually his babysitter's parents' house as she was only 16. Those curtains were a burnt orange, like the insides of cheap fondants. He used to hide between them and the window, cold glass on his back and scratchy fabric on his front, the comforting claustrophobia of his own caught breath. She'd pretend to search the room for him, looking behind the flap of the video player, inside vases, up the chimney, places he couldn't possibly fit. Finally she'd whip back the curtain and scoop him up, giggling so hard he felt sick, safe and found, never really lost at all. You'd think, considering his line of work, that he'd get used to these sudden swoops of nostalgia, but they got him every time.

Sidney opened the empty cupboard under the stairs to stash the curtains, but it was unexpectedly not empty. Crouched on the floor in the middle of the cupboard was a large red dial-phone.

Sidney flinched, but the phone did not ring. He went to throw the curtains on top, but was then seized with a surety that the fabric would somehow catch on fire in the night. Besides, the phone looked vintage. He put the curtains in the corner and lifted the phone. The cable trailed after, a dog's hopeful tail.

He put the phone on the hall table, plugged it in to the wall and lifted the receiver.

Silence.

Of course the line wasn't hooked up yet; he was lucky there was electricity. Ah, but they would have needed that to light the place so prospective buyers could look around. There'd be gas too, for the oven – everyone knew those estate agent tricks, baking bread and brewing coffee to make a house smell like a home. Just the thought of that made him hungry. He closed the door to the cupboard under the stairs and went to make himself some dinner, cheered by his twin, the Sidney mirroring him in the windows, following his every movement.

After dinner, Sidney channel-flicked. He got engrossed in a film before realising it was about a missing child, and quickly changed over. Then he changed it back and kept watching. It was, from his experience, unrealistic, and he found that fact strangely reassuring. The missing child was a moppet; too cute to die, but with appealingly large eyes that carried tears well. Listening to the film's dialogue, Sidney heard someone refer to the child as Cotton, and for a moment his blood stopped flowing. Then he realised he'd misheard; the name was just the sound of the mother catching a sob in her throat. His blood moved again.

Sidney watched the film to the end, even though he knew it wouldn't make any difference. The child was not called Cotton, and anyway they found him and he was still alive.

Sidney woke from the depths of night. A loud sound had just stopped. An alarm? Building site security. Thunder, hail. A fox killing something, the dying shriek. In his dream, a phone had been ringing. He itched to answer it.

Sidney slid from bed, feet cold on the bare floors. Tomorrow he'd get a rug. Slippers. Adult possessions. Down the stairs in the dark, the house's held breath. He didn't want to switch on the light; it would wake him up, and he'd always had trouble getting back to sleep. In the soft night, he padded down the stairs.

There was the banister. There was the bottom step.

The door to the cupboard under the stairs. The hall table. The phone.

He knew that the phone could not have rung. Last night there had been no dial tone, and the BT engineers certainly didn't hook up phone lines at midnight. He'd made a fuss about keeping his old phone number, so he knew all about the intricacies of BT.

He knew no one had called. But he lifted the receiver. You have to answer the phone.

Silence. Of course, silence.

It was a sun-through-the-rain Monday afternoon and Sidney was just counting the pieces in a recently-bought Rugrats jigsaw when the bell over the door jingled and the man walked in. Sidney nodded politely and the man nodded back, then went to browse a display of Gameboy cartridges. Sidney had commissioned a special bookcase for them, all reclaimed wood, the shelves quarter-height so the cartridges could sit face-out but in proportion, like a dollhouse bookcase; he was proud of that idea, and many a hipster had squealed ironically and asked to buy it, the whole thing, shelves and cartridges, presumably to display ironically in their ironic living rooms.

Sidney's shop sold everything you remember from your childhood, and some things you don't. But every single thing was from between the years 1990 and 1999. He scorned remakes, reissues, faux-vintage kitsch; in his shop, it was genuine or nothing. If you wanted a DreamPhone board game, a pink inflatable backpack, a jungle-pattern Adidas shell suit, a box of red floppy discs, a Global HyperColor colour-change t-shirt, platform Buffalo trainers, a Right Said Fred cassette single, Tamagotchis, Trolls, Goosebumps, Gak, Boglins, Milky Pens, a box of Cherry Coke Lipsmackers still sealed in plastic – Sidney had it. An entire childhood, both real and ideal.

Sidney observed the man without the man realising he was being observed. It was a vital shopkeeper skill, part of his arsenal against shoplifters. The more he watched, the more uneasy he felt. The man looked like a 1950's greaser, like the one in the film you're meant to think of as the bad boy – but a Hollywood bad boy, not a real one; borrowing cars and returning them later, maybe smoking a joint or feeling up a girl in the backseat. Leather jacket with a popped collar and wide shoulders, fastened a shade too tight over his belly, oily-looking black t-shirt, grey hair styled into a duck's ass. There was something unwholesome about the man. He seemed stiffly relaxed, too self-conscious, like he was an actor playing a role but could easily switch into another. Sidney sensed that the man was about to look up at him, and quickly looked away.

'Looking for a Nokia,' said the man. His voice was low, as if mid-seduction. 'One of the old ones.'

'Everything I've got is old. I don't do replicas. But no phones.'

'No Nokias? I don't mind which model.'

'No phones. At all.'

'Well, are you going to get any in?'

'No. Don't do them. Don't even have a shop phone.'

'Mate.' The man paused until Sidney looked up from his jigsaw; with the bright cartoon pieces in his hand he suddenly felt ludicrous, like a child playing shops. 'You've got all this shit.' The man motioned at the Megadrives, the floppy denim hats, the Maid Marian VHS, the Fisher Price extendable skates, the Cadbury's Dairy Milk dispenser, the Pogs. 'And not a single phone? Mate.'

Sidney shrugged, and felt even more like a child. He cleared his throat and felt even more ridiculous; what was he going to do next, smooth down the moustache he didn't have?

'Sorry. Too many of them around, and I like to keep things special.'

The instant Sidney said the words, he regretted them. The man's gaze raked down and up Sidney's body and his smile split wide; his teeth were straight and white. For a second Sidney thought he had a toothpick between his incisors, but he must have imagined it. He'd been watching too many films. Jesus, next he'd be expecting the guy to take off his leather jacket, unroll a pack of Lucky Strikes from his t-shirt sleeve and clack open a Zippo. Put the cigarette between his teeth. Grin wide and white. Call him a good boy.

'Special, huh?'

Sidney stood up. This had the disadvantage of revealing more of his admittedly not very lech-worthy body to the man, but at least now they were the same height; Sidney might actually have been in inch taller.

'Write your email down,' said Sidney. 'I'll let you know if anything comes in, okay?' Anything, anything to get the man out of the shop.

The man leaned in – a smell of maleness, aftershave and outside air – and wrote a series of numbers on a piece of scrap paper on the counter.

'You can call me.'

'Thanks,' said Sidney, though what he meant was no.

'Thank you.' The man's wink was implied rather than literal. He opened the door and the bell jangled.

Memory lurched in Sidney. He had to sit down and count the jigsaw pieces from the start before he could convince himself that the bell over the door was not the same one that had rung in his sleep last night.

When Sidney's little brother Cotton had been snatched from his babysitter's house, no one saw anything. There was no evidence. No trail to follow, breadcrumb or otherwise.

Police swarmed the house. Days of fingerprint dust and room searches and TV appeals and lists of everyone they'd ever met. Days of interviews with every neighbour and teacher and family friend. Days of badgering the tearful apologetic babysitter, who had been in the kitchen making the boys a snack and was certain, absolutely certain that she'd locked the front door.

Cotton's face was repeated on a thousand posters, pasted on every shop door and lamppost and noticeboard. It was an appealing face, moppet-like, a face made for an easy life. His unexpected curls, his tiny cleft chin. None of it helped.

Days and days and days. Weeks and weeks. Everything, everything except for Cotton.

The police set up a tip line, and people called the station every day with potential new leads. Now it wasn't that there was no evidence. There was plenty: an avalanche, a glut. It was a small town; the police brought in officers from other towns, but there was still too much. So many helpful citizens out there, helping. Calling to share every detail they could possibly think of.

I saw a boy at the shops. He looked a few years older than the missing boy, and his hair was a different colour, but you never know what those kidnappers can do, surgery and all sorts. I wrote down the number plate so you...

My cousin is acting suspicious. I tried to show him a picture of my little son but he didn't want to look. Don't you think it's strange? I think he has something to do with that missing boy...

I overheard a guy walking past my house say something about a boy and a van. I didn't get his name but I drew his face. You could make posters...

The next morning, Sidney opened his front door, then shivered and closed it again. Summer was definitely over, though he couldn't remember it starting. Sidney opened the cupboard under the stairs, his mind already on the endless list of tasks that the shop seemed to bring up every day, and stared dumbly at the pile of orange velvet within.

Coat. Coat. He should have made coffee; his brain felt fuzzed, mossy. But of course his coat wasn't in the cupboard. It was upstairs, in a stack of cardboard boxes with all the rest of his clothes. He raced upstairs and dug through the boxes, then pulled on the coat. As he pounded back downstairs, without thinking he put his hand in the pocket for his car keys, which he had left on the hall table beside the phone. He hadn't worn this coat since the previous winter, and the pockets were tiny time capsules. He pulled out a crumbling piece of gum, three receipts for pumpkin spice lattés – repulsive things they were, just the memory of the smell of them turned his stomach; he'd only bought them because the woman he was seeing at the time was inexplicably obsessed with them – a tissue hard with old snot, a small black button with a snapped thread tangled in its eyes. He put the things on the hall table and picked up his keys instead. Then he put down the keys and picked up the red receiver. It wasn't silence, he now realised. There was no dial tone, but there was something. Static. A held-breath hum. And somewhere in the distance, just under the sound of his flowing blood, when he pressed the phone hard against his ear and really listened hard, something else.

By the time he got out to the car, he knew he'd be late opening the shop. But it wasn't his fault. You have to answer the phone.

The Rugrats jigsaw had sold almost immediately – and at the ridiculously high price he'd put on it too – almost as a challenge to his customers, some of whom he realised he was actually starting to resent. Sidney was pretty happy to have found a job lot of retro jigsaws online. The downside, he now realised, was that counting all the pieces was a right pain in the arse. As it was a job lot, too, clearly from the same household and probably forgotten in an attic for decades, there was no way to know for sure that the pieces weren't mixed between the boxes. What if someone bought a *Teenage Mutant Hero Turtles* 1,000-piecer only to find that instead of April O'Neil's face, the only piece left was Marge Simpson's left shoe? Sidney felt life was far too short to have that conversation. So there was nothing else for it: he would have to make up each jigsaw individually, to check. All nine of them.

He had just finished making the edge of an *Aaahh!!! Real Monsters* 800-piecer, the rain was scattering a lullaby on the front window, his favourite song had just come on the shuffled playlist, and he was thinking that life wasn't such a downer after all, when the bell over the door rang and the 1950s greaser came in. He shook his lapels to get the rain off his jacket; his hair was so slick the rain didn't seem to have touched it. Sidney held the tip of his tongue between his teeth and gave the man a shut-mouth smile, then carried on with his jigsaw. He felt like he'd been tricked into a role-play, but didn't know how to play something else. He knew he should collapse the jigsaw and put it back in the box. Get to his feet. Pick up a pricing gun or the credit card machine. Something adult-like. But he stayed behind the counter, head bowed, toying with a piece showing Oblina's inviting, red-painted mouth. That made him think about his ear, which still throbbed from holding the phone for so long. He hoped that wasn't red too.

Sidney looked up to steal a glance at the man, but the man was already looking at him, mouth quirked up at the side flirtatiously. He looked as if his clothes covered not a body, but something else. In the shape of a human, but not.

'You been listening?' the man said, which made it seem like he was asking Sidney if he was listening to him, but Sidney was sure he hadn't been talking. When he spoke his face twisted and sagged, mask-like. It was age, Sidney told himself, age and wrinkles and loose skin and a flabby body. He was old. He was old. He was normal and old. 'On the phone.' The man motioned to Sidney's head. 'Your ear. Looks sore. That'll happen if you listen so hard. I bet you never thought about not answering.'

'I don't know what you – I don't sell phones. I told you that.'

'Noble tradition, it is. Listening. Did you know that Thomas Edison tried to invent a machine that would communicate with the dead?'

'I don't –'

'He failed, of course. The dead have nothing to say. And in Italy, another guy – I forget his name – recorded mysterious voices with an old tube radio. Spent his life trying to figure out what they were saying to him. But they weren't saying much of anything, I bet. Then in Sweden, another guy recorded birdsong in the forest, but when he listened back to the recording it was his mother's voice saying: 'Friedrich, can you hear me?''

'I don't want –'

'Then in Latvia, another guy made over a hundred thousand recordings of the dead, including his mother. Isn't that strange? Why is it always the mother?'

The man stepped closer and Sidney couldn't help but flinch back, jolting the counter so the jigsaw pieces all ticky-tacked down on to his shoes.

'Have you heard of anything like that?'

'I don't. I don't. No.'

'Still looking for that phone. Got things to say, you know?'

The man winked at Sidney. Then, incredibly, he pulled a pack of Lucky Strikes from his pocket and clacked open a Zippo. He put the cigarette between his teeth. He grinned wide and white. Don't say it don't say it please please god don't call me a good –

'Call me if you hear anything,' said the man, and he lit his cigarette and opened the door and the bell jangled. Long after he was gone, Sidney could smell the smoke. His ear ached from the echo of the bell.

After weeks of people phoning about Cotton, the police had so many tips that dozens of them were working around the clock to investigate them all. It was too much – but nothing could be ignored. The truth was a needle in a stack of needles. The police put a special tip-line phone in Sidney's parents' kitchen, so that they could deal with the tips and the police could get on with investigating them. The phone was red and plastic and when it rang, Sidney's parents had to answer it and write down the tips in a special folder. And when Sidney's parents were out, Sidney had to answer.

At first the tips were okay. Hearing that it wasn't a policeman's voice on the end of the phone, but a child's, people were kind. They spoke softly. Reassured him that Cotton was surely fine, surely would be home soon.

Listen, darling, I saw a man… Can you write this down? He was at the supermarket and he was buying kiddie things. Little boxes of raisins and lollipops and potato waffles and chicken kievs. I bet you like those, don't you? If you can write it all down and show the policeman…

The P.E. teacher at the primary school is strange. Don't you think he's strange? My boy forgot his kit once and the teacher made him do it in his underpants. It's just not right, it's not proper. Would you play games with the other boys in your underpants?

For a while, Sidney wrote all the things down in the special folder to give to the police. He wore a pack of pencils down to stubs. But the calls kept coming, all day and all night, and Sidney was almost a teenager now and so his parents couldn't be there all the time.

I saw that boy, that missing boy. He was locked in a shed. It was my shed. If you come and look I can show you…

My dad hurts me and I don't like it and he could have hurt your brother too, and at night he comes into my room…

I know why your brother got taken and you didn't. He's so little, so pretty and sweet, his cleft chin. I wanted to suck it into my mouth…

Sidney wrote it all down in the special folder. He listened and he wrote it down because you never know. Someone knew about what happened to Cotton and he couldn't miss it, he couldn't miss it if Cotton or the man who took Cotton was on the other end of the phone.

I had a dream about that little missing boy. He's near water and he can't see. I think he's been blinded. There's water though, perhaps he's been drowned? Perhaps someone took him and drowned him? You should check all the water, the river, drains even, he's definitely blind and drowned…

I took him. I took Cotton and I put a gag in his mouth and he couldn't speak any more. But you can, can't you? Speak to me, little boy. Tell me about how…

When I was your age, a man took me and he hurt me. I need to tell you, I think the man took that boy too. I'll tell you all the things he did to me, the things he's doing to that boy, I'll tell you all of it…

And then Sidney stopped answering the phone. It rang and he turned the TV up louder and it rang and he put his spongy orange headphones on and turned his tapes right up and it rang and he felt the sound in his throat and it rang and his ears ached and it rang and he couldn't sleep and it rang and he burned the special folder in a metal bin in the back garden and it rang and he thought of the cold glass on his back and scratchy fabric on his front and it rang and it rang and it rang.

Sidney did not answer the phone again. Cotton never came home. And Sidney knew, knew with a certainty that filled his head with a constant sickening buzz, that he had missed the one call that mattered.

The next day at the shop, Sidney didn't even pretend to make the jigsaws. He stood and waited with his fingers clutching white on the edge of the counter. He couldn't stand to look at the thing he'd bought; he'd wrapped it in layers of black bin-bags to hide its shape from himself.

When the bell over the door rang, he knew it was the man. He was barely even pretending to be human now. He had the leather jacket and the greased hair and perhaps at a very quick glance he looked okay. But if you looked for more than a second, the thing inside bumped up wrongly against the inside of his skin, making strange lumps and hollows. His face shifted. When he spoke, his voice came out wet and echoing like from the bottom of a well.

'You got something for me? Something nice?'

Wordlessly, Sidney held out the package. The man smiled. His teeth were straight and white.

'Well now. That is nice.' The man took the package from Sidney. His nails were ragged as knives and cut straight through the bin-bags. They fluttered to the floor, revealing a Nokia 3210, an original from 1999, fully charged and with one phone number programmed in.

Sidney kept his gaze down on the counter, not looking, the exact opposite of what he'd done when the man had taken his brother Cotton and he'd hidden behind his babysitter's orange velvet curtains and watched and done nothing and never said, never said a word, not even when the man had looked right at the gap between the curtains and said to him –

'You're a good boy, aren't you?'

'Yes,' said Sidney.

'This is our secret, isn't it?'

'Yes,' said Sidney.

Sidney closed the shop early so he wouldn't have to drive through the estate in the dark. He drove to his brand-new house, which had no ghosts and no curtains and nowhere to hide.

He opened the door to silence.

He picked up the red phone and took it into the cupboard under the stairs.

He wrapped himself in the orange velvet curtain and sat on the floor.

He waited for the phone to ring.

He picked up the red receiver.

He listened.
You have to answer the phone.

A Few Things I Miss About Skeletons

Tom Offland

It's been a couple of years now, since they made skeletons illegal. It happened on a Saturday. In the morning. And mine was taken whilst I was sleeping. Other people lost theirs at work. Whilst they were out shopping. Or on the dilapidated trams into town. There were raids at breakfast tables. In the strip malls. The bagel stores. The ocean dog-walking trails. Where everybody's skeletons were confiscated.

Finger clicking. Star jumps. Piggybacks. And *cycling.* Are a few things I miss about skeletons.

And I can't help but dwell on those earlier times. When we all had skeletons. And it's so recent but it feels almost mythological. So distant and so unreal. And I am pining for those days. And I remember them as contented and perfect and endless. And filled with a sort of sturdy love. Because everything is so much harder, for all of us now. But also softer. Without our skeletons.

I miss *gloves. Rings. Sock puppets.* And *shoes.* Now we no longer have skeletons.

And I think we all feared that it might happen eventually. Losing our skeletons. There were signs and rumours and those people who tried to warn us. But none of us really believed it. So it was quite a shock when the interventions started, and our skeletons were plucked out like feathers. Bad teeth. Or like eyebrow hairs. *Reappropriated* was the term that was used.

And I miss *calligraphy. Playing marbles.* And *shaky hands.* And I miss *stairs. Escalators.* And *step ladders.*

And nowadays, the main difference between humans and

animals is that animals still have skeletons. And my favourite animals are snakes. They have the most bones in their skeletons. But they look like they have the least. And I used to feel disdain for slugs and worms. But now I respect them. Because they do so well.

Without skeletons.

Propping up the bar. Sitting on deck chairs. And *queuing for the bus.* Are some more things I miss about skeletons.

And I worry about the animal kingdom, and its precious skeletons. Birds have the lightest skeletons, so they need to take the most care. And rhinos have the sturdiest, so they should be fine. And I like to look at fossilised animals in the museum. At their old skeletons. Turned to stone. They make me sad. Reminiscent of things lost in the past. The ancient animals. And times long ago. But mostly I miss skeletons.

I miss *using cutlery.* And *opening mail.* And I miss *finding the end of the sticky tape.* And I miss *pulling champagne corks.* And *looking through binoculars.*

And if I'm honest, I hardly thought about my skeleton until it was gone. I took it for granted, in fact. And I hate to admit it, but there were times I doubted I even had one. And in the old world, they used to say 'grow a backbone', to mean be courageous! And they'd wish one another luck by saying 'break a leg!' But none of that means anything anymore. And it's hard to have courage or humour or good fortune without a skeleton.

Posture. Body language. And *careless swagger.* Are some more things I miss about skeletons.

And at least graveyards are better now. They're no longer spooky. Or strange. Or sad. They're happy places. After all, it's only in graveyards that we can be close to skeletons. So people congregate there. Sliding along on the spongy grass. Above all the buried skeletons. Remembering how it used to be.

A few more things I miss about skeletons are *sprinkling salt. Turning steering wheels.* And *putting on sunglasses.*

And nowadays people really like to rent those old films. About graveyards. Where the skeletons rise out the earth. And everybody does it, not to be frightened, but to rejoice. And to wish that it was reality. Because those films seem like a beautiful fantasy now. Like our skeletons are returning to us. Clawing themselves out of the ground. In a creaky and clambering and loving reunion.

I miss *taking off sandals* and I miss *touching smartphones* and I miss *putting in earplugs.* I miss *chopsticks* and *bicycle chains. Typewriters* and *trousers.*

And I'd like to own a skeleton key. Just for old times' sake. I'd like to look at it. And I'd like to lock the front doors for my neighbours. When they've forgotten. I think that would be soothing. Because it seems so unfair. That we're not allowed skeletons. The way I see it, buildings have girders and buttresses and foundations. Computers have circuit boards. Machines have pipes and springs. Even books have spines. Why can't we have skeletons?

Some more things I miss about skeletons: *Shuffling playing cards* and *pressing buttons.* I miss *band-aids. Arm slings.* And *leg casts.*

And I look forward to a time when we no longer miss our skeletons. When we are satisfied. But that time seems a long way in the future. I don't know. And I suppose I can imagine, after very many years, a kind of collective dementia. Where we are content, as we have forgotten. That we ever had skeletons. But it would be a confused contentedness. A panicky and drunken time.

And I miss *ring pulls* and *rollercoasters* and *reclining chairs.* I miss *fistfights. Handshakes.* And *opening jars.*

And often when I first wake up, I think I still have a skeleton. It is a beautiful moment. And then it dissolves. But it is worth sleeping for. Just to have that instant. It is worth living for. And sometimes I dream that I have some sort of super skeleton. Made out of crystals, or future metals. And other times, I dream that there is just one skeleton in the entire world. But that's okay, because we all share it. And in the dream I am happy. Because it is my turn. And I am stepping into the skeleton. And it feels like putting on clean, warm clothes.

Why Aren't Millennials Continuing Traditional Worship of the Elder Dark?

Matt Dovey

In a generational shift that some claim threatens the fabric of existence and the sanity of all humanity, surveys show that worship of the Elder Dark is at a record low for one particular group – millennials.

Bob Rawlins is worried. "When I was growing up in the 1950s, I made my obeisance before the Manifold Insanity every night, uttering the invocations to satiate the Watchers Just Beyond and keep them at bay for one day longer. But young people now aren't prepared to make the necessary sacrifices."

I remind him that human sacrifice was deemed unnecessary and illegal in 1985, and animal sacrifice in 2009.

"Well I don't mean *literally*," he says, though there's a note of longing to his tone.

Bob is showing me round his inner sanctum, a converted basement given over to the worship and appeasement of the Unknowable Gods. He's the Grand Dark Supplicant of his local chapter, and is continuing a long family tradition: men of his bloodline have been bound to the service of the Elder Dark since the days of the Pilgrims.

"Our ranks are already thin," he says, resting a hand intimately on an idol of the Ten Thousand Staring Eyes. "I worry the world I'll leave behind will be overrun by the gibbering horrors of the between spaces, ushering in a never-ending age of nightmares and insurmountable monstrosities. It breaks my heart to think of the Eight Palms golf course getting swallowed by a roiling pit of blackness. Hole five's a real beauty."

In town, I talk with a group of twenty-somethings working in the local coffee shop. Aren't they anxious about the impending immolation of mankind and the eternal night of the Elder Dark?

"Well, I guess," says Luiz, shaking chocolate onto my cappuccino in a cephalopodan design. "But it's hard to get worked up about such a distant prospect when I'm mostly worried about making rent next month."

"Yeah, yeah," agrees Deema, another barista. "And even if I had the brainspace to worry, I haven't got the roomspace in my apartment for a shrine. I make my obeisance when I visit my parents at the weekend, but my apartment's so cramped the shower's in the kitchen. Where am I meant to find the space for the Eighteen Forms of Frozen Madness?"

"Not that I have any time for the complete incantations anyway," says Luiz. "As soon as I finish here I start a shift at the Midnight Dark Bar on 8th. Do you know how much mess is made by people burying the futility of their infinitesimal existence in drugs and debauchery? By the time I get home from cleaning that up, I've only got five hours before I'm back here. It's hard to muster the energy for self-flagellation on four hours' sleep a night."

These responses may sound cynical and resigned, but talking to Luiz and Deema, there's a sense of frustration: they *want* to be doing more. But some millennials have other reasons for abandoning the worship of the Elder Dark.

"These old dudes – and they're always old *dudes*, you notice that? – they're all caught up in this spiel, like, 'If you don't perform the rituals of devotion then the world will fall to lunacy', and I'm like, dude, look around already!"

Ace shakes their long dreads dismissively and sips a green tea, looking over the gray ocean from their dilapidated RV. Their parents were members of the ultra-orthodox Church of the Nineteenth Insanity; Ace left home at seventeen, sent on their mission to witness the madness of the wider world. It was meant to reinforce the importance of keeping to the convoluted strictures of the Nineteenth Insanity, necessary to resist the influence of the Watchers Just Beyond.

But instead, says Ace, they saw only human madness.

"Like, all the suffering and hurt and injustice, that's not coming from beyond the Pierced Veil, ya know? It's caused by politicians and corporations on this side! People are blind to the roots of their problems, blaming it all on these creatures they've never even seen, right?"

"It's sad to hear," says Kathy Halton, Honorary Senator for the Sunken State of Hggibbia. "I represent the Many Drowned Dead, so I know better than most what the cost of failure is."

Senator Halton looks up at the huge oil-on-canvas that hangs behind her mahogany desk, *The Sinking of Dead Men's Deeds*, that infamous night when eighty thousand souls were lost to the sea. The eye is drawn irresistibly to the dark slash that hangs in the sky, the Pierced Veil itself, and the indescribable creatures of the Entropic Menagerie that spill forth – and it is surely an unparalleled artistic feat to paint a creature that cannot be described – and there is a strange sensation of being drawn into the painting, as if the soul itself is being pulled out through the eyes and reeled into that perversely dark hole on the canvas. Only Halton's smooth voice breaks the spell; she seems used to the painting, immune to its attraction.

"Some people are so desperate for a mundane explanation they'll ignore the evidence of their souls," she says. "The irony is many of this country's problems can be traced back to a disturbing lack of faith in the younger generation."

But isn't there an increasing consensus on grassroots social media that neoliberal government policies of the last thirty years are to blame for irrevocably leading us to this point of critical failure, where the very substance of the multiverse is threatened with annihilation by wage stagnation and an untenable housing market leading to unrealistic work expectations?

"If only it were that simple," she responds. "We're doing everything we can to encourage participation despite the economic downturn, including state-funded glossolalia lessons and mandatory flagellation breaks for government employees. But we can't force a free soul to act."

Two days later we're standing on the windy beach at Chatham, Massachusetts for the annual Sunken Memorial, facing the steel-blue Atlantic where Hggibbia once stood. Senator Halton leads a group of representatives through the Silent Evocations of the Eighteen Forms, their dark trench coats snapping in the wind like ravens fighting over scraps. Two assistants have to help the elderly Health Secretary Johnson through the movements, sometimes physically lifting him to position his limbs correctly.

Fifty yards away, behind a mesh fence and a police line, there's a protest taking place. I'm not surprised to see Ace at the front, leading a chant of *WE'RE NOT INSANE, WE'RE JUST MAD, WE BLAME YOU FOR A WORLD GONE BAD.*

"It's all a distraction!" they tell me to a chorus of agreement from their fellow protestors. "They're using the myth of the Elder Dark to stop you noticing their corruption!"

"Yeah," interjects another protestor, her pink hair straggling over a loose-fit chunky sweater. "Like, did you know they used this stuff to justify some *super* racist ideas? Most people can't spot the subtext now, but if you read the old stuff they basically claimed Jews were in league with the Watchers Just Beyond, right? It's unbelievable!"

Ace picks up the argument, a real bitterness in their voice. "They like, try and handwave that racism away now, ya know, claim you have to understand it in the historical context, but it just proves how they fit it to their agenda at the time. It's all bullshit. You can't trust them."

I go back to see Bob Rawlins. He's invited me up for the traditional orgy that marks the Approach of Winterdark, more commonly called the fall equinox. He prepares for the night by stripping naked, beating his tattooed skin raw with a branch of Hggibbian driftwood, and pulling a tight red hood on that covers his eyes.

He offers me the branch and a spare hood, but I respectfully decline.

There's fifty or more participants gathered at the edge of town for the ritual, all naked bar that same red hood. It's meant to evoke a feeling of insignificance, reminding supplicants they are only anonymous flesh to the Watchers Just Beyond, but the effect is undercut somewhat by small town America: everyone is easily identifiable from their voice and body shape, and Bob chats casually about DIY projects and school district elections as the sun sets.

Once dusk grows dark and a chill settles in, Bob climbs onto a flame-lit stage set up for the event, reminds everyone to stick around for the barbecue afterwards, then begins the Rituals of Unending Vigilance. I find myself talking to a late arrival: Eric Rawlins – Bob's son.

"I'm only back for the weekend," he explains, shuffling uncomfortably. "It means a lot to Dad that I get involved." He's eschewed the naked dedication of his father and kept his jeans on, a single Screaming Gshvaddath tattooed in Shifting Ink just below his red hood, dancing wildly in contrast to Eric's diffidence.

Presumably his father is grooming him to continue the family tradition?

"Yeah, he's really enthusiastic about the whole thing. Dad's worried that if I'm not ready to continue his work the next time his back gives out, then the Elder Dark will flood the world and shackle humanity to an eternal yoke of madness while he waits on his pain relief prescription. He honestly believes he's the only one holding it back right now."

Does Eric think participation is down because people are

coming to terms with the history of it and stepping away? I repeat some of the theories I heard at the rally.

"Yeah, I've heard those ideas too. I agree with them, to be honest, with the people saying the Worship has racist underpinnings, but don't tell Dad. He thinks the texts are sacrosanct, and it's like, if you criticise them, you're criticising him. But there's a growing online movement to embrace the original truth of the Unknowable Scriptures, peeling back the layers of human influence and prejudice. We're all just meat to the Watchers after all, regardless of our skin or beliefs, beneath the notice of an unfathomable Universe made of madness and unending time. I can show you some really interesting subreddits after this."

On stage, Bob is in an awkward crab position, thrusting his flaccid penis towards the night sky and howling in ecstasy. Blood drips from his back where a bed of nails beneath him pierces his flesh over and over; volunteers in hi-viz jackets wait at the edge of the stage with antiseptic cream, stood before signs reminding participants to PRACTICE SAFE SUPPLICATION.

Eric looks anywhere but the stage as the crowd shrieks back, lacerating their own flesh with a variety of pointed implements. There are spiked paddles in ornately carved mahogany, hand-sharpened sticks of blasted elm, and one Hello Kitty cat o' nine tails.

"Dad worries too much, to be honest," says Eric. "I've met a lot of people at college, and at the end of the day people are decent. They do what they can when they can, even if it's just carving Escherian shapes into their avocados at breakfast. We're not gonna let the world run to shit with shambling horrors at the bus stop and tentacles blocking up the plumbing. We've gotta live here too, after all."

Eric finally responds to his father's exhortations with a self-conscious howl, and pricks his thumb with a pocket knife. Bob looks out from the stage, and spots his son; he lifts a hand in greeting, then, unbalanced, slips and lands heavily on the bed of nails. His scream of pain is answered faithfully by the crowd, but Eric runs forward and clambers on stage. He eases his father off the nails and they limp to the side, where a volunteer frantically unpacks a first aid kit.

A brief yet intense exchange follows. The body language is clear: Bob wants Eric to finish leading the worship. The crowd is wavering, their flagellation tools drooping like their middle-aged bodies. I see the moment Eric takes the burden on: his back straightens, his jaw clenches, his shoulders square. He's doing a good impression of being ready for this, and I find myself hoping it convinces Bob.

Eric strips off and positions himself over the nails. He picks up the chant perfectly from where his father left off, closing out the ceremony with vigour, athleticism and rather more – shall we say – *rigidity* than his father could manage.

Off to the side, Bob stands with his legs wide as his bleeding scrotum is gingerly nursed by the volunteer paramedic. He's removed his red hood, and he watches Eric lambaste the crowd with a final chant of "Yhiu! Kaftagh falln!" and receive the answer of "Engibbigth valectia!"

His face shines with paternal pride.

Mr. Fox

Heather Parry

Peter moved to a new town when he was seventeen years old, which is about the worst time of your life to move to a new town. Peter's mother had died, and in their home city there was too much of her; she was in every gallery, every theatre, every vintage clothing store that she'd loved. To Peter, these visions of her were comforting, but to his father they were vicious. Peter's father grew tinier and tinier under the weight of his grief, until the city seemed too vast and feral. The new town was small, ever so small, and lots of the buildings there had wood against the windows, but it was empty of their mother. The houses there were on sale for one or two pounds each, so Peter's father sold their city flat, paid off their debts, and had some money left to turn the house they'd purchased into a home. All that Peter had of his mother were her furs.

Peter had one year left of college so he was enrolled at a grey, brutalist sixth form. On his first day, wanting his mother's warmth, he threw one of her red furs on over his raincoat and walked to school. The fractured groups in his year all turned as he entered the gates and padded up to the front steps. They watched him, sneering and giggling, until someone threw a rock and he ran into the building. In the corridor, a boy tried to tear the coat from his back, so Peter ran to the bathroom and bundled the fur into his rucksack, stroking it as if it were alive. For the rest of the day, he was teased and called names. The next morning, Peter left his mother's furs safely stored in his wardrobe, and set off from home, saying goodbye to his father. But instead of going to college he spent the day wandering through the small streets, looking at the quiet people in their quiet homes. If he was to be lonely, then he would be alone.

The town was a clockwork toy set, with its identikit terraces and its grey-brown brick. The colours were scratched off the playgrounds, with only charcoal-coloured metal left. It was all angles and jagged edges, with clockwork people going from work to home and home to work, all at the same time, moving in lines. On Saturday mornings they went to the library, on Sunday evenings they went to the pub, and on bank holidays they packed their small brown suitcases and took the grey train to the coast. Peter's father was always amongst them, keeping his face to the floor and shuffling along with few words.

Yet there was a man in the town that was unlike the others. The man was red-haired and freckled on the face, with a thick square jaw and shoulders so large they left him no neck. He wore workman's boots, old Levi jeans, an array of jumpers with holes at the elbow, and always, always an orange-red fur stole. He lived on the outskirts of town, in a flat one flight of stairs down from the road, behind an orange-red front door that had black paper taped over the windows. Peter started to watch this man every day, heading straight to his street in the morning and following him wherever he went.

The man always left his house in the late morning, his eyes half opened, blinking rapidly. He kept to the shadows as long as he could, the stole around his shoulders never quite settled but never quite falling off. He went to the butcher's daily, the post office sometimes, the greengrocer's once a week, but never to the pub or the library or to the coast. He never spoke a word to anyone else, and if asked any questions, he folded in on himself and scurried home.

He never left in the afternoons or the evenings, as far as Peter could tell, though Peter had to be home before dinner so his father wouldn't become suspicious. The man must have been an early riser, though, because no matter what time of the morning

Peter made it to his spying-place, the doorstep milk had always been taken in.

The man did washing on a Wednesday, hanging out his clothes on a line at the bottom of the stairs. But never, Peter noticed, did he wash the fur stole.

The end of college came, with little complaint from Peter's father about his lack of qualifications and little complaint from his teachers that he did not sit exams. The greyness was seeping into their household and draining Peter's father of all his colour. Peter worried that it was affecting him too. He got an afternoon job and moved into a one-pound flat of his own, two flights of stairs up, behind a blue door with no glass in it at all, just three streets away from where the man lived. He took his mother's furs with him. He settled into a new routine, getting up early no matter the season, leaving his house every morning at the appropriate time, and watching the man go about his daily rounds.

One day, as winter came around and the mornings grew colder, Peter combed his hair neatly and put on his raincoat. He set off from home and headed straight to the butcher's. He arrived fifteen minutes before the man was scheduled to arrive, and he anxiously waited outside, playing with his cuffs. As the man finally turned the corner, Peter darted inside and stood staring at the prime beef and pig's knuckles. As the man slid in beside him, Peter did his best not to stare.

The butcher nodded at his fur-swaddled customer, going into the back to retrieve a pre-placed order. The man stood by the glass-covered counter, his feet twitching, and Peter could have sworn that the stole was moving, loosening and tightening itself around the man's upper arms and wide back. There was no breeze inside the shop but the fur was moving, bristling against bicep and chest. Despite himself, Peter glanced up at the man and couldn't turn away. The man felt Peter's gaze and moved further from him. The butcher returned with a paper-wrapped item, or rather, two items, their unskinned legs and dangling paws visible just beneath the edge of the paper, their long ears just visible above. The man slid two uncrumpled fivers across the counter, took the parcel underneath his fur, and left.

The next day, Peter went to the butcher's again at the same time, leaping inside as the man arrived. This time, he waited until the butcher went to fetch the rabbits, then turned to the man. He said something about the tougher meat that time of year, the smaller animals. He mentioned his own taste for the tender flesh of rabbits, stewed or barbequed. How many people wouldn't eat them, through superstition or sensitivity. The man neither responded nor ignored, but was clearly spooked by the attention. He simply stared forwards, gently trembling, and when his meat came and he paid his money, he ran out of the shop.

The man did not return to the butcher's shop. Peter assumed that his orders would be delivered from then on, and he was right.

The man stopped going out in the mornings. Peter quit his job in the afternoons to watch over the man's house, but he didn't appear then either. After a week, Peter went home, to his grey things behind his blue door, and he took his mother's furs out of the wardrobe and wore them all at once. But still Peter felt scooped out, bereft. He was missing the warmth he'd started to get from knowing that the man was there. He put the furs away and went out and spoke to people in the town, bringing the conversation around to the burly man in the orange-red fur stole, but none had seen him nor cared to speak of him. It was a bleak and cold winter in that small town, and Peter felt more alone than ever.

It turned January. Taking sandwiches, flasks of Ovaltine and all the blankets he could carry, Peter set up a den for himself in the bushes across from the man's door, hiding down in the ochre, the dead leaves, the frozen soil. He ate and drank through cracking lips, wishing for a stole of his own. As night fell, he squinted, adjusting his eyes to the dark, barely daring to blink for what he might miss.

It was after two when the man appeared. The door opened just a few inches and the man stepped out. He moved quickly, sprinting up the one set of stairs and down the road. Peter threw off his coverings and followed behind in the blackness, close enough to see, but far enough to stay undetected.

They turned one corner, then the next, then the next. The man struggled to stay silent, letting out a yap here and there, an odd sort of barking. Suddenly he tripped, fell – no. He dropped to all fours and he began to run, perfectly balanced, quicker than Peter could keep up with. The man's stole slipped from his neck and, suspended in the air, it followed behind him, resplendent and full and tipped with pure white. The man took off into the night and Peter couldn't hope to follow.

Peter was back in his bush-den when the man returned, his barking quieted, his gait once again human. In his fists were bleeding creatures, rats and such like, the fur stole safely back where it belonged, around his neck. Peter sniffed a droplet of snot back into his nose and the man whipped his head in Peter's direction. Nestled as he was and wrapped in darkness, Peter was sure he couldn't be seen. Yet the man's gaze held on him for minutes. He slowly, quietly, went down his one set of stairs and behind the orange-red door. Peter stayed there until he was sure he wouldn't be seen again, then gathered his things and bolted for home.

Peter stopped watching the door. He started making visits to his father, who was greyer and more opaque by the day, and asked the older man to show him how to sew. The old man brightened slightly, his cheeks flushing pink. For hours each day, Peter sat at the sewing machine with his father, watching how his hands worked, how the needle went into the material and fixed everything together. Peter went to the library, taking and returning book after book from the nature section. He started visiting the butcher, and taking cuts of meat he'd never bought before. Finally, Peter opened up his wardrobe and took out his mother's furs.

Three months passed by. Peter was ready.

He chose a night in March, the first fair night of the season. He took the piece that he'd worked so hard on and stepped into it. He pulled up the patchwork fur outfit around his legs and over his bottom. He wrestled his arms into the arms of the costume, feeling the scratch of the underside of material against his skin. He'd sewn a zip into the front of the one-piece so he could close it easily from the crotch to the neck. He flipped the hood over his head. The fur around Peter was not a steady red, but ranged from yellow to grey to brown to white, with flecks of orange where he could find them. The funk of old clothes was constant, but inescapable. Alongside the smell of dust and darkness was the smell of his mother.

Peter rubbed the outfit against himself, felt the warmth it brought. He turned around; it was a snug fit, but it suited him. From his buttocks hung a weight, an old stole that had been repurposed, but one that did not float in Peter's wake. Some things just cannot be faked.

Peter closed his blue door behind him and set out into the night, warm and swaddled and bathed in cold sweat. He turned the three corners to the man's street and stared down the one set of stairs. He stopped. The outfit would not be enough.

An hour later, Peter stood at the top of the stairs, breath heaving, the fur stuck to his skin with perspiration and dripping blood. His cheeks were red, his teeth bared to show what was trapped between. He held his tongue back in his mouth, so as not to rub against the damp skin of the rats, and held back a retch whenever their two tails scratched his neck. He stepped to the orange-red door and knocked firmly. The black paper was peeled back. A pause. The door opened.

The man looked at Peter. He took in his mottled pelt, the costume of a feral creature, the colour it brought. He took in the bouquet of two dead rodents between Peter's teeth, their blood running down Peter's chin, his lips drawn back in an unnatural snarl. He took in the wild eyes above the creatures, the way they looked at him. Peter said nothing, but continued to pant, standing in front of the man, asking for nothing but asking for everything.

The man pulled his lips back, tilted his head and pressed his face into Peter's. He took one of the rats in his own mouth, let the blood flow over his chin and onto his neck. The man's lips brushed Peter's. Peter felt his balance topple. The man took his hand and led him inside, and, as he did so, the man's tail fell from its hiding place around his shoulders and followed behind him, tickling the floor.

Joss Papers for Porcelain Ghosts

Eliza Chan

"Nothing followed you?" Harriet's mother said, peering up and down the corridor.

"No, Mum," Harriet replied. She looked pointedly at her suitcase, hair clammy around her forehead and neck. She hadn't slept in nearly twenty hours thanks to the baby next to her on the plane. "Can you let me in?"

She had to duck under the white banner draped above the doorway: the Chinese calligraphy done hastily, acknowledging death within, the spidery script dripping black ink downwards. Like raindrops on a car window, growing heavy as they merged. There had been so many long journeys in childhood.

Her mother finally nodded, ushering her in, notching the double locks behind her before she acknowledged her daughter. "Shoes off ah!"

Harriet was halfway to the enticing fan before shuffling back to remove her footwear. She had fallen out of the habit. Steven had been brought up in a household that only removed their shoes before bed.

"Who would be following me anyway?" she asked.

"Not who – what," her mother said over the hissing kettle from the diminutive kitchen.

Time had stood still in the last four years since Harriet had visited her por-por's flat. Or more likely, the last three decades since gong-gong had passed away. The wall of family photos had grown slightly. She recognised her daughters, Lucy and Mia from last year's Christmas card. Next to it was her own faded school photo: face beaming under thick rimmed plastic glasses and badly cut fringe. None of Steven. It was bad enough her mother moved overseas and married a gweilo, but Harriet had gone one step further and had kids with one without even stopping to marry him first.

Harriet went to the household shrine to light her joss sticks before she got told off. The imposing mahogany unit had a carved roof like a tiered pagoda and shelves underneath filled with books and knick-knacks. Por-por had brought Guanyin with her when she came to the UK. No crucifixes and hymns needed but instead food and flowers. Egg tarts, fresh fruit, and hot cups of tea were left daily. Today there was a pyramid of oranges, a large pineapple and flowers in a blue and white vase. She remembered that vase. Por-por had moved over when Harriet was nine and things started to go wrong for her parents. Slept in Harriet's bed whilst she fumed on the floor, listening to the motor of an old steam train heaving in her sleep. But to make up for it, at the Chinese supermarket, her por-por had let her choose her own chopsticks and rice bowl, even pick the vase for Guanyin's flowers that her gran took back to Hong Kong nearly a year later. There were plenty of vases in China, but only one that had been handpicked by her granddaughter, she had explained. And so they had to visit, Harriet and her mother, to check in on por-por, on the vase and on the goddess.

The statue was covered with a cloth, and Harriet was about to remove it when her mother came from the tiny kitchen with a screech. "What are you doing? Don't touch that!"

Harriet flinched like she had been slapped, her nerves shot through. Her hand jumped back and knocked the vase over. She watched it teeter on the narrow base, water slopping from the brim as if she was not even there, a spirit without any means to stop it. When it smashed on the tiled floor, Harriet felt an odd sense of relief.

"Aiyah," her mother said, crouching to pick up the shards.

"Sorry, I'm… tired I guess. But why is Guanyin covered?"

Harriet said.

"It's bad luck for the gods to see leh… because of por-por." Her mother had already cleaned it up, like there had been no mess in the first place. She snatched the joss sticks from Harriet, shaking her head as if she had been brandishing a knife. Returned to folding the heap of laundry. She held up a beige polo shirt. "How about this one for tomorrow?" her mother asked, staring past Harriet.

Harriet turned to look behind her, but it was only por-por's empty chair in front of the TV. Two strokes in the last year and a stubborn refusal to move into a nursing home. Her mother had flown over to Hong Kong six months ago, their roles now reversed. A phone call at one in the morning, her mother's voice robotic as she told her it was too late. Por-por had gone. No, she didn't need to come, it's fine. Harriet felt a hollow guilt in her stomach that had nothing to do with the tepid aeroplane meal or jetlag. She had been going to visit, she had always planned to. All through late primary and into high school, she and her mother visited every year. Then Harriet had wanted to try something new: a girls' holiday in Spain, a European break with a boyfriend. She was studying, she was working, she was saving… Mia happened. Lucy a year later. And Harriet never knew what to say to por-por over the phone with her broken Cantonese. Could never find the time, putting it on the back burner along with decorating the spare bedroom and learning Spanish.

Her mother looked at her – pouring Harriet a mug of boiling hot water from a thermos – exactly what she wanted in the local humidity. She bit back her complaint, blowing until the heat steamed up her glasses and she drank it down in thirsty sips.

"I told you not to come," her mother said, the laundry now in one tidy pile. Her hands couldn't keep still. Wiping one spot on the coffee table over and over.

"It's okay. Steven's parents said they'll help. He can survive for a week," Harriet said, reaching to squeeze her mother's arm. "I wanted to be here for you."

"Hai ah, hai ah. There's so much to do. Your uncles and auntie are arriving tomorrow, we need to meet with the monk and…"

"Mum, let me help," Harriet said. "What can I do?"

Her mother patted her hand. "I don't think you will understand."

Harriet bristled with the defensive spikes of every "gweipor" snigger from shop assistants; every Chinese New Year greeting she stumbled and faltered over on the phone as a chorus of relatives lined up to correct her intonation; every look of pity when she asked for the English menu. Her arm stiffened beneath her mother's touch. "I can help," she insisted.

"Hor ah, you want to help. Look after your por-por," her mum said.

Harriet heard the laughter from next door's TV through the wall in the silence that followed. "What?" she said finally. The happy jingle of an advert was playing now from the unseen TV, the low tones of the narrator droning under Harriet's skin.

Her mother pointed at the small dining table. Only then did Harriet notice that her por-por's place was still set, chopsticks, spoon and all. Her favourite cushion was plumped up and her purple buttoned vest draped over the chairback. "We still have to look after her wor."

She was getting delirious with the lack of sleep. There were only two beds in the flat and these went to the elder uncles and their wives. Harriet had offered to book a hotel but no, her mother said firmly, if she was here now, she would stay with family. Space was tight and privacy lacking. She slept on the unpadded wooden bench that was her grandmother's sofa, above the ratchetting snores of her mother and auntie on an airbed below. Ornate dragon clawed handles may be beautiful to look at, but they did nothing pushed against her forehead as she tried to stretch and turn on the narrow seat. And when she woke, she saw things in every shadow: a man at the dinner table, hunched over a bowl of soup; a woman's shoulder just visible beyond the open bedroom door; a head glaring at her from the shrine ledge.

"Haven't you seen her yet? She probably doesn't forgive you," Uncle Lei said. He had seen por-por this morning. At five in the morning when he woke to go for tai chi in the park, he had seen her. Uncle Lei was rather pleased with himself since the others had all seen por-por already and he was sick of being lumped with Harriet. He had been heading out of the door when he felt someone touching his shoulder like she used to do before giving him a lecture. And when he turned, he saw something, just out of the corner of his eye, for a second. Her ghost.

Auntie Pui-Ling decided it was high time to tell her story again, because she hadn't repeated it in the last three hours. She had shut the kitchen door, definitely, because of the oil smells she always shut the kitchen door, but it opened, completely by itself! That was definitely por-por. Por-por didn't approve of spring onion pancakes when auntie was supposedly losing weight. So they put the stack onto por-por's plate instead and the whole family yammered encouragingly to the empty chair, telling her spirit to enjoy them whilst they were still hot.

Her mum opened the window and turned off the air conditioning because por-por had scolded her about the waste of money. Uncle Freddie bought salted fish for dinner because of a whisper in his ear she was craving it.

It was no good talking about coincidences and delusions. Harriet had tried that, but they just shook their heads at her, sad at her disbelief. It had to be Steven. He hadn't even paid for dinner that time he came to Hong Kong and he even had the audacity to cross chopsticks with por-por. Didn't show her any face, no respect for his elders! And living in sin with Harriet: she was in the bad books, the only logical explanation why she hadn't seen por-por's ghost.

Harriet had to excuse herself from the dinner table, pretending to look at her phone with her back to them. She stared at a vase of flowers. The blue floral motif looked like frilly lion heads, recurring in a spotty pattern that reminded her with a pang of potato printing with her own daughters. Wondered if Steven would remember their ballet lessons and drive with the noise of insistent singalongs from the backseat. Lucy would be louder to make up for her lack of tone, glancing at her older sister and copying every mannerism she could see. Tapping out a short message, Harriet noticed something moving out of the corner of her eye.

Gwei

She froze, resisting the urge to look. Her relatives were yammering in Cantonese, gossiping about her as if the language barrier would be enough to hide the conversation. She tried to tune out, easy enough with her limited language skills. Still, she could not ignore the pointed looks her Uncle Lei threw her, the gesticulating chopsticks, that whatever she had done, they disapproved. Her mother's face was a mirror to the stern door god at the entrance of the apartment block. She spooned some fish atop por-por's untouched white mound of rice, her silence blacker than a starless night.

Gwei ar

This time the voices were closer. Whispers that breathed lightly on her arm like limp mosquitoes. Her eyes strained with the effort of keeping them still, calmly focused on her phone. The words she had typed blurred and migrated across the screen as if tipping out of the corner. She would not succumb to the suffocating hysteria in the room. No matter the jetlag, the migraines pushing at her temples, she was not that person.

Gwei ar, gwei ar, gwei ar

Very slowly, she inched her eyes up from her phone. Past the bowl of oranges, the spiked stems of burnt out joss sticks like needles in a pin cushion, past the screaming faces on the flower vase and up to the…

Harriet looked at the vase again. Chrysanthemum heads, that's all they were, chrysanthemum blooms. But she had smashed that vase. The one she had chosen when her parents had been screaming the house down at each other. The one her por-por had nodded at, the language of hand gestures and folding paper cranes; the chicken drumstick fresh from the chopping board for a hungry stomach; a warm hand towel rubbing her face clean of tears.

The open-mouthed ghouls looked back. Mouthed the taunt at her.

Gwei ar

"Lei, that's enough," her mother's voice cut through. "Steven is Harriet's partner, lah."

"Gweilo don't know how to do a hard day's work. All they do is complain and give up!"

"You talking about Harriet's father?"

Auntie Pui-Ling pretended to spit on the floor, cursing loudly. "Don't you bring up that sei gweilo! He divorced you as soon as there was trouble."

"That's enough. He's still Harriet's father."

"Deem ar? Look at her? Her Cantonese is rubbish and she had kids without getting married! What side of the family do you think she picked that up from?"

She was nine years old again, a tug of war rope in a game with only one possible outcome. Harriet dropped her phone, the corner smacking off the tiled floor and cracking the screen. The table of relatives erupted in a fuss of advice and condolences, the argument forgotten.

She was coaxed back to the table, almost at the plastic stool, when she remembered the faces. Harriet turned, glaring towards the shrine in defiance of any mocking screams. The vase was gone.

"What's wrong ar?" Uncle Freddie asked.

"Did you see something, did you see *her*? The gwei?" said her auntie.

"No, I... it's nothing," Harriet replied, swallowing hard.

Harriet had burned joss papers in the barbeque pit with her por-por when she was younger. It had been fun, rolling up the gold sheets and tucking in the corners to resemble the boat-like gold ingots. She would fan out the joss paper notes with their multiple zeroes, money for the afterlife, and throw it onto the fire. And would it just appear in the afterlife on someone's lap, in their spirit bank account or raining from the sky? The details were never very clear, even when por-por tried to explain.

But the scale of things was different here. The street was full of religious goods shops, the smell of sandalwood pungent in the air from the bundles of joss sticks. Paper signs in red and gold for double happiness, studying, health and everything in between, decorated the walls between each small shop, advertising their wares on every available space. It was chaotic on the surface, piles and heaps of goods spilling from shopfronts onto the pavement. But there was pride in it. Cardboard lined the ground and cellophane covered delicate items. One shopkeeper was cleaning with a dog-eared feather duster and another wiping each statue's face.

An elaborate papier-mâché house – a doll's house her Mia would've wanted – sat on a low table: candy floss pink over three floors with a balcony, twin turrets and external columns. Next to it, but not on the same scale, were card and paper TVs, smartphones, a hot tub, mahjong table, massage chair and tea set. Child-sized cars lined streets outside the next shop: Porsches, BMWs and Audis with lucky license plate numbers of 18s and 88s. Cardboard handbags and shoes, perfumes and make up sets, gold and diamond watches and banquet meals: all boxy facsimiles but as good as the counterfeits in the market.

If she didn't know why they were here, she might have

presumed they were Christmas shopping for kids.

"Is this all for burning?" Harriet asked her mother incredulously.

"Yes, I have a list of things your por-por definitely wanted, but you can choose the extras. A few nice outfits, some jewellery. Not the cheap stuff leh, I want to treat her," her mother said.

The row of red-faced Guan Yu statues watched Harriet as she drifted over, her mother's words rattling inside her head. Treat her? Not the cheap stuff? She looked down and sure enough, there was a price difference between the cardboard watch sets dependent on brand. Her voice broke in a sharp laugh. Great – days of insomnia, an upset stomach due to change in diet, not to mention washing herself with buckets of tepid water because her relatives had used up all the hot water – had rendered her into a hysterical madwoman.

The old woman dusting looked at her suspiciously, moving forward. "You Chinese?" she said in way of a greeting.

"My mother's from Hong Kong, my father's British," Harriet responded in Cantonese, the phrase so often repeated that it was etched into her skull.

"Oh, half, you're a *half* wor!" she pronounced. Harriet grimaced and closed her eyes. No matter what side of the world she was on, people always thought this was the best way to describe her. Like a made-to-order pizza, split down the middle and dissected: the liver and left kidney for England, the stomach definitely Chinese, lactose-intolerance and all.

Harriet smiled through gritted teeth and moved on. Down the street, drawn towards the shop with ceramics. A whole two shelves were blue and white porcelain: vases with round bellies like a laughing Buddha, others tall necked like thin saplings, ones with a nipped-in waist, lidded jars and tiny teacups that could only be held with finger and thumb. They were patterned with dragon and phoenix pairs, willowy fairy ladies and plum blossom branches. Her eyes roved, looking for one with a pattern like the one she had broken.

There had been flower heads on it, small petals connected by curved stems that she remembered tracing with a finger. She would start at the top of the vase and see if she could make one unbroken trail to the bottom. If she could, if she could manage it, then everything would be okay. Mum and dad would get back together, she wouldn't have to go to Chinese lessons anymore and her por-por could be a normal gran who made roast chicken rather than chicken feet for tea. As long as she could make a line – it would be true.

Three rows deep, she saw a vase with a familiar shape. The light did not quite penetrate between the shelves but she felt it in her bones, calling to her. Carefully she began to move the other porcelain to one side, the bases scraping on the metal shelving as she inched them away. Her fingers could just about touch the cool surface. See the shadow of a pattern.

The darker patches weren't quite the flower heads she had thought. Clouds? She turned the vase with one outstretched finger. Turned and saw it now. A face. A decapitated head lolling on the shelf.

"Shit!" Harriet said, jumping back.

"What are you doing?" the stall holder shouted, sandals slapping down the aisle. "You break, you pay!"

"No, no, I just saw…" Harriet shivered and looked back. Nothing but dust.

"Gwei? You see a ghost?" he asked, crouching beside her. Harriet shone her phone light left and right, but there was no third row of porcelain, just some cardboard boxes and empty space.

"No!" Harriet said, the negative burning her mouth. She saw the faces of her disappointed uncles and aunties lingering in the air. Then there was just the face of the exasperated stall holder, arms folded as he yelled at her to stop wasting his time. "Chi seen gweipor!"

They stopped for soup noodles and fishballs. The server waited for them impatiently, tapping her pencil on the table as Harriet's mum translated as much of the menu as she could from the peeling signs on the walls. The cook stared from behind his glass prison, steam wafting up as he pulled off the lid from a vat of soup and shook handfuls of noodles into wire baskets. Roasted ducks and strips of marinated meat were displayed like a hanging.

"Wonton noodles," Harriet decided finally.

"I translated all of that and you *still* pick wonton?" her mum said, frowning. "This place has stewed tripe!"

"No way," Harriet said. "Besides, I like wonton noodles. They remind me of childhood. And por-por…"

Her mum relented, ordering for them both as the server repeated the order in a loud bark to the cook and threw two cups of lukewarm tea down on the table.

Por-por had made pork and prawn wonton. Taught her how to squeeze the little yellow squares into parcels and watch them bob on the surface of the hot water. And she remembered trailing water around the table with her finger unnoticed as everyone's attention was on her father, two bulging suitcases and a door, not slammed as expected, but politely and firmly closed behind him. His house keys still on the breakfast bar next to her elbow. How will he get back home? How will he get in when we are asleep? Harriet had asked and asked, following her mother around with the questions that rolled into her head and could not be ignored, like a small stone in her shoe, rattling and jagged no matter where she went. Por-por had made Harriet a distracting bowl of noodles and let her eat them with a fork. Come home, come home, what's left for you here, por-por had said. I'll look after Harriet, she won't be a burden to you. We can teach her how to be Chinese. Soft but persistent, the message continued through the remaining months of her stay.

Harriet looked around the place, distracting herself from the tight lump forming in her throat. The old man in the corner had a simple plate of choi sum and was enjoying an unwieldy newspaper, folding and tucking it down to size so that he could bring it close to his face as he was reading. The aunties were washing the chopsticks in hot water, each shouting over each other about their sons' school grades. And there was also a young family sharing two portions of ho fun between four bowls.

It could be normal for her, easy if she knew just a little bit more of the language, the culture, the people. Instead, it was like she was on a rickety old lightbus, hurtling through the Hong Kong streets and being dazed by the neon lights, but never stopping long enough for her to orientate herself.

"Have you seen her?" her mum asked.

"Her?"

"Por-por."

"Not this again," Harriet said, burying her hands in her hair.

"You didn't want to see the body. This is the best way to say goodbye!" her mother insisted.

"I'm not a child," Harriet replied. "You can't just make up stories about river dragons and a rabbit on the moon. You can't honestly tell me you've seen her ghost. A real gwei."

"Does it matter?"

"Of course it matters."

"Uncle Lei is talking about something other than the money he lent Uncle Freddie two years ago. Auntie Pui-Ling has not criticized my weight once whilst she's been here. We remember your por-por together, that's what's important."

Before Harriet could respond, their conversation was interrupted by the server dumping the two bowls of soup noodles. Harriet stuck her finger in the puddle of spilt water. She didn't know what to say. A reflection of the bowl blurred as she trailed a track through the liquid as she had done as a child. The angry child with no clear outlet for her grievances other than a mother who wasn't like all the other mums at the school gate.

"It's different for me. It will always be different," Harriet said. Her chopsticks had twisted themselves up a little, crossing over in the way that por-por would have scolded her for.

"Only if you let it be," her mother said.

The blue and white border on her soup bowl was inching very slowly around the rim. Hiding from her. Harriet turned it, hot broth scalding her hand although the pain barely registered. Ornate symmetrical patterns swirled before her, just out of focus as she turned and turned to follow the blasted thing, the mocking laugh just around the corner. Chasing it, head down near the table, following the trail.

"Harriet?"

The eyes looked frightened, por-por's eyes, hiding from her around the next curve.

"Harriet!" her mother said, grabbing her arm. "What are you doing? Can you see her?"

Harriet released her hold on the bowl, suddenly aware the other people were looking at her, whispering that ubiquitous word under their breaths.

Gwei

"No, I can't see anything."

"See lah," her mother said.

"That's your thumb obscuring the camera lens," Harriet said, glancing at the photo.

"No, that's your por-por's spirit wor. We need to help her cross over to the other side," she said adamantly. It was hard to argue when she and all the other close relatives were wearing the traditional funeral clothes Harriet had only seen in TV dramas. A bandana across her forehead and a shapeless white tunic. They were in por-por's village for the funeral, at the old family home that Uncle Lei had inherited. It was like a different country out here in the rural dust, the houses large and sprawling compared to the boxroom flat they had been staying in.

"Okay, okay. Tell me what I need to do," Harriet said.

"Here's the thing," her mother said, suddenly dropping her gaze and finding her jade bangle very interesting. "You aren't actually allowed to do the ceremony."

"What?" Harriet said. Her voice came out shriller than intended. They had been up all night making dish after dish in the sweltering kitchen for por-por's afterlife feast. Lack of sleep had worn her patience to nothing. Her vision pushed in a little at the edges, pressing on her temples.

"The monk said so."

"Because I'm half?"

"No lah, because you aren't married," her mother said.

"How is that better?" Harriet heard herself snap. She took a deep breath.

Her mother sighed, shrugging her narrow shoulders. "Your por-por's spirit might be jealous, might want to come back. And... an unmarried woman is easier to possess."

"And if I was married, I'd *belong* to someone else, you mean?" Harriet said pointedly.

"Look, I don't make the rules! Best not to risk it lor. You can stay out here and burn the joss papers."

"It's just stupid. Stupid superstitious nonsense, and you know it!"

"This is part of *your* culture. Chinese tradition."

"Only fifty percent," she said. The words lingered in the humidity between them.

Only the cicadas broke the prevailing silence. Her mother made a strangled sound of frustration and turned to join the other aunties and uncles around the trefoil coffin. Uncle Lei whispered urgently to her, rolling his eyes a little. Harriet knew exactly what he would be saying. *Gwei. Gweipor, gwei sing.* Like chattering pigeons peck, peck, pecking at her. Harriet thought about leaving. She imagined the whole process in her mind's eye: getting a taxi, picking up her passport, buying an earlier ticket home. But her feet remained firmly planted, her limbs refusing to leave the shade of the trees.

The funeral started, the Buddhist monk leading in low stylized Cantonese that could have been Russian for all Harriet recognised. Her uncle's shoulders were shaking and for a moment Harriet was going to call out, scared he was having a fit. But then his wife starting weeping loudly, like she was wringing the tears from a face cloth. Soon everyone was crying, howling wails and ugly hiccuping sobs filled with bubbles of snot smeared on cuff sleeves. Only her mother was silent. Her eyes were wet, but her fists tightly pressed to her sides and she kept her lips pressed firmly together. Harriet remembered now where she had seen that expression before, the night por-por had finally left the UK.

The monk told them to turn away, not to look lest the hungry spirit seek solace in a still warm body. Harriet looked instead at the trees behind the house. From low hanging branches dripped heavy roots, fingers digging down into the earth. The aerial roots swayed like curtains, the darkness between the forming shapes. It pulled at her, dragging her down with it as she heard them lower the coffin into the ground. She swayed forward, stumbling as she pinched herself on the inner arm to stay awake. The smell of incense, ripe fruit and the dishes they had cooked mingled in the growing heat, the heady concoction swirling in Harriet's sinuses. She dragged her glance away from the shifting tree, from the faces she could see watching her there, and stared instead at the backs of heads.

They started burning the bigger items in a huge bonfire. The joss papers caught fire, bright flashes of light before withering into grey soot. Ash rose, dancing coyly into the air above the large burner before tumbling like first snowfall into her hair and eyes. After the third cardboard flatscreen TV, Harriet began to wonder which room por-por would put it in, and if her afterlife mansion had enough plug sockets. The threads began to unravel the more she considered it: glasses, a toothbrush and traditional Chinese medicines. Did ghosts need a safe for valuables? Banks? For a woman who had lived plainly in life, por-por's funeral offerings were decadent beyond reason. There were piles of paper notes to burn, skyscraper columns like the harbour skyline, and they had to be burned as individual sheets. After a while, Harriet's admiration of the handiwork, her morbid curiosity, gave way to numb reflex and her hands fed things into the flames with the barest of recognitions.

With a sense of inevitability, Harriet looked for the blue and white among the piles of cardboard. The more they burned, the more she could feel its baleful gaze. Eyes had winked at her but disappeared when she turned to look. Among the clothing sets, a wide smile snapped shut when she grabbed it, holding only a joss paper handbag. But when she finally found it, the faces on the vase stared straight back at her. Deep blue eyes, one bigger than the other, held her gaze as they drooped on the surface of the cardboard. One, no two, three of them, drifting downwards with absurd crescent moon smiles as if to ooze onto her feet. She dropped it, flinching as if the flames were already alight.

"Harriet?" her mum asked, suddenly at her side. "Did you see something?"

"Ghosts aren't real," Harriet whispered. The paper vase was just flowers and leaves. And there was a body burning on the pyre. A woman with preposterously pink skin in a simple cheongsam, her skin blistering in the heat and peeling off in layers. "Tell me you see that," she said softly.

"That's just a paper servant," her mother said.

Harriet started laughing. Unrestrained laughter punctuated by exhaustion, tears rolling down her cheeks as she continued. Laughing at the absurdity, the heat, the isolation she had felt as soon as her plane had landed. Faces. All she could see were faces, uniform in their difference from her own.

"I'm glad she wasn't crying in the ceremony like that," Auntie

Pui-Ling said. "You'd be fired as a professional mourner for that performance!" They had emerged now, her aunties and uncles in the white garb, surrounding her like clucking hens.

"I can see her," Harriet finally admitted to no-one in particular. She wasn't talking about the body burning in the fire. That was no more than paper and card like the rest. She meant the real ghost. The one who pulled the blanket over her shoulder after she had cried herself to sleep. That had sent her letters she could not read and never had the energy to decipher. That hung her photo on the centre of the wall, in the biggest frame. That had kept every childhood gift she had sent on the shelf just below Guanyin's shrine.

Harriet picked up the paper vase, meeting the eyes of the faces.

"Yes," her mother said. And a press of bodies surrounded her, bony shoulders and soft limbs pushed in close. Comforting.

Harriet rubbed her eyes, stinging from the tears and the smoke. When she looked up, the courtyard had changed. Gone was the bonfire, the relatives, the noise. Her vision was unclear, like gazing through a crack in the door. Stacks of gold ingots were laid out like bamboo steamers on top of each other. Two lines of servants formed a path in front of her, each with a tray before them: tea and rambutan and tongyuan all on offer. Harriet moved forward towards the mansion at the end. It had jade green dragon-spine ridges and flying eaves curving upwards. The cars they had burned were parked outside, with the showroom gleam on their bonnets.

The pink sky rained with fluttering bank notes like snow and Harriet reached out to catch them. The money was warm to the touch and smoky, some still singed with holes that mended themselves before her eyes. Inside the house, half a sofa was forming, and a small dog bounded across the polished tile floor. And there, in the kitchen, looking through the cupboards was a familiar figure, bent over and making pleased sounds under her voice.

"Por-por?" Harriet said. She reached out. A vase, blue and white porcelain, appeared in her hands.

"Por-por?" she repeated.

The old woman turned.

Harriet blinked, suddenly facing the bonfire, her eyes smarting. The joss paper vase watched her from the ground where she had dropped it. The chrysanthemum flowers had por-por's eyes. Her mother stood beside her, the soothing weight of her presence giving Harriet a certain calmness.

She placed the vase within the flames.

The Fisher

Melanie Harding-Shaw

It was Wednesday and a man was standing on a small rock jutting out of the ocean a few metres from the beach in Oriental Bay. He had a fishing rod in his hands and an old paint bucket by his side for when his luck found him. He was wearing a tatty blue and purple jacket that looked like it wouldn't keep the water out at all.

Neil disguised himself in his wife's old jacket and came down to the beach to fish one day every second month. His wife thought he was at work and his workmates thought he was at home. The stresses of both were lost in the noise of the waves crashing and the anticipation of success. At the end of the day, he would take his catch to a local homeless shelter, change back into his suit and go home for dinner.

His wife was grateful that he came home early every once in a while. They were more like flatmates than husband and wife these days. She would try not to start up old arguments that day, although her mind couldn't help but save them up for the next. Maybe this was the Wednesday she would bring up having children again. Surely a child would close the gap that had grown between them.

In two months' time, his wife would go for a walk along the beach and see him standing on a rock fishing. She would feel betrayed, but at least they would have something new to talk about.

Jack lost his job three months ago, right around the time his fourth child was born. He'd suffered a brain injury at work and never gone back. His jacket came from the free bin outside a thrift store and his hands ached from the cold. He walked an hour to the beach to fish every day. His wife was breastfeeding and needed the protein. He'd heard fish oil could help with depression. Sometimes he thought if he ate fish one more time he would scream.

Each night as he walked up to his front door, he wondered if his family would still be there to greet him. His wife was exhausted and kept asking him to stay home and help. She glanced sideways at Jack as they sat on the couch watching tv, but only when she thought he wouldn't notice. She wondered if he would ever be the man he used to be.

That Wednesday, she took the kids down to the beach to see him. They dug for pipis in the sand and pestered their dad to sing. She rolled her sweatpants up and waded to his rock in the ocean to take his hand.

"Come on. Let's go home," she said.

Steve's Grandmother taught him about kai moana, the foods from the sea, when he was a little boy. Her tangi was two weeks ago. He had not been home for years and he cried almost as much for the memories he had lost as for her death.

He'd called in sick from his city job to stand on that rock and fish. It was a different ocean to the one at home, but if he closed his eyes the sounds of the waves and gulls calling started to restore his memories. He hadn't worn the jacket in ten years. Even all these years later it still smelled of teenage angst. Its scent mixed with the smells of bait and seaweed to make him feel slightly ill. That brought memories back too.

His boyfriend was reading a book further up the beach, wrapped in the red picnic blanket they always carried in the boot of their car. When Steve grew tired of standing on the rock, he waded back to shore and sat with him. He told him about the fragments of his childhood on a wild coastline that had returned to him, and his boyfriend added his own. They had never realised they had this in common.

Two years later, Steve would propose at that same spot and six months after that they would exchange vows and rings with the sea breeze blowing around them. The rock sticking out of the ocean was just big enough for two men to stand with arms wrapped around each other, smiling into the wide-angle lens that would capture all 180 degrees of memory-restoring ocean.

Poseidon was far from home and searching for his lost trident. He was hoping if he stood out of the water in disguise that Tangaroa would not notice his encroachment in this ocean. Who would think a God would wear such a tatty jacket?

He had followed the trail of earthquakes up New Zealand from Christchurch, through to Hurunui and Kaikōura. Now he stood on a rock in Wellington harbour hoping he could get the trident back before the next earthquake struck. He wasn't against earthquakes generally, unless someone made them happen with his stolen property. He didn't know who had stolen the trident. It could be Tangaroa for all he knew, but he hoped it wasn't. That would be awkward.

As he stood there fishing, the rod bent and he started reeling in the line. His muscles strained and his eyes narrowed as he realised whoever was holding the trident might be as strong as he was. He'd been reeling for 10 minutes when he felt a tremor travel through the rock underneath him. He looked across the harbour just as the pier in the main business district crumbled into the ocean.

"Fuck," he said, and started reeling faster. The water around him receded out into Cook Strait, leaving him stranded on a rock surrounded by sand. He could feel the ocean preparing to lever itself up to flood the city quays lined with high-rise buildings. A tsunami-warning siren wailed in the distance.

He sighed in frustration. He may as well make the most of it, though. He fashioned himself a surfboard from the sands around him, melding it into golden glass. Then he rode the 20-foot waves into the city as if it had been his idea all along.

Kate lies on a smooth hard surface. The man, the fishing rod and the bucket aren't even real. They are just a virtual construct created for a woman who yearns for the days when the oceans were full of life; days she hadn't been alive to see.

Does the jacket have special meaning to her? Perhaps it came from researching her family history. Or perhaps it was just made up by the author of the construct to give authenticity to an environment he had never experienced. Just another line of code.

The ocean and the sky start to flicker and then disappear. Kate sits up in a room with plain white walls, ceiling, and floor, and pulls off her headset.

"I wasn't finished. I didn't even see a fish," she yells to the empty room. "And why the hell did you make me a man?"

Only static comes from the room's hidden speakers. The door opens to tell her it is time to leave.

"Bloody budget VR companies," she mutters as she returns to her apartment.

It won't stop her coming back month after month though, spending her savings to search a virtual construct for anything that might make her life more real.

Jeremy lies in a hospital somewhere. The scene at the beach is part of a years-long timeline that plays through his head in the hours between when he loses consciousness and when he regains it.

He stands on the rock with his son, teaching him how to fish. It was a spur-of-the-moment trip. He'd grabbed the jacket from a bag of old clothes they had cleared from his mother's house after she died. He should have taken it to the dump months ago, but he couldn't bring himself to throw it away. They only stay ten minutes before the cold gets to be too much and he piggy-backs his son to the shore.

In a few hours, he will wake in the hospital to find he has never had any children. He will stifle his great heaving sobs in his pillow until his chest aches and he is dizzy from lack of air. One of the nurses will find him sobbing and hold him tight to her, even though she knows she shouldn't.

Their first child will be a boy. Jeremy's mother will come to stay for three weeks when he's born. She will snuggle the baby close under her jacket to protect him from the wind when they take him for his first trip to the beach.

It was Wednesday and a man was standing on a small rock jutting out of the ocean wearing a tatty blue and purple jacket that looked like it wouldn't keep the water out at all.

Canst Thou Draw Out the Leviathan

Christopher Caldwell

John Wood boarded the *Gracie-Ella* ahead of the crew. He carried his sea chest on his shoulder. In a satchel slung low on his hip were his tools and the three things most precious to him: a lock of his grandmother's hair, a shaving from the first cabinet he had built as a boy, and his freedom papers. No light but the moon, but John could walk the length of the *Gracie-Ella's* decks eyes closed and barefoot without placing a wrong stop. She was named for the daughters of two men who held her title, and at sea she belonged to the captain, but John reflected that she was his as much as anyone's; his hands had shaped her and healed her, cosseted her and kept her afloat. He ducked down below decks. In the dark he made his way midship to a space he and the cooper shared. The smell of sawdust and resin was a comfort. A few strikes of a flint and the lantern overhanging his workspace was alight. John set about arranging his tools. The work here was sweet. He ran his hand over words he had carved on the underside of the vice-bench. "I hereby manumit & set free John Wood. He may go wheresoever he pleases."

The sixth night out from Nantucket, John woke to find William Harker looming over him in the darkness. John sat bolt upright in his hammock. William put a calloused finger to John's lips. William's voice was silky. "I've been thinking it's been a mighty long time since I've been ashore. Man can develop a thirst."

John groaned, half in anticipated pleasure, half in exhaustion. "Not even a week yet. Ain't your wenching last you a fortnight?"

William bent close to his ear. John could smell salt, armpits, ass. William's breath was hot on his cheek. "T'aint wenches I'm after. I was hoping the ship's carpenter might lend us some wood." William put one big, scarred hand on John's crotch.

John felt himself stir in response. "Captain'll make you kiss his daughter if I'm too ill-rested to swing my hammer come daybreak."

William put his other hand on John's neck. "My harpoon will be all the keener for it, and I can give you practice with your hammer."

John sighed. "Best get on with it. It's summer and the night's nowhere near long enough." He slid out of his hammock and led the big harpooner by the wrist from steerage towards the foretween decks.

John shoved William against the bulkhead and fumbled with his breeches. For all his talk of rest, John was every bit as eager. In the darkness, he traced William's form with deft, curious hands. The body was familiar: the taut belly, the ropey scar high on one hip. He found William's mouth with his own, hungry and biting. They rocked as the ship rocked. John felt the crest of a wave, and in its deep trough heard William cry out. Warm, sticky wetness splashed against his thigh. Slick and sweaty, the two men clung to each other. William whispered, "I'll make you pretty baubles from the bone of the next whale I kill. I'll spend my lay to bring you spices and silks. I'll –"

Light pierced their quiet darkness. John saw the earnestness in William's eyes, before William shoved him away and pulled up his breeches, slipping back the way he came.

John shaded his eyes. Pip, one of the cabin boys, walked past wide-eyed towards the forecastle with a stinking little lantern and a beaten tin cup. If he took any notice of John near naked and smelling of sweat and spunk, no sign of it showed on his dark, intense face. John laced up his breeches and followed after.

"Hoy there, Pip."

The boy spooked. "Hoy, sir."

John laughed. "Ain't no one never called me sir. And you ain't 'bout to start. Name's John, or John Wood if you have to keep formal. Bought my own freedom, and I won't let you give me yours."

The boy gave him an owlish look. "Hoy, John Wood. Never bought my freedom. I suppose I might have stolen it."

John clapped Pip on the back. He pointed with his chin at the tin cup. "What's that, boy?"

"Corn meal." Pip pinched his lips together. "I ain't steal it. Cookie gave it me."

"A nobbin-hearted old skinflint like Cookie gave you near a half cup of it? You must got more charm than I know."

The boy cradled the cup close to his narrow chest. His eyes were wide. "La Sirene knows ways to soften the hearts of men."

John ruffled the boy's hair, as coarse and kinky as his own. "What you doing with that this time of night?"

"Watch."

John watched in the flickering lamplight as the boy wet a finger with his tongue and traced with precision a little boat on the deck. Pip finished his drawing by writing a word strange to John, "Immamou."

John said, "I learnt my letters soon's I got my manumission papers, but what's that word for?"

Pip said, "Protection."

John laughed. "I don't know about that. Ain't no charm against the captain if he catches you sleep on first watch. Get to bed, boy."

Pip blew out the lantern.

Two more days out and early morning John was dumping wood shavings into the cold furnaces of the try works when he heard a foremast hand's thin voice cry from the hoops, "She blows! There she blows! A cachalot!"

The Captain roared, "A sperm whale, aye? Where boy, be

quick? She alone?"

"Leeward, Captain! One spray. No more'n a league out!"

"To the boats, boys!" The Captain cracked a rare smile. "Mr. Wood! You keep my ship in order."

John looked among the bodies scrambling over the deck for the other shipkeepers, Cookie, the cooper, the blacksmith, and the steward. He saw they were all awake and above-deck. "Captain sir, all's ready for your return."

The Captain beckoned at the Kanakan harpooner named To'afa, whom everyone called Gospel. With measured speed, they headed to the first whaleboat, four crewmen in tow.

William ran to the third whaleboat swinging from its davit, his boatkeeper, the portly second mate, close on the lean, blond harpooner's heels. William looked back at John once and shouted, "I've not forgot me words to you."

The Captain's boat launched first, and the boat with William soon splashed down after.

John heard the Captain cry out, "Take care, you louts, any of you gally this whale and she sounds, I'll stripe you with nine lashes!"

Four whaleboats set out leeward after the whale. John stood for a moment at the railing midship watching them row, each boatkeeper urging their crew on faster in low growls. Cookie stood at John's shoulder. He spat a thick gob of phlegm over the side. Cookie sucked at his gums. "Whale brains the night instead of salt horse."

The sun was high when John first heard the crew again. Echoing over the waters, rough voices sang obscenely about the ladies of Cuba before the first of the whaleboats came into view. Towed behind them by the fluke was the carcass of a sperm whale nearly half as long as the *Gracie-Ella* herself.

John yelled for Pip to attend the returning crew. The ship pitched and listed as they lashed the massive beast starboard for

Best of British Fantasy 2019

the cutting in.

The crew were wet and boisterous, although, to John's eyes, tired and the worse for wear. William's whaleboat was the first. The second mate's face was red. "Grog!" He shouted. "Grog for the harpooner!"

Pip ran over with a tin cup full of drink slopping over the edges. William took it from him with both hands and drained it in a single pull. He looked over at John. "That old bull was meaner than my granny, but I keep me promises."

The Captain supported one of his rowers around the shoulder. John ran to help. Ethan, his name was. John knew him to be a serious, quiet boy from Pennsylvania. His thin, white arm was bent at a ruinous angle. He slumped into John's arms, his face grey. John thought Ethan would have need of his saw. The boy whimpered. John looked to the Captain. "He well?"

"Struck by the blow of a fluke. Plenty of grog and full barrels of parmacety will help him forget, I reckon. Time he comes to collect his lay, he'll be smiles again."

John half-carried the boy down into the darkness of the forecastle. He lifted him into his hammock, the boy yelping and shuddering. Ethan's eyes were large and tearful, but John knew he was needed on deck to erect the cutting stage. He stroked the boy's hand. "I'll send the Steward to come look after you."

The sun was low to water when John, stinking and calloused, hammered the last plank of the cutting stage into place. The hands' voices were hoarse with hours of filthy shanties – Gospel abstaining. The whale was held fast to the *Gracie-Ella* with great chains. John remembered the injured boy, but knew the Captain would see pulling an able worker away to tend to Ethan as coddling. Every hand was turned to cutting in the whale. The harpooners peeled its skin in spiralling strips known as blankets with long-handled cutting spades. Each blanket piece was so heavy it took John and six others to haul it up. Men already sore and tired with rowing and killing chopped those pieces into smaller sections, to be yet again minced into paper-thin slices known as bible leaves.

William was back in the water with a monkey-rope tied around his waist, passing up buckets full of spermaceti to the two cabin boys, who ran the pearl-colored waxy substance over to barrels, which when full, were hammered shut and sealed under the watch of the cooper. The deck was red and slick with blood. On one of his last passes, Pip slipped in the gore and fell on his back. John tossed a horse piece of blubber to the blacksmith and hurried over to the boy. Pip's eyes fluttered shut as milk-fragrant spermacati from his bucket pooled around his narrow frame. John lifted the boy up and staggered against sudden weight; in an instant Pip felt heavier than one of the blanket pieces. He kneeled under the tremendous burden. Pip's eyes snapped open. The boy's expression was hard and made him look far older than his fourteen years. His voice was like thunder. "John Wood. You know me not. But you I know. Your kin called to me for safe passage across my waters."

John groaned, struggling to keep the boy upright. "Pip, this ain't sensible. You struck your head."

The boy's look was pitying. "Pip? No. I am the storm and the wind hard behind it. I am the wave and the darkness below. I, the white foam and the shifting sea sand. Do you know me, John Wood?"

John whispered, "Agwe?"

"The blood remembers. Destruction follows your present course. You have until the moon waxes full and wanes again." Pip shut his eyes. John felt the weight vanish from the boy.

The first mate, a tough, wiry man with a parsimonious mouth and thinning sandy hair stood over them. "You niggers pick a fine time for resting. Work to be done, and that spilled parmacety will come out of your lays, so I swear."

Pip squealed. "Sir, t'ain't the Carpenter's fault. Sir? Mr. Wood was just helping me on account I'm so clumsy."

"That so? You'll pay double penalty, then."

John stared hard at the deck so as not to give the First Mate a reason to call him out for insolence. "Sir, now Pip's up and about, if I have your leave, I'm needed elsewhere."

The First Mate scowled. "What are you looking poe-faced for? Back to work!"

That night the fires in the tryworks burned hot. Foul smoke, black as ink, curled up and blotted out the stars. The crew pitched bible leaves into the try pots for rendering. The cutting in had slowed after the sunset, and John turned his hand to the Captain's whaleboat, which had seen some damage from the flailing whale. It had needed bailing out with a piggin on the way back, but John assessed the boat as being in fine condition, all things considered. He was sanding out a new board to replace one that had been cracked in the hunt, when a shadow distinct from the roiling clouds of smoke fell across him. Without looking up, he said, "William, your mama was no glassblower."

William's smile seemed to beam in the lantern-light. He was wrapped in a moth-eaten old bear hide and held out two cups full of grog. "Looks like thirsty work there."

John accepted one of the cups. He took a deep pull, relishing the burn down his throat. He gazed up at William. Shivering cold. Bedraggled. Ridiculous in that bear hide. Reeking of stale blood, salt, and sweat. Beautiful. He said, "You stink. You ain't think to splash some of that ocean water on you whilst you was splashing around with that big fish?"

William smiled and squatted next to John. "That whole time I was fighting that mean old bastard, thinking what you'd say to me when I came back with a mouth full of teeth to carve into something for you kept me going." He rested his hand on John's shoulder.

"Careful. You'll get old Gospel to come over and give's a

sermon 'bout the evils of sodomy, and I don't know about you, but I prefer my sinnin' in quiet," John said.

"Be days before a whale this size is barrelled and tucked away, unless the sharks find it first. We won't have any idle hands for the devil's tools, I reckon."

John swatted William's hand off his shoulder. "The devil! You think I'm old scratch?"

"You are a mighty temptation." William's voice turned serious. "That little negro cabin boy? What happened with him? There's been some whispers that he's touched."

"He fell. That's all. Ain't none of you hoodoo-fearing whaler men never fell?"

William pulled John's hand to his mouth and kissed the knuckles. "I just know you're fond of him. I wanted you to beware if things go sour."

"A great big whale out there in less than a fortnight's time, and you all are muttering about things going sour?" John laughed, but thought of the word 'destruction' and all his mirth drained away.

Three days after the cutting in, John was working at the vice-bench, when Ezekiel, the other cabin boy, rushed in, flustered. John looked up from his work. "What is it, boy?"

"Mr. Wood! Mr. Sherman sent me in to find you. He said to bring a saw!"

"Bring a saw? Where?"

"The fo'c'sle! Ethan Anderson's arm's gone all wrong!"

John nodded, took a moment to select his sharpest and a yard of clean cloth, and followed the boy. The forecastle, never a sweet-smelling place, was rank with the smell of sick and rot. Ethan's twisted arm had turned black. It wept pus through a poultice. Ethan moaned. His face in the lantern-light was pale. His lips were grey. John pressed gently on the arm near the wound and heard a crackling sound like logs splitting in a fire.

John pursed his lips. "Zeke, get the boy whiskey."

Ethan's eyes were dull. "Don't mean to gainsay you, Carpenter, but I dreamt of a black dog. Death's coming, and I'd rather go into the sea intact."

"If that arm don't go, death will surely come. You had a misfortune is all. Don't mean the end."

Ethan managed a smile. "My fortune ended the day I signed up to the *Gracie-Ella*."

John looked over to Simon Sherman, the Steward, who stood striped by shadows just beyond the dying boy. He wiped a thin hand across an ungenerous mouth and sniffed. "Well, Mr. Wood? You heard the man. Leave him to die in peace. Go find Gospel; he'll want to say some prayers for his soul, I imagine."

John put away his saw and found his way to the deck where he saw To'afa looming over the Captain. The harpooner was six and a half feet if he was an inch, and the expression he wore would fit a desert prophet. "Sir, may I have permission to speak plainly?"

The Captain winked at John. He stroked his salt-and-pepper beard. "To'afa, you seem about to burst if I say no. So out with it!"

"Sir, I have served you with the best of my skill. My arm has been yours. Why have you chosen to imperil me with the placement of an unrepentant sinner?"

"Imperil is a strong word." The Captain beckoned to John. "Mr. Wood, what's your perception of sin aboard this ship of mine?"

"Seems to me like pumping the bilge and repairing rotten boards occupies my time in a way that I ain't really considered it, sir."

To'afa wheeled on him. "This is no matter for sly jests. I have seen how you coddle that little heathen. You ought to talk sense to him!"

"Who ain't got sense, now?"

"That cabin boy, Pip. I know you feel a fondness for him out of your shared bondage. But he invokes heathen gods! He makes offerings and worships idols. This cannot stand!"

The Captain stood. Even at his more modest height, he struck an imposing figure. His voice was low and calm. "I trust your objection is to my choosing to have Pip crew my whaleboat? Do you have a suitable replacement for Mr. Anderson? Will you perform the laying on of hands to heal his ruined arm? Or would you prefer I take that half-wit moon-calf Ezekiel to row? I would take the devil himself over that weakling and poltroon. If you have any objections to Pip and his savage worship, I suggest that you live up to your moniker and convert him, Gospel."

To'afa looked thunderstruck. The Captain turned his back on him and walked slow and stately aft.

To'afa looked to John as if he could spit. "Does my faith amuse you, Carpenter?"

John's voice was soft in reply, "It is your faith that has sent me forth. Ethan Anderson is not long for this world. Mr. Sherman has sent me to ask you to say a few prayers for his soul in the next one."

To'afa nodded. "I shall collect my Bible." He looked in the direction of the Captain. "I hope the Old Man does not regret taking no heed of my words on that devil-worshipping boy."

On the day they buried Ethan at sea, one of the foremast hands caught sign of whales. Right whales this time, two, mother and calf. As the crew made muster again for the whaleboats, William pressed something hard and cool into John's hand. It was a sperm whale's tooth, carved into scrimshaw. John recognized his own face carved into the surface, rough edges smoothed away, and surrounded by fanciful flowers. He watched William bound across deck to his whaleboat and smothered a rueful smile.

It was after nautical twilight when the whaleboats returned. The crew sung no work songs, and the slapping of the oars against the ocean struck John as sepulchral. It reminded him of the creaking of a hearse. Once aboard, the Captain's face was pinched and Gospel walked behind him with his head down, muttering prayers beneath his breath. William found John and embraced him in sight of God and the crew. "I'm sorry, I'm so sorry."

John grabbed William by the chin. "What you sorry for?"

"The boy Pip – he..."

"Where is he?"

"The hunt was good at first. Old Gospel got right into her with his whale iron, she were fastened, and –" Tears and snot streamed down William's big honest face. "Whale sounded and snapped two lines. The sea churned into froth. All the whaleboats rocked, mine nearly overturned. Pip. He just dove into the ocean after the whale. It must be a fit of madness. We searched until it was half-dark, but he never surfaced."

"I see," said John in a cold fury. He looked over at To'afa's broad back. "You sure he ain't had any help?"

William shook his head. "Gospel's a sanctimonious bastard. But he wouldn't bring no actual harm to a child beyond sermonizing."

"Ain't needed for the cutting in, am I? Reckon I have work to do below-deck," John said.

John was not settled at his vice-bench for more than a moment before William's shadow fell between him and the lamp. Chisel in hand, he said, "Thought I told you I had work."

"Thought maybe you could use me in grief as you do in joy." William's tone was bashful.

"You think that? We sailing together on a ship for two years, but after that I ain't so sure I'll sign back on. Seems a short time for you to be studying my grief."

"Six year we sailed together since I was a green hand and you..."

"Bought myself free from a cabinet maker?"

William's voice was patient, pleading. "And you came aboard to be this ship's carpenter, even if you are too skilled by half. What I mean to say is, I don't see no future for me without you in it, John Wood. I keep my lay by, don't spend more than necessary. I've set aside some money. I could set you up a shop to work your trade, buy land for a house and –"

John sighed. "William, I like you. I likes your body. I likes my body when it is with yours. But future? Ain't no future for any negro and a white man in the goddammed Union 'cept as master and slave. I been a slave, I'll be in my grave before I return to that." John looked down at his lathe to avoid the hurt he knew was in William's eyes.

"You're wrong, John Wood. I love you as any man loves his wife. More. I love you so much that it is the filling up and making of me, and sometimes feel like to shatter when you're not near."

John made his expression stony. He crushed down the part of him that wanted to recite to William the Song of Solomon, that wanted to cradle him in his arms and rock him to the rhythm of the boat. "We have sweetness here. Sweetness never lasts. Let it linger on your tongue while it can."

"Do I mean nothing more to you than the cockroach-ridden molasses you sweeten your coffee with?" William clenched his fists.

John looked at the lathe. "What I mean is, we got two years. Ain't no point in expecting more."

"I knew what you meant," William said. John watched him walk away. When William was out of sight, John pulled out the scrimshaw portrait from under his shirt, where it had dangled on a cord to rest next to his heart.

Restless, late to bed, but too tired to find himself elsewhere, John headed midship where he had his hammock. Across from him, the blacksmith snored. Above the blacksmith, William slept. His arms hung down limply, and the careworn look on his face had vanished. John put out the lantern. He settled into his hammock, turning to face away from William. His mind raced darkly, but sleep took him in moments.

He dreamt of the poor lost cabin boy Pip sitting at the right hand of a handsome brown-skinned youth with green eyes and wavy hair. The youth rested indolently on a coral throne. His full-lipped mouth pouted prettily, but the sea green eyes were piercing, knowing. An enormous mirror, gauzed over with black crepe, rested just beyond the throne. All else was darkness. Pip spoke, but the voice was like the roar of the ocean, and John knew the words belonged to the melancholy youth. "You break bread with thieves. They seek to plunder my seas the same as they have plundered the land before them." He gestured behind him. John knew without seeing that there were hundreds, perhaps thousands of shuffling figures in that unspeakable darkness. The youth nodded. Pip spoke again. "You *feel* them. The whales sing to keep them calm, to prevent them from despairing of never seeing Guinea. These the plundered lost in crossing. I have given them homes and solace."

John felt himself transfixed by those green eyes. Pip spoke in his own voice. "Ain't right what they done to us. Ain't right what they do to the whales. They'd burn us both up for lamp oil, and then when we's gone, seek to take more."

The dead, John knew they were the dead with certainty, began to shuffle into almost visible ranks beyond the coral throne. They cried out in languages that were strange to him.

The voice of thunder issued from Pip's mouth again. "Until the moon is dark."

John awoke, the visions fresh in his head. He saw that William had already arisen and left his hammock empty. After washing his face with cold seawater, and finding the vision did not fade from memory like most dreams, John resolved to see the Captain.

The Captain had just finished taking breakfast in his cabin with the Mates. The First Mate cast an ugly look at John when he asked if he might have a moment of the Captain's time, but the Captain agreed and bid John to sit at his table. The Mates cleared out in silence. The Captain was still hale at nearly sixty, but John noticed a sag in his shoulders. He looked at John with something like regard and asked, "What troubles you?"

John put his head in his hands. He knew the Captain to be a man of no great faith in things unseen. "Sir? Would you say I am honest?"

The Captain inclined his head. "I know you to be an honest man. And one who never has shirked from toil."

John swallowed. "As I am honest, and for the love I bear you as one who has served under your command for six years... I —"

"Out with it, man."

"Captain, this ship must return to its home port."

"Are you mad? We're less than a month out. We had good fortune with that cachalot bull, but the ship's holds are nearly empty."

By instinct, John fell back into the flowery speech he knew appealed to white men of rank. "Sir, I swear by my life that death and perdition overhang this ship. My only care is to save the *Gracie-Ella* and her crew from this fate. And if I be honest —"

"Enough! I had not thought you to be a fool, John Wood. But if I hear that you have repeated this half-cocked notion of curses and witchcraft to any soul aboard, I swear by my life I'll clap you in irons." He thumped the table with a short-fingered fist. "Am I clear?"

"Yes, sir."

"You may leave."

Another fortnight before the next whale sighting. It was an ugly, overcast afternoon on choppy seas. John was ill-tempered and worse rested. The night before, he had troubling dreams of voices calling out to him in the darkness. He and William had scarcely spoken. But he caught William by the arm as the whaleboats swung on their davits. William's face was unreadable. All John managed was, "Take care."

William pulled his arm away. "Take care?"

John felt his cheeks burn hot. "I love you, too."

William grabbed John then, pulled him close to his chest and kissed him hard and deep and slow. Gospel squawked in protest, and John heard noises of disgust, but his heart thundered in his chest loud enough to drown out the roar of the ocean and he kissed William back.

"I'll take care," William said. Then he bounded over to his whaleboat with a joyous whoop.

The moon was a sliver in the sky when the whaleboats returned. John heard the Captain cursing and spouting imprecations across the water. When all the whaleboats were pulled up, John's heart sank. The Second Mate's boat had absent both its boatkeeper and its harpooner. William was nowhere to be seen.

He overheard one of the hands from the boat talking to the steward. "Bad hunt. Lost two. The Second Mate and his harpooner. Harpooner got caught in the line, Second Mate went to cut and got carried over. Whale rammed him up against the boat."

John felt a great shudder of grief. The Captain passed by without meeting his eyes. A choking sound died in his chest, and he ran to the railing and vomited.

To'afa crossed his arms across his chest and surveyed the smashed timber. Without looking in John's direction, he said, "The wages of sin."

Another hand said, "And after all that loss, damn whale sounded before we could bleed its black heart away."

The next morning a squall came hard out of the west. Waves battered the ship. Its creaks and moans sounded like cracks and wails. Listless but dry-eyed, John made his inspections, filling in leaks with oakum, yelling at Ezekiel to help him pump water out of the bilge. The moon would be dark tonight, he knew. He carried out his tasks diligently, with dread growing in his chest like wet rot. He remembered William telling him he saw no future without him and laughed without humour.

That night, the storm quieted abruptly. John went above-deck to examine the masts and the yardarm, when in the night's stillness the ocean roiled. Whales in their multitudes flanked the ship aft and starboard. No foremast hand called out this sighting. The Captain himself was left speechless. Right whales, humpbacks, sperm whales, fin whales, in numbers beyond counting were a phalanx of the sea. Some hand, not clever enough to be terrified, broke the silence to opine that these whales represented riches beyond the dreams of avarice. It began shortly after. A sperm whale rammed the boat with his large square head. There was a crunch and crackle as wood splintered. The ship, over a hundred foot long from stem to stern, rocked and shuddered. The Captain screamed, "Mr. Wood! See that you keep us afloat!"

John ran down below-decks and into the hold. The ship shuddered with repeated assaults. A great fracture ran along the keel, and John knew the situation was hopeless. The hold was taking on water fast, and oakum wouldn't slow it down. Still, he picked up his hammer and rolled an empty cask over to the worst leak in an attempt to slow it. Another heavy crash and the ship listed hard to port before righting itself. Thunder pealed. John set to breaking apart the barrels in an effort to shore up the ship. The thunder spoke to him. "John Wood." The voice was Pip's. "You ain't gonna save them, but you can save yourself. You bought your freedom once, and I give it back to you now."

Hearing the truth of this, John reached inside his shirt for the piece of scrimshaw and, clutching it, abandoned his task, tearing out of the hold and onto the deck. For a mad moment, John thought to go back, grab his satchel with his grandmother's hair, and his freedom papers, run his hand over the words on the vice bench. Then the whales struck again, and the deck listed, causing John to slide into the mast, where he clung for dear life. There was a scream, and he saw the First Mate tumble overboard into the churning water. The Captain kept his footing, and shouted for whale irons. The last John saw of him, he thrust a harpoon into the air and vowed to the heavens that he would fight and kill every last fish in the ocean.

When the ship righted, John scrambled over splintering wood and dodged falling debris. Crab-walking midship on the port side, he tucked himself into a spare whaleboat, cut it loose from the davit, and trusted fate during the long drop into the night-dark water. A bull sperm whale, black as obsidian but with green eyes, breached nearby, and the force of his splashdown pushed the whaleboat away from the doomed *Gracie-Ella* as she sank out of sight.

He was adrift for two days and a night before a merchant vessel came across him. With kindness and care, they rescued him from the leaking whaleboat and brought him aboard their ship, *The Lady Elise*. After he was given fresh water to drink and wrapped in warm blankets, the captain, a young, amiable-looking man with freckles, asked him to tell his story. John did, with some careful omissions. *The Lady Elise*'s captain furrowed his brow. "We picked up another castaway from your ship two nights gone. You must have the devil's own luck."

He saw him then, wrapped in an Indian blanket. Staring up at the star-shattered sky was William.

John fell to the deck. "How can this be?"

William hobbled towards him, his movement slow and aided by a cane. He said, "Leg's seen better days, and I've been pummelled all about like a sack of rotten fruit, but I live." William winced. He dropped the blanket. A red welt the breadth of a thumb was raised around his neck. "Nearly strangled to death and dragged into the sea. But when I was down in the briny cold, I heard a voice tell it weren't yet time, that I were given a second chance. Queerest thing, sounded the near exact twin of that poor lost little cabin boy."

John rose to his feet and closed the space between them. When William took his hand, John was still clutching the piece of scrimshaw carved with his image.

What the Sea Reaps, We Must Provide

Eleanor R. Wood

The ball bounces off the tide-packed sand and Bailey leaps to catch it with lithe grace and accuracy. He returns to deposit it at my feet for another go. It's nearly dusk; the beach is ours on this January evening. It stretches ahead, the rising tide low enough to give us ample time to reach the sea wall.

Bailey's devotion to his ball is second only to his pack. He is never careless with it, relinquishing it only at my command or to give Bernie the occasional chase. Bernie brings up the rear, my shaggy bear, staying close but lacking Bailey's fierce duty to his ball.

The town belongs to us now, half a year from holidaymakers, the beach winter-rough and devoid of summer's candy-brightness. It will return soon enough, buckets and spades hanging from shop awnings, a time for ice cream and fish and chips eaten from the paper as gulls watch for their opportunity. A time when locals lend our beach to the tourists and day-trippers, avoiding the bustle and crowds, longing for autumn's return. It is a town of two seasons, of excitement and peace, of light and dark.

The dark is buried deep.

We don't discuss it. That yearly sacrifice to keep the summer safe, to protect our town's lifeblood. But winter's rawness reveals the primal undertow, much as we pretend otherwise.

It awes me.

It terrifies me. The town's need. The sea's power.

We reach the end of the beach and head up the ramped walkway to the sea wall. The tide is too high to return along the beach, but the wall's safe height gives us passage. A moment of doubt nags me as we ascend. Darkness is falling, a light rain with it. The sea wall's sheer drop one side and railway line on the other has always unnerved me. The waist-high wall to separate pedestrian from train has never seemed enough. A woman was hit and killed one year trying to retrieve her dog who'd gone over. I clip leads onto Bailey and Bernie. That year's sacrifice was a harsh one.

Gazing toward the distant harbour mouth, I'm reminded of the ill-prepared yachtsman who bargained his livelihood on a madcap voyage but ultimately gave himself to the sea to save his family's shame and destitution. He never sailed home to the town whose balance he reset.

Not every balance tips so heavily, though. The far end of the sea wall now has a gate, erected a few years ago when some fool drove their car along the wall, crashing over the edge onto the beach. They sacrificed only pride and a vehicle, although the council takes no further chances.

We walk, the rain increasing, the sea rising, the occasional train thundering between us and the cliffs that loom above all. Halfway to the promenade, I glance left and freeze. The tide is far higher than it should be, all trace of beach gone, water lapping the wall's base. I increase my pace. So does the sea. A sudden wave crashes over the wall ahead of us, stopping me dead. Bernie tries to drag me back the other way.

But this is the only way.

The tide shouldn't be this high. The lights of the promenade seem miles away through the wet gloom. Another train rushes past and I flinch, caught between dangers.

Another wave booms up feet away, soaking us in spray. And I know. Sacrifice is due, and I am subject to its demand.

I clutch the leads tightly. *No*. Not my boys. Never.

We're almost doused by the next wave, and I know it'll take us all if I don't give freely. I have nothing else to give, nothing else here that matters to me.

"No!" I shout into the rising wind and know I'm out of time.

Bailey looks at me, unspoken communication between us as ever. Bernie lives in his own world, but Bailey *knows*. He has always understood my moods. He has always known what's required of him. His gaze meets mine and my throat closes in fear.

"Bailey, no." The words are a strangled noise he doesn't comprehend. He steps towards the wall's edge even as I tug his lead back.

He leans over the edge. The sea roils. I scream.

He opens his mouth and lets go of his ball.

The rain patters on my hood as the waves draw back. Bailey stares into the calming surf for a long moment. The lead stretches taut between us. A small whine of longing leaves his throat before he looks at me, his sacrifice made. Perhaps only I will ever understand what it cost him. Relief drives me to my knees on the wet stone and I open my arms to him. He leans into me.

"Good boy. *Such* a good boy."

The town will prosper for another year, but as I start back for home, I know I'll never walk this wall again.

No Children

E. Saxey

My unmarked tatty white van carries the two of us along the coast road: not sea-side, but scrub grass and wind-chill in no-man's land.

It's best to be cautious so I let the van stutter to a stop in a layby some distance from our client's house. We skulk there between heaps of bramble bushes until my phone pings, and a moment later, a red car shoots past us in the other direction.

"Was that Mr Jones?" asks Bronwyn.

"Better hope so."

Our clients' house is a modern white bungalow, flimsy as a holiday cottage, not sturdy enough for the weather we get round here. I notice the lead flashing pulling away from the roof-tiles. I'm a builder, but we're not here to fix the house. That would be simpler.

The sea is at an extreme low tide, a twisting white ruffle, right on the horizon, twenty minutes' walk across the sand.

Bronwyn, my cousin and my painter, sighs as she clambers from the van. "It's so much easier at high tide." She stuffs her curls into a hat, and buttons her overalls across her wide chest, hiding knitted roses. I hop into my own overalls, turning us both into nondescript grey tubes.

"The tide'll be back in by midday," I tell her, grabbing my tool kit.

"Will we not be done by then? What about that wet-room job in Llanelli? We could get started this afternoon."

"I don't think this will be quick. The husband built this house." The shoddy bungalow could hold a lot of secrets, which will make for a long day's work. "That's why we need your Marie."

A chugging roar tells us our final crew-member has arrived. Marie, Bronwyn's kid, halts her much heftier vehicle and hops down onto the grass. She's got purple hair, which makes her overalls look deliberately punk. "Where's the husband off at, then? And where the fuck has the sea gone?"

Bronwyn tuts at the swear-word. I don't mind the swearing, but I could do without the tutting.

"Husband's just left for a family funeral," I tell Marie. "Other side of the Brecon Beacons."

Marie whistles. "That's stone cold, that is."

"Got to make sure they're out of the way," says Bronwyn. "Learned that on the Porthcawl job."

Bronwyn has a habit of mournful reminiscence. I don't join in.

"So he just comes home, and *bam*?!" Marie asks.

"He's had his chance," says Bronwyn.

Marie's been working with us for a year – mostly tiles and plastering – but this is her first side-job. I'd wanted someone young on the team. Bronwyn and I are nearing fifty, now. Our clients are younger. That is to say, our clients look younger.

"No children, though?" Bronwyn asks.

"Aw, so are you the heart of the operation, Mam?" mocks Marie.

"She's also the common sense," I say. "And I'm the muscle. So I don't know why we brought you along. And no, there's no children."

"What's the legal position, then," asks Marie, "if there's children? What about the dad?"

Bronwyn fetches her tools to avoid the conversation. I lower my voice. "The legal position is he can fuck right off out of it."

Our position is only legal in as far as our side-jobs are so wildly improbable. We don't go mob-handed to the house, in case there's still company. We wait until the door opens, and the wind snatches it and slams it back against the wall. Is this Mrs Jones, her ankle-length dress flapping in the wind? I've not yet met her. When she comes closer to the van, I'll see her face, and I'll know.

"Don't you stare," says Bronwyn, elbowing Marie in the ribs. Then she sighs. "Oh, Sal. It's so soon after the last one."

"You know I didn't pick the date." Our clients come in an uneven trickle. Through the women's refuge in Swansea, through a network of barmaids, my phone number ends up in the hands that need it. "And the last one was hardly any trouble."

"It's not the attention I'm worried about, Sal." She nudges me with her big shoulder. "It's *you*. You're not as tough as you think you are."

Family always want to take you down a peg.

Mrs Jones pushes against the wind as she walks. I move to meet her. Bronwyn is half-right, in that this job has come sooner than I expected. Most clients call me three or four times before they set a date. Sometimes, when I call back, the client pretends not to know me: "We don't need any work done, goodbye." Or she'll turn us away at the doorstep and tell her man we were charity collectors. I have to have the patience of Job.

By contrast, Mrs Jones has been frighteningly decisive. One phone conversation to set the date, and here – close enough to touch – is Mrs Jones. She looks no older than Marie, maybe twenty. Her eyes are inky and wide, almost circular, her hair slate grey and glossy.

"You're Sal?" she asks.

"That's me." I smile. Behind me, Bronwyn will be smiling too, and she's better at it.

Mrs Jones holds out one arm in invitation.

As we cross the patchy lawn, young Marie is silent, perhaps for the first time since she was born. Last week, when I explained these side-jobs to Marie, she asked, "How do you know they're not ordinary housewives? Pissed off at their blokes?" Now Marie has seen Mrs Jones, and the sheen of her skin, and her bottomless eyes, she won't ask again.

We tramp across Mrs Jones' threshold in dusty work-clothes. Ordinary clients tolerate our invasion because they want a loft extension, or a nice new open-plan lounge, and they still get testy, fretting at us to wipe our feet. I never saw a homeowner less bothered than Mrs Jones. I suppose we may be the last people she ever welcomes into her tasteful modern kitchen.

I catch Bronwyn surreptitiously checking the fridge for kid's drawings. Soft-hearted, and she never takes my word for it. I also spot Marie placing thumb and finger on the metal knob of a cupboard door, starting to unscrew it. I kick her and she stops. Does her Mam know she's bloody light-fingered?

"What happens first?" asks Mrs Jones.

"We look through all your storage. Sometimes that's enough."

"I've searched..."

"Always in the last place you think of looking," pipes up Marie.

Sometimes our clients back out at this point, particularly the ones who've been married for longer. They flinch at our mucky hands rifling through their belongings, with no promise of success. Even half a life is worth keeping.

"We'll be careful," I tell her. "You don't have to be here, while we work. You can wait in the garden." That scruffy garden, clinging to a saline incline.

Mrs Jones stays.

The drawers are the most distasteful part: shoving aside bras, mementos, bills marked *FINAL NOTICE*. I prefer to search the impersonal spaces, like the gap under a chest of drawers, the inches behind a wardrobe. The places that kids find when they play hide and seek, or hunt treasure.

Marie is small and bendy enough to wriggle right in under the bed. Her questions, slightly muffled, keep coming. "Couldn't she leave him, anyway, even if we don't find it?"

124

"That's not how it works," I say. "You want to go up in the attic, look there?"

Marie holds up a bedside photo on the way out. "He looks like a weaselly little scrote. She's a good-looking woman, hey, Aunty Sal?" She tries to wink at me like a woman of the world.

"Don't start," I say. "And don't pocket the kitchen fittings."

"I was just seeing if they were proper pewter."

"We can't risk you gleaning." We get away with this line of work because our crimes are too strange to report. Stealing is ordinary, stealing will bring us down. "Bugger off and check the attic."

Left alone, I fish with a long slim stick in the cavities of the built-in bedroom set. There's a snag, a tug of resistance, and I work my hand in deep. My fingers tingle, brushing something warm, firm, supple.

A figure moves between me and the window. Jesus, is it Mr Jones? I jump back, yank my arm free.

Mrs Jones stands silently behind me.

"Might be something back there," I say, keeping my voice level. On the third job, I found something this way, and now I always let the client pull it out. It felt indecent to touch it. And it was hard on my heart, to pass it over.

Her arm is longer than mine. When she brings her hand back out, between her fingertips is an ordinary heather-coloured jumper. She flicks it away like a dead thing.

Marie bellows down through the attic hatch. "There's nothing here! Can I rip up the insulation?"

I look to Mrs Jones. Mrs Jones nods.

I pace around the outside of the house, to see if we've missed a garage or a boat-shed.

I stop in the sloping garden and look out to check the tide, but the wind makes my eyes water. I grew up in a seaside house, with salt ghosts on the windows and everything corroding. There's another white bungalow further along the road, and a figure in the doorway. They turn as I watch and the door slams behind them. My van, and Marie's truck and trailer, disturbed the neighbour, and the site of me has put the seal on it. I know with sinking certainty that Mr Jones, on his way to his uncle's funeral, will be getting a phone call. I hope reception is bad over the Beacons. I very much prefer not to be interrupted.

I hurry back to the kitchen for the next stage. With Mrs Jones' permission, we set crowbars to the kitchen tops and lever them off, prise the sides from the fridge-freezer cabinet. "He's done it shoddy," scolds Bronwyn. "Look at that, it's all spit and glue."

Not much dust, I notice. House-proud, Mrs Jones must be, but she stands coolly by and lets us peel her house like a satsuma. While I work, I watch her. I see a family resemblance in her snub nose and short upper lip. Then I look away before I get caught staring.

We work well together, a real family business; Uncle Justin, Bronwyn's dad, taught all three of us. We yank plasterboard free, show the spaces inside the walls. There's one tricky corner, and Bronwyn raises a sledgehammer to knock a hole.

"It's not there," Mrs Jones says. "I'd have felt it." She holds out her hands, like she's warming them on a fire.

Is that true? None of our other clients have mentioned it. The sledgehammer wobbles in Bronwyn's hands, and she looks to me, uneasy. Is this just an excuse to stop, the first sign of Mrs Jones getting cold feet? In a panic, I calculate if we can replace everything we've torn away, before Mr Jones returns, summoned by the Neighbourhood Watch. Whether we go forwards or back, the clock's surely ticking.

"Go ahead," says Mrs Jones, and Bronwyn swings, and then I step up next to her to rip the hole wider. Our hands are clumsy with eagerness and relief, but the thing we need isn't there. Mrs Jones was correct.

I have to maintain a professional demeanour, not sweep our

client along with my plans, so they can always back out if they need to. It's very hard to hide my satisfaction as Bronwyn and I go wild on the floorboards: putting your whole back into it, rewarded by the first creak, then a gratifying shriek as the nails pull free. All the better for knowing that Mr Jones probably hammered them down himself.

But every space we reveal is empty.

"What's that?" There's something fluffy at the tip of Bronwyn's boot. Only a mouse's nest, and the husk of a mouse. "Oh. Poor thing."

Marie marches in, soot in her purple hair. "Awright, Mary Poppins! There's fuck all up the chimney, I gave it a good rodding."

"Is there a chance Mr Jones buried it in the garden?" I ask Mrs Jones.

"It's in the house."

"Can you feel it? Can you…" I wave around my hand like a metal detector.

"No."

I blush. She looks about twenty, but I feel her disdain like I'm a child clinging to her knee. "Then the next steps, we discussed…"

"Do it," says Mrs Jones.

"I'll turn off the water and gas," says Bronwyn.

When I broached the subject of this job with Marie last week, I asked, "Do you know about the other jobs? What your Mam and I do?"

"Is it smuggling?"

"What?"

"I reckon it's illegal, and you go down the coast road to do it. Never up the valleys."

She's sharp as a whip, is Marie. Now I have to stand back and trust her as she trundles a mini-excavator away from its trailer and right up to the house. I've previously only seen Marie handle a wallpaper steamer.

"She's got a good light touch," says Bronwyn, soothingly, as Marie bops around like a muppet at the levers of the JCB. I hope that isn't a motherly over-estimate.

"Still, maybe I should have done it."

"On the Rhossili job," says Bronwyn mildly. "Didn't you drive that digger into the quick-sand, then whinge about it?"

"Where first?" I ask Mrs Jones. She raises her hand and points, the seaward side of the house. Her dress in the wind ripples like kelp in a current. Marie rocks the machine back and forth, an ugly eight-point turn, graunching great scars into the pitiful garden.

Marie flays the side of the house with precision. The sharp teeth break the skin of brickwork, deafeningly loud. Water sprays briefly from a sheared-off pipe. Electrical cables snag and then snap. The bricks don't fall apart smoothly but stick, like a box of Lego holding shapes from the last game.

"Break it up, Marie," I shout out.

The JCB rakes its scoop back and forth, Marie swaying to match it and cackling. Bronwyn has a tattoo on her ankle with Marie's name and a rose. I wonder how she expected her kid to turn out?

Marie asked me, last week, "Do you ever just punch them?" Meaning the husbands.

"No."

"I would."

"Not if you work with me, you won't."

"How do they think they'll get away with it?"

"I don't know. You know, the factories closed. The women went to the cities where they can get work. The men turn to the sea." It's a fairy tale my aunties told me, Bronwyn's Mam, Marie's Gran. I'm surprised to hear it come out of my own mouth.

"They can turn to a sock full of liver," suggests Marie. "And stick their nob in that."

What can you tell a teenage girl about companionship, or wanting a family?

But why would I argue that you can build a family on an act of kidnap?

The digger lifts its triumphant head and freezes in that pose. Mrs Jones walks in under it, the maiden poking about the dragon's hoard, and Bronwyn follows behind.

Something moves in the corner of my watering eye: a car? No, it's the vigilant neighbour, striding over to us, a pillar-of-the-community type, pristine in her pastel sweater. "What's all this, then?"

"We're under Mrs Jones' instruction."

When we started in this line of work, I used to say: we're helping Mrs So-and-so move out. That always set off an avalanche of moaning.

"He's not a bad husband," objects the neighbour. Even when I say nothing, some people hear condemnation. "I know there were a few unfriendly comments. Because she isn't from round here."

"She is from round here," I say. There is nobody who is more from round here, *right* here, than Mrs Jones. The neighbour scowls, perhaps noticing that I don't look quite local myself.

Mrs Jones is picking through the rubble of her own house like a beachcomber. Marie runs over and mucks in with her Mam, the two of them heaving aside the bigger blocks.

"You can't do this, you know!" the neighbour yells. "It's illegal!"

"Am I his wife?" calls back Mrs Jones.

I'm surprised. The clients don't usually like to talk, once they've made up their mind.

Her question flusters the neighbour. "It's none of my business whether you're married."

"If I'm his wife, this is my house!" calls Mrs Jones, and goes back to the search.

"She's gone mad," offers the neighbour. "Because of her kid."

My breath catches. It's as though the tide has finally come in and filled up my lungs. Mrs Jones said there were no children.

"Losing the kid, it's sent her mad," the neighbour confides. "But it couldn't live. Deformed, it was."

I find my breath again, and use it. "Piss off and drizzle your bile into someone else's ear."

"He'll be back here, soon," she gloats, before she stalks away.

"*Hi ho*," I hear, "*Hi ho...*" Marie is singing while she and Bronwyn haul up a lump of brick-work, letting Mrs Jones dart in to search beneath it.

The red car swings around the corner and skids to a halt on the grass. Mr Jones jumps from his car, jerky with shock and anger, a wiry man past forty failing to fill out his funeral suit. His mouth hangs as open as his home.

"What? What the hell is this?" shouts Mr Jones.

Mr Jones has come back to catch his wife cheating, or leaving, and he's found his place turned into a doll's house, its insides displayed to the world.

Bronwyn runs up to form a wall beside me, between Mr Jones and his bride.

"What is this? What?"

"We're acting on behalf of Mrs Jones," I say.

"Well, I'm *Mr* Jones," he replies, like he's playing his trump card. He has a smoker's mouth, lips like a cat's arse. He moves to the left, we lean to the left. He sees he shouldn't try to dodge to the right. Marie was right: he's a weaselly scrote. "You're telling me I can't talk to my wife?"

I shrug. I look big when I shrug. "Talk yourself hoarse."

He calls to his wife. The wind plucks his voice away. She could plausibly ignore him. But she raises her head, fixes her great dark eyes on him. He starts bellowing, vile things, foul things, touching on everything from her face to her sexual propensities.

I can't show it, but I'm scared. With Mr Jones hopping mad at ground level, Marie can't use the JCB. He could run forward and have his head knocked off, tidy. Could we restrain him? I could punch him, and Bronwyn could hold him down, but a small crime like assault is a tool in the hands of a petty man.

Then Mr Jones' insults are drowned out as loose roof tiles drop in a deafening shower.

Marie screams, and my heart jumps, because she could have been hit. But I see her at once, jumping up and down and pointing upwards: "Look! Look there!"

There's mineral wool insulation, in clumps and strands, flapping around. But there's something else, dark and supple like a sheet of suede. It whips back and forth, lithe in the sea wind.

"I'll get it!" calls Marie, and before I can stop her she's shinning up the neck of the bloody JCB. Foot on a piston, hand on a hinge, like she's spotted a fiver growing in a tree.

She tugs and yanks and the sheet-thing comes free. It billows into every wild shape as it falls down into the arms of Mrs Jones.

I shout cautions as I run towards her: "Mrs Jones, wait!"

She is elated. I saw Bronwyn hold Marie, when she was new-born, and her face looked this way. "Not until you're near the water!" I swear the tide has come in early, to rescue her. It's streaming and foaming only two hundred yards away.

(And Bronwyn is hanging back to protect Mr Jones, just in case. We learned to do that on our messy third job, down in Porthcawl.)

Mrs Jones nods. She holds the thing we have found, and we walk together towards the water.

The foam rushes over my boots and her feet, which are bare now. She wrings her hands, like someone miming regret, but then holds out the ring she has removed, offering it to me. I shake my head; who'd want a souvenir of this marriage? She drops it and it winks out of sight in the foam.

I tighten my fists, feel the slight webs between my fingers

strain. I no longer need to be professional, or carefully neutral. There is no chance, now, that Mrs Jones will back down. Now I might bring out one of the hundred questions I carry in my chest. I draw in a lungful of briny air.

Simultaneously, the yelling starts up again.

"Gwen, don't do it!" Mr Jones has decided he can bellow her back to him. "We were happy! We were going to try again, for a family!"

Mrs Jones changes.

She sheds her dress like a wet dog shaking, stands stark and fearless. She swings the skin up over her head, high like dark wings. The fierce wind can't take it from her, it strokes her shoulders and won't let go. It clads her arms, which are shorter than arms now, and covers her head. The dark hood becomes a powerful thick neck. The skin clings to her torso, cloaks her legs. She falls to her knees, and that sharp drop turns into a sinuous roll.

I want to hold her. I'm ten years old again, and I want to cling to her and drag her back up the beach. Of course I don't, but of course I cry.

She lollops towards the water. It only takes a couple of undulations before a wave comes in to scoop her up. God it's freezing, but she quivers joyfully all along her dark body, from her muzzle to the tip of her tail. A twitch of her fins sends her scooting off into the blue-black water. We watch her round head bob, and then dive, and her flank curves after it, curling in a perfect arc. She doesn't resurface.

I walk back to my crew. Bronwyn squeezes my shoulder.

Mr Jones is sitting in a crumple on the ground. Bronwyn and I climb into the van and belt up.

"It'd be a nice house, in the summer," says Bronwyn of the building we have just demolished. "Can we get lunch in Llanelli?"

Maria sticks her head through the open van window.

"I want those nobs, Marie," says Bronwyn. "You get paid by

the hour, same as when you're plastering."

"Aw…" Marie, shamefaced, starts to decant handfuls of pewter doorknobs from her overall pockets.

"Leave that, now." I want to move off before Mr Jones notices my van has no number-plates. "I'll buy you a drink, later, down the Red Lion."

Marie stomps away, to drive the JCB back to the plant hire company.

"She's got a good heart," says Bronwyn. "Just needs a firm hand."

I pull the van back onto the road, thinking: we need a better plan. What if there had been a kid?

I do hope anyone would want their mother to be free. Even if it meant never seeing her again and being raised by heavy-handed aunties. Even if it meant going off the rails a bit, until Uncle Justin stepped up and taught you bricklaying. Eventually, you'd want the best for your Mam.

But it's too much to ask of a kid. If they held their mother's freedom in their hands, warm and firm and supple – what kid would willingly pass it over?

Bronwyn turns on the radio, finds Abba, and gives me a nudge which nearly knocks me over. "Come on, you know it! *Nothing more to say, dah-dah dah-dah play…*" She warbles the chorus as our van trundles through Pwll.

Today, at least, there were no children.

The Colossus Stops

Dafydd McKimm

When the Colossus stops moving, the silence hits the island like a thunderclap. The creak and screech of its enormous limbs have been a constant companion to each of us since birth, a lovingly cooed lullaby, now so suddenly, so violently, absent. As far back as anyone can remember, the Colossus has patrolled the waters around our island, hurling boulders the size of houses at menacing pirates and invading fleets, never tiring, never stopping, until the day before yesterday it slowed, making two rounds instead of its usual three, and then, a day later, grinding ponderously to a halt.

We gather on the cliffs and, biting our lips and wringing our hands, watch for any signs of movement from the metal giant.

"Perhaps it's resting," one of us says. "It will wake up soon, well refreshed, and everything will be back to normal."

We murmur in agreement, none of us wanting to curse its waking by speaking our fears aloud.

Three days pass, and the Colossus remains motionless, the nooks of its helm cacophonous now with baying gulls, who have already begun to populate its body, mistaking it for a sea stack.

We send some men in boats to inspect it, and they return with grim faces. The Colossus is not sleeping. The great gears of its heart turn no more.

Panic burns the island like a fever. "Who will protect us now that the Colossus is gone? How will we defend ourselves with only hoes and paring knives?" Soon enough, scaffold is erected around the giant, and piece by piece they tear away its shining flesh. The metal brought back in the boats is unlike bronze or iron, stronger by far than both, yet so light a child could lift it; the swords forged can cleave a shield in two as if it were butter, the spearheads pierce armour like a weasel's tooth popping an egg. There is talk of reviving the army, after all these centuries. There are whispers of taking the boats and these new arms and raiding the nearby islands. "We should attack them before they attack us," is the logic wielded by the men holding the unblockable swords, the unstoppable spearheads. "We should strike now, before they realise we're vulnerable."

The Colossus, its bones bare to the sea wind, a carcass, picked clean by scavengers, looms over our island still. Its eyes, two giant orbs the colour of the sun, look down at the surface of the ocean, as if unable to meet our gaze, as if it cannot bear to see us like this.

The army gathers on the shore, bands of men bearing sun-coloured swords; they prepare the ships, raise flags emblazoned with a metal giant, grimacing as the Colossus never did. "We will bring back riches," they say. "Each of you shall have a house of gold and a retinue of captives to do your bidding."

When we say we are happy with our houses of stone and are quite capable of living without slaves to wait on us, fattening our bodies with food and our souls with guilt, they say instead: "We do not do this because we want to; we do this because we must, to keep you safe."

As they turn from us to hoist their sails, the wind wails through the shell of the Colossus, howling for the dead the swords made from its flesh will create.

When the last of the ships disappears over the horizon, we who remain on the shore take action of our own. We will not be a part of this betrayal; we will not have it done in our name.

The boats have all gone, but the strongest swimmers among us swim to what remains of those giant legs, as thick once as a cluster of trees, now withered and ravaged by termites. They climb its trunk, their hands finding holds in the wounds made for sword-metal, and lash the strongest of our ropes around the pocked torso.

We pull, and we pull, and down it falls with a crash that sends the waves halfway up the cliffs. Its bones as light as poplar wood, the Colossus floats.

We clamber aboard, making our bunks in its body, taking refuge from the wind behind its ribs or in the hand-shaped bowls of its hips. Its eyes no longer look at the sea; now they point upwards at the sky, as if to say, *I will guide you, my children, by the stars to better lands.*

Wake the Dead

Maura McHugh

"If you're running from yourself you'll always come in second."

Donnacha didn't understand this cryptic statement when he'd heard it as a kid, impatient and bored, in his Gran's kitchen. She'd been counselling his father about his restless job-hopping. Yet a haunting vision lodged in his mind, despite his desire to return to his Mam's house and his unfinished Zelda game. He imagined his Dad being pursued by a better, fitter version of himself in a long race, but dream-like, his father's faster self outpaced him, and drew away until he disappeared into a hazy horizon. Uncatchable.

Red-faced and panting, his father slogged on, alone. Too proud to admit defeat.

In the car ride home, Donnacha puzzled over it, and concluded Gran was implying his Dad was a loser. And looking at him, compulsively wringing the steering wheel, crumpled, unshaven, and permanently broke, Donnacha reckoned she was right.

Now, after a month of driving around rural Ireland, trying to evade his cracked adult life choices, Donnacha had a grudging new insight to her meaning, and unexpected empathy for his Dad.

But he wasn't ready to admit he couldn't dodge his demons.

"I'll run them ragged first."

He glanced guiltily around his car. Talking out loud wasn't a good sign.

He signalled, and drove into another small town that existed half in the past and half in the present. A shabby, boarded-up hardware shop cringed next to a shiny Thai street food restaurant. A statue of the Virgin Mother and Child cast a shadow over the town square that pointed at the lingerie store opposite. Teens loitered together on a street corner with their individual faces illuminated by their mobile phones, while a tractor motored past them and the auld fellah in a cap driving it waved at the older locals.

"He even has the sheepdog on the passenger seat," Donnacha marvelled. The collie lolled his tongue at him as Donnacha pulled his car around the slowpoke driver.

This was typical of his impromptu tour of the cultural blindspots of his homeland. Ireland had emerged from its colonial chrysalis, but its new form was not yet set. It was malleable and shifting. Underneath the wet flesh some of the old bones were resistant to change. They could establish the new form from their obstinacy.

Perhaps there were even more ancient shapes that might re-emerge. From when people chanted to stone and paid respect to trees. When blood was spilled for nature's tribute. And primordial forces responded to such offerings...

Donnacha blinked rapidly, surprised at the strange direction of his thoughts. Luckily, he spotted the B&B he had booked for the night, and made a quick turn into its driveway. This owner had a quixotic array of statutes and potted plants in the small garden. A gnome wearing sunglasses held court with a duck dressed in a raincoat. A hedgehog in a Hawaiian shirt lounged beside a dancing, piping satyr.

It was another in a series of cheap, unassuming B&Bs he had picked for his wandering. He avoided hospitable homes with cheery fireplaces, chatty guests, and reminders to review the premises kindly online. He preferred the old-fashioned, reserved host, who took money without questions and offered a spartan experience.

Donnacha craved their cell-like rooms. He read books, anything abandoned in the lodgings he occupied briefly, and never turned on the TV. Perversely, the world continued to turn without his attention. He heard snatches of news via the radio in his car, but he thought of them as stories. Fantastical yarns of tyrants, villains, and beasts, wrangling in distant kingdoms.

Each day he got up and drove, over drenched rolling hills, past indistinct villages, through tangled, black-boughed woods, and over swollen rivers. Dependable Ireland rolled out a sepulchral chill as October deepened, and around him every dark rock and huddled glade was damp and glistening.

His funds had ebbed. What remained from his share of the house – Mairead had done well out of that showdown between solicitors – had paid for petrol and a frugal month of roving around a landscape he had never explored.

He could get work as a barman. That well-honed skill was ever needed. He wasn't the best at feigning interest in customers, but his supply of sardonic commentary was limitless, and there was nothing his countrymen liked better than banter, especially if it skewed bleak.

That evening, Donnacha fired up an antique computer in the beige living room of his current residence. He browsed through job ads on local towns' forums, and noted some likely contenders. It meant he had to log into his email account, and endure the few concerned messages from old friends. The ones that knew him from his happier days in Boston, before he and Mairead returned home, or those childhood mates who stubbornly believed there was some spark of that original kid left within his chest. The most difficult was the patient reminder from his younger brother Fintan that a room was available at his home. He responded with a one-line thanks, but he knew that Juanita wouldn't welcome him. She and Mairead has always been tight.

He scrawled a couple of addresses and numbers on the complimentary notepad by the asthmatic PC. His pay-as-you-go phone was a primitive plastic savage. His address book was slips of paper in his wallet.

Donnacha didn't notice the lady of the house enter the room until her shadow obscured his writing. He startled and turned.

She could have been in her twenties or her fifties: a tall, thin grey woman with big plastic spectacles, and a smile that hung on her long face like a titled picture. She wore some orthodontic contraption that gave her a slight lisp and added to her indeterminate age.

"Buster Mahon needs a hand."

He blinked at her, a variety of interpretations crossing his mind, including a joke about prosthetics.

She pointed at his scrawl. "You're looking for work?"

"Depends on the job."

"Pub. Town's so small if you sneezed while passing through you'd miss it." She snorted a laugh. "It's the pub, and the grocery shop, *and* the funeral parlour. They used to do petrol too, but gave that up when the big companies took over. Traditional place. Old men in wellies and caps. Young people go elsewhere."

"And I'm not young?"

"You'd fit right in there. They want pints pulled while they read papers and complain about the weather or the price of sheep."

"Is the pay as attractive as the company?"

She shrugged. "Buster has a room above the place. It could be right for someone minding his own business."

Donnacha stood up. The landlady was half a head taller. "You've come to some conclusions about me."

She met his direct look without any caginess. "I know people." She held out a piece of paper with an address.

His bitterness rose like addictive bile. "That's impossible. We're all pretending."

But he reached for the paper anyway. She held onto it for a moment longer than necessary, and he met her gaze again.

"I see you Donnacha Sweeney."

Her knowing stare pierced his bravado. A shiver rippled down his back and his hand jerked back involuntarily with the paper.

She smiled, and the row of metal bands covered her teeth so completely it was as if they were fashioned from iron. "I'm away early tomorrow. Busy day. I'll leave a cold breakfast for you, and you can let yourself out."

He watched her leave the room as soundlessly as she entered.

It was one of the occasions he cursed not having a smart phone. The town wasn't on the map which lay in a crumpled mess on the passenger seat. He had been circling through a series of winding boreens at a crawl because of the silvery rain shroud. The car clock said it was 1 p.m., but he had set out at 11 a.m., and the place should only have been 30 minutes away. Through the haze he spotted the smudged shape of the apex of a stone church he was sure he had passed twice before.

"Fuck's sake!" he shouted, and gripped the steering wheel to knuckle-white tightness.

He pulled the car into a scrap of earth by the barred gateposts, beyond which lay the outline of a church after a long, gravelled path. Listing headstones and ivy-strangled vaults studded the mist.

He hoped some farmer's son in a souped-up Honda Civic wouldn't bash into him while he consulted his map. His finger traced along the creased page for a tell-tale cross that would indicate the church, but there were only a squiggle of lines. They met in a crossroads where he suspected the town was located.

A bell tolled, oddly muffled. He glanced up. A figure moved down the path toward him.

Donnacha reached over to roll down his passenger window, and plastered on a bewildered smile. It appeared to be a man in a dark suit, who walked steadily but didn't get any closer.

He squinted. The mist had already seeped into the car, and a fine film of water beads clung to his face, obscuring his vision. He wiped at his eyes, trying to focus properly on the approaching person.

It walked, but it gained no ground.

Warmth leeched out of him, along with his enthusiasm to meet the person. The bell clanged again, dully.

At this, the figure blipped forward on the path. Donnacha could make out a translucent face with black voids for eyes that radiated malevolent triumph. Long-figured hands hung loosely from the sleeves as if the suit was badly fitted. A costume for an intruder.

There was no other sound. No crunch of gravel, or the complaint of crows.

Again, the bell rang out strangely.

The manshape was almost at the gatepost. His pretend mouth was a vicious slash, curved up in the delight of the predator. His arm reached up as if to hail him –

Donnacha put the car into gear and slammed his foot on the accelerator.

The car caught on the mud and the back swerved slightly, to scrape against the stone post. The grind of metal merged with the bell. Donnacha refused to look at the path, despite the freezing gust that swept through the window, causing his rapid breaths to materialise before him.

With an anguished shriek his car surged onto the road and sped forward quickly, but he had to slow immediately because of the mist.

Donnacha glanced in the rear-view mirror for any sign of his pursuer, but all that was evident was the concealing rain.

His heartbeat slowed down again, and he broke into a stuttering laugh, mocking and congratulatory.

Then, he spotted the signpost, at a drunken angle, pointing at an obscured road, and the name of the hamlet: Rathdearg.

He turned the car, and heard the protest from the back wheel, relieved he was only a couple of miles from his destination.

Rathdearg was a collection of houses rather than a village, yet the road widened to accommodate a small green area with benches and a saint's statue. Everything was tidy, with walled gardens up front. The pub/shop was called The Haunt. Next door what looked like a home also had the green flash that indicated it doubled as a post office. A bus stop pole punctuated either side of the street.

He parked the car in a small concrete space at the side of the building and got out. He wilfully ignored examining the damage. What did it matter when he couldn't afford to fix it?

At the entrance to the pub sat a collection of turnips, carved with deranged faces, and with a light flickering inside each one. The hanging sign depicted a revenant dressed in a 19th century black suit, sitting inside the pub holding up a pint of porter in a perpetual toast. A skeleton in an apron grinned from behind the counter.

He pushed open the door which had wavy glass inset, and it squealed loudly as if griping about its use. Inside, the dimly-lit room was narrow due to an ancient counter running along the left-hand side. It was composed of glass and wood, and displayed a variety of canned goods, including baked beans, peas, and spam. Behind it were shelves with toilet paper, washing powder, and giant boxes of tea. A small fridge containing juice and milk hummed. An old-fashioned register sat unattended. A rack of newspapers, containing national and regional publications as well as *The Farmer's Journal* and *Ireland's Own,* finished off the row.

After the shop a swinging half door opened into the pub itself.

It's the Wild West, Donnacha thought as he entered.

This space was roomy, with a smoke-stained counter at the back which looked like it had been worn smooth by generations of elbows. The array of tall stools didn't have padding or cushions. *The townsfolk have hardy backsides.* The usual pumps for the dominant breweries were on display, but he was surprised to see a craft beer from a nearby town given a prominent spot. Glass shelves behind the bar displayed the selection of spirits, and rows of glasses. He noted the lack of dust on the bottles of Babycham – someone had professional pride. A turf fire blazed in the large stone fireplace on the right. In front of the hearth lay a grey, grizzled hound. It raised its head at Donnacha's appearance, and watched him with wise, brown eyes.

A faded, hand-written sign pasted on the back of the bar proclaimed, 'No Cappuccinos!', but underneath that it offered a WiFi password.

He crossed the tiled floor toward the counter. The dog stood up, revealing its height. It was a cross, but with a strong wolfhound pedigree.

"Hello," he said, and cautiously extended his downturned hand.

The dog sniffed from a distance. A tag dangled from his collar, and Donnacha sank down on his hunkers to read it.

"Joxer," he read out loud. The dog's ears twitched.

"I'm Donnacha."

Joxer walked right up to his face, licked it once, and returned to his post by the fire.

Donnacha straightened, and looked around, but no one appeared. He walked to the counter, leaned on it, then coughed politely. An old clock hanging among black and white photographs ticked loudly.

After another minute crawled by, he noticed the black door at the back of the room. No doubt it led to the toilets and some quiet room where people retired for the lock-in.

He walked to it and placed his hand on the old-fashioned metal handle, but before he opened it he glanced back at Joxer. The dog regarded him placidly. He clicked the door open.

The short corridor beyond was icy cold, and he was glad again for his parka. A fragrance of lilies and beeswax lingered. He cautiously opened another black door, and formed his mouth

146

into a "Hello?" as he entered.

The word died in his mouth when he took in the tableaux before him.

It was the funeral parlour, and it was in session.

The first thing he saw in the rectangular room was a huge, ornately-framed picture of the Madonna hanging from the wall facing him. It was painted in a modern – or primitive – style. Her radiating halo – perhaps gold leaf – glowed in the subdued candlelight cast from four huge wrought-iron standing candelabras positioned in the corners of the room. Her skin was blue, and her raiment red, but her yellow eyes contained compassion despite their eerie, direct gaze.

A plain, wooden coffin, painted black, sat in the centre of the room on top of a plinth covered in maroon velvet. Donnacha could not tell what was in the open coffin from this distance, but a skin-creeping horror of dead people shivered through him. He could still remember the waxy, lifeless features of his grandmother when she had been waked, in the old way, in her home. Donnacha had been eleven, and his father insisted he kiss her goodbye. He had practically dragged Donnacha to the coffin in her old living room, where the gathered neighbours drank cups of tea and glasses of whiskey. His lips only grazed her forehead, but he'd had to choke back a retch.

The old revulsion, and the shock at intruding in such a private ceremony, paralysed him.

The room was lined on all sides by seats, and they were occupied by people wearing traditional black. Their faces, grey with grief he supposed, turned to stare at him.

A wide man in a coal black suit emerged from a darker part of the room and walked up to him.

"I'm so sorry," Donnacha began in a whisper, "I was looking for Buster Mahon. I had no idea –"

"I'm him," he said in a quiet tone, and held out a square hand. Donnacha took it, and Buster gave him the shake that implied with one extra pulse of pressure he could crush his hand. Buster had the gait and carriage of someone who used to be a rugby player, or a soldier. Someone not afraid to apply force if provoked.

"You're Donnacha Sweeney, I'm guessing?"

Donnacha nodded to cover his surprise.

"Connie warned me you might be dropping by."

"Ah..."

"Constance Harte. You stayed in her B&B last night."

"Yes, of course!" He never remembered the names of any of the people he stayed with. "Tall lady," he added, idiotically.

Buster smiled in a neutral way, and titled his head back slightly as if appraising him. "Yes she is. Good judge of character."

Donnacha looked about, unsure what to do. The people in the room were standing now but remained fixed on him and Buster. He could not tell who the lead mourners were. They all seemed equally... morbid.

"You're looking for work?"

"Yes, but I don't have a CV —"

Buster waved him into silence. "Paper doesn't tell the tale of a man. Work does. Anyway, you got past the dog."

"I'll have to thank him."

This time Buster's eyes crinkled along with his smile. "He likes avocado."

Buster gestured to the door back to the pub. "Let's see how you handle yourself. After that we'll know what you can deal with."

"Now?"

"There's an apron behind the counter. A tradition of my father's. He always liked us neat."

"Okay."

Buster nodded at the door. "We'll be coming through in a minute, and you can begin."

"Connie said something about a room."

"No matter how it goes tonight, you can stay in the flat upstairs. Tomorrow we can assess."

Donnacha inclined his head, glad he'd thought to wear his black jeans and shirt, which he considered his uniform for bar work. He turned his back on the room and felt an unnerving vulnerability. A sibilant drone began, but Donnacha could not make out the words or even the language. He imagined it was a decade of the rosary or some other chanted prayer. He was relieved to depart and return to the vacant pub. Joxer didn't even raise his head from his paws when he entered.

A black apron hung from a peg behind the bar. He swapped it for his coat, and tied the apron around his waist. It hung to mid-shin, and he felt more like a European waiter than a barman. He spotted a dishcloth by the sink and began a wipedown of the counter even though it looked perfectly clean. It was his ritual for getting into the right mindset for the job: clean down the space and prepare for the array of mad ones and saints: always in proportion of ten to one.

Joxer got to his feet and gazed at the door. Buster walked in and the dog gave him a tail wag before he sat down, looking like a regal stone statue.

Buster noted Donnacha's final polish of the counter.

"Good habits," he said with approval.

The sea of mourners washed in behind him, and soon Donnacha had no time to think. It was a pints-of-stout and balls-of-malt crowd, with a sprinkling of shandys and white wines. A tab was established – no one's hand was allowed near a wallet. All the seats were full, and people milled around the bar – none obstructing orders. A buzz of conversation built up, but even illuminated by the cheery fire, which Buster kept feeding, the customers' faces retained a greyish cast.

After an hour, a sturdy woman in an old-style housecoat and a crocheted cap knocked through the swing doors with a big tray of sandwiches in her muscled arms.

"Delores! Just in time," declared Buster. A muted cheer rang out from the assembly. He relieved her of the tray and set it down on the nearest table. Hands grabbed the offerings in moments.

"Two more trays, and cake coming," she told him, before she swung out again.

Within minutes, most of the bar were chewing contentedly. Buster snagged a few for himself and for Donnacha. He deposited a plate bulging with ham and cheese sandwiches and moist tea cake behind the counter for Donnacha.

"Get these in you boyo, quick. They'll call for another round once they've scarfed that lot."

At the same time Delores returned with two china plates covered in tin foil, and left them on the corner of the counter. Nobody touched them.

"Delores, my beauty," Buster began, and curled his arm around her shoulders affectionately. She beamed at him. "Meet Donnacha Sweeney. Tonight's attendant. Connie sent him to us."

She eyeballed Donnacha the way a farmer appraises livestock.

"You seem competent."

Buster laughed. "Steady on, Delores! Such praise. It'll be offers of matrimony next."

She raised her eyes in an exaggerated eye roll. Clearly they were old friends.

"Delores is our hamlet's postmistress, professor of all the town's legends and gossip, and our establishment's provider of pub grub when required."

Buster was opening his mouth to say something else when a disturbance from outside the pub slipped in between the mumble of conversation.

Drumming; whistles; chimes.

The pub hushed, and the cacophony drew closer.

Nobody moved, or took their eyes from their drinks.

Joxer stood up.

Donnacha glanced at Buster, ready to ask a question. But the expression on the man silenced him. Buster looked like someone with a sombre duty. Next to him, Delores had her hands stuffed in the pockets of her housecoat, and her lips tightly held, as if holding back an alarm.

Three knocks hammered on the front door.

"You!" Buster said with quiet urgency to Donnacha. "Come with me."

A path through the bodies opened, and the two men pushed through the swing doors.

Through the wavy glass of the front door Donnacha could make out three figures.

"What –?" Donnacha started, but Buster clamped a big hand on his wrist and the pressure quietened him.

Buster opened the door.

Outside waited three capering characters, resplendent in suits of gleaming straw, wearing rough animal masks of straw: a goat, a hare, and a bull.

The goat played a battered tin whistle in an eerie melody that stuck to the minor keys, while the hare shook an old-fashioned tambourine, and the bull banged an ancient, stained bodhran drum.

They danced in the light cast through The Haunt's windows, and the flicking candle light from the carved turnips in front of the door. Behind them, darkness and fog. It was as if the town had melted away, and nothing existed except for these players and Buster and Donnacha.

The trio became stock-till, and struck up a folk tune that sounded familiar in a warped way. They sang a chant:

"Hungry we stand before your door
No food nor drink since the year before
Give us whiskey, give us bread
Open the door, let's wake the dead!"

They performed it three times, increasing their volume after each turn, until their last version was a shouted demand.

Silence again except for their excited breaths through the masks. There was only darkness behind the eyeholes.

"Welcome to our hearth, Mummers," Buster said. He carefully handed each one a coin.

He jerked his head at Donnacha to indicate he should open the door. Donnacha stood inside and held it. The three Mummers swept past him, bringing the smell of a field of barley bending to a wild wind under starry skies.

When Donnacha pushed through the swing doors after the entourage, he froze.

They had brought the coffin into the pub. It stood on six stools, parallel to the hearth, but not close to the fire. Joxer had vanished. The three Mummers stood in a half-circle around the head of the coffin.

Everybody was standing. Delores was stationed on the left of the coffin with a plate of cake, and Buster was at the counter collecting the other plate. He waved in an underhand manner to Donnacha to urge him to his side. Donnacha had to swerve by the coffin and Delores. This was his first chance to see what lay within. He darted a glance, and could only make out a dark shape. Something glinted into his eyes when he tried to see the face. Further unnerved, he almost hopped forward to reach Buster.

The big man picked up a china plate filled with thinly sliced pieces of meat, cheese, fruit, and soda bread. He pointed at a small silver salver, on which sat three glasses of whiskey. He pointed back at the coffin.

Donnacha picked up the tray, and followed his boss, who took up a position opposite Delores. Buster titled his head to indicate that Donnacha should stop at the foot of the coffin.

Donnacha kept his attention firmly on the glasses, concentrating on keeping the tray level, and halted where indicated. Immediately, the Mummers struck up another tune, the weirdest disharmony so far, accompanied by occasional cries, squawks, and yelps that were more animal than human.

The sound bounced off the walls in the room and magnified it. Donnacha felt like he was *inside* the song. An updraft caught the flames in the hearth and they roared and leaped, pumping out tremendous heat. The din began to reach intolerable levels and, at some unknown signal, the crowd joined in, stamping, clapping, and crying out encouragement.

The clamour became a great beast whipping around the room, seeking a prize.

Donnacha squeezed his eyes shut against the fear and the overwhelming sensory overload. A chilly breeze zipped past his neck and he nearly dropped the tray in shock.

He opened his eyes. The glasses were empty, the food taken from the plates.

Silence fell like an anvil dropped from a great height.

The Mummers spoke in unison:

"Look now, don't wait,
Learn your New Year's Fate.

One heartbeat: past
Two heartbeats: truth
Three heartbeats: dare
Four heartbeats: death."

Delores lowered her plate, and leaned forward slightly to stare into the coffin. Donnacha found himself counting a slow beat, and it seemed to him that she pulled back after two seconds. A line of people formed behind her, and they repeated her action.

Most only attempted a moment or two. One man slumped after three, and staggered away helped by a friend in the crowd.

Donnacha remained motionless, the tray of glasses balanced

on his hands. His mind stalled; the black eyeholes of the goat, hare, and bull remained fixed on him, unwavering throughout the parade of questers.

Finally, Buster stood in front of him, his solid face serious. He removed the tray from Donnacha's hands and gestured to the coffin.

Everyone else had looked. They waited on him.

He moved forward stiffly, and his trembling right hand clamped on the side of the coffin. He could almost smell his grandmother's perfume, and feel his lips brush her lifeless forehead.

The shape of a body, wrapped in a black shroud, lay in the coffin lined with black silk. An aged oval mirror covered the face. Its surface was dully reflective, and splattered with ink blots of tarnish.

Donnacha leaned forward so a dim version of his face appeared in the mirror.

One heartbeat: *he was with Mairead, dancing and laughing at the Irish Cultural Centre in Boston.*

Two heartbeats: *he staggered, blindfolded, after a version of himself dressed in gleaming white who walked arm-in-arm with an ethereally happy Mairead.*

Three heartbeats: *he stood behind the counter in The Haunt, Joxer by the fire, with a small group of contented customers; but once a year the Mummers would call...*

He tried to pull his gaze away from the mirror, and he sensed the moment stretching into what came next. A memory of the grinning spectre in the graveyard reaching out to him rose in his mind. A cool mist settled against his face, numbing it and blinding his sight. A dreadful bone-deep understanding of the constant proximity of death settled into him. During this night, as the tissue between worlds became as soft as dandelion down, the illusions of life were easily rent, and the reality of time's quick passage revealed.

The race existed to be run, not won.

He tried to say something, a gasp, a grateful cry for the unbearable beauty and doleful duty of living, but his body was locked as if bracing an anticipated blow... until a sudden pain at his ankle yanked him out of that vision, and he fell, clutching his leg.

"I've got you, lad," he heard Buster say, and his hands held Donnacha's shoulders, offering support and comfort.

Under the coffin, Joxer watched him alertly.

"It's over," Buster said, and he drew Donnacha up.

The Mummers were gone. Delores and the crowd had departed.

The coffin lay empty.

Donnacha heaved in a ragged breath.

By the counter, Connie saluted him with a glass of whiskey. "Happy Hallowe'en," she said with a solemn expression.

Donnacha turned to look at Buster.

"I want time and a half for that."

Buster slapped him on the back. "Let's talk terms and conditions. But first, how about a drink?"

Donnacha shook his head. "I need to get that dog some avocado."

Both Buster and Connie laughed, and Donnacha lurched forward, his feet awkward and unsteady. He could not sprint yet, but he could shuffle to the counter.

Around him reflections abounded: in a copper coal scuttle, the mirror over the fireplace, in the glass case of the clock, and the glint in the eyes of his patrons.

And in each one a hazy hand stretched to seize him.

Tilt

Karen Onojaife

If Heaven truly was a place on Earth, Iyere wondered, who was to say that that place couldn't be a crappy little casino on the top floor of a shopping centre in Shepherd's Bush?

If she really thought about it (and generally, she tried not to think about it), she understood that there wasn't all that much of a difference between her and the patrons of the betting shops that seemed to sprout in every empty space on the high street. And next to the betting shops were the pawn shops, their windows emblazoned with bright posters depicting people inexplicably joyful at the idea of having to put prized possessions in hock. But those places, grubby with daylight and disapproving glances from passers-by, could make a girl feel like she had a problem, whereas a casino at two, three, or four a.m., while not necessarily a sensible choice, at least made Iyere feel like she had taken a considered decision to court decadence.

'Decadence,' she could imagine her sister, Ivie, scoffing. 'This place is called *Barry's Casino*.'

Which is fair enough. But until Iyere could figure out a way to make it to the neon lit hiss of the Bellagio's fountains, Barry's would have to do. Besides, she had come to appreciate the fake solicitude from the liveried doormen; the powdery sweet scent of carpet cleaner that perfumed the tired shag pile lining the mirrored hallway; the complimentary warm, sugared pretzels that staff brought round on silver platters, presumably on the nights that Barry was feeling especially generous, and the unpredictable choice of soundtrack piped onto the casino floor, this early morning's selection being a run through of Gloria Estefan's greatest hits.

What she liked most of all was that the two, three or four a.m. crowd at Barry's Casino knew what it was about; a loose camaraderie of sorts but, essentially, people would mind their own business. No tourists wanting to distract with chatter, or rookies taking up valuable space at a table while they fumbled over their chips and mixed up their bets. No, the early morning crew just hummed like a hive; gentle sighs and sometimes light taps on the back from a neighbour, either in celebration or commiseration, depending on the cut of a deck.

"What the fuck is it?" Ivie had asked her once, simultaneously incredulous and despairing on one shameful afternoon when she had caught Iyere rifling through her handbag for money. "What is it that you get from doing this? From being at that place?"

Iyere, face flushed and eyes bright, hadn't known what to say. To explain that she liked the sweat of cheap plastic chips in her hand seemed small. She liked to stack these totems upon the green baize of a table, liked to listen to the rattle of the ball as it skittered across the wheel as lightly as a girl skipping rope, liked the swish of cards through a croupier's gloved hand as they fanned the deck this way and that, the flicker of white edges like breaking waves.

She could have spoken to the science of things; the ticker tape parade of dopamine lighting up in her brain and the rerouting of neural pathways.

Or she could have dealt in practicalities; for example, the fact that she had been borrowing money from the petty cash account at the community college where she taught so she needed to win some back and win big, so that she could replace it all before anyone found out.

Or perhaps this: you and your little girl, Ofure, are in a local park one day and she is playing on a swing while you are reading a book. This playground is nothing special, just something that's there on the walk home from school and there's no way of telling, just from looking, that somehow the local council has missed the last three annual inspections, or that screws in the swing's frame are coming loose, or that when Ofure clambers to a standing position on the rubber tire, mittened hands clutching metal chains, the whole structure will groan and pitch forward, tipping her, your little girl, onto the hard ground, head first. Bright red blood splashed across snow.

Iyere had always liked the things she liked too intensely. If it wasn't gambling, it would have been other things. It *had* been other things – food, sex, or telling lies just because. But after Ofure died, the casino seemed the only place where Iyere could comfortably exist in time. It wasn't that she enjoyed the losses – in fact those made her panicked and sick, and aside from an ephemeral flare of glee, she didn't really much care for the wins. But these swings of fate either way seemed at least conceivable and therefore manageable, and matters that she had a hand in, as opposed to the loss of Ofure, which had been so complete, so profound and so unexpected that even years later, she could scarcely allow herself to accept that it had in fact occurred.

So Iyere had said nothing, and Ivie had just stared at her. Iyere had known that if her sister hadn't been tired from chemo, she might have tried to fight her right there in the hallway until, as Ivie had put it once, "You see some fucking sense!" As it was, Ivie had been exhausted, giving a mirthless chuckle before sliding onto the nearby sofa in defeat.

"Whatever you're looking for, it's not there," Ivie had said, fixing Iyere with a hard gaze. "*She's* not there. Not in a fucking casino."

"She's not anywhere," Iyere had said, and then she had walked out, a stolen twenty pound note still in her hand.

Iyere always knew what time it was, despite the casino's attempt to dissemble by the regular flow of free drinks and the complete absence of clocks. Even without her watch she knew because she had always preferred the night hours, enjoying their relative quiet and the softness of possibility that sunlight tended to burn away.

She had been there for about an hour, having had a couple of uninspired rounds of blackjack and Texas Hold'em when she noticed the croupier standing at an empty roulette table across the room.

Iyere knew all the croupiers there by now and this one was definitely new. The woman's hands darted into the thick fall of her locked hair, fingers moving swiftly as she arranged it into a messy bun. The action made the crisp white of her shirt draw tightly across her breasts and Iyere scolded herself for noticing, so she looked away, her face feeling warm and her thoughts suddenly scattered. She made herself count to ten, made herself engage in boring chitchat with the dealer at her table, and then counted to thirty before she allowed herself to look again.

The croupier was already looking at her, her head tilted to one side, one corner of her mouth beginning to lift in amusement. She let her gaze travel the length of Iyere's body before it returned to her face, and then she nodded once, mostly solemn but that half smile hinting at a degree of mocking in her assessment, or her invitation, or whatever this was.

"Morning," the woman said as Iyere neared her table. Iyere just nodded, not entirely trusting her voice to speak until she had taken a sip of her drink. "And how are we today?"

"Oh, you know," Iyere shrugged, letting her eyes fall on the woman's name tag; '*Essy*'.

"Oh, I know," Essy said, allowing a grin to bloom across her face, leaving Iyere bewildered enough to glance behind her to see if Essy's smile had been directed at someone else. But everyone else seemed far away, somehow, although she could still see them and hear them, everything dulled as if with a thick veil. And when she turned back to the table, Essy was closer, leaning forward slightly with one hand positioned either side of the wheel.

"Bets, please," Essy said, looking at Iyere expectantly.

Iyere placed a chip on a numbered square, barely even checking where she'd left it, preferring instead to watch the flick of Essy's hands as she spun the wheel one way and tossed the tiny ball the other. They both watched the ball stutter and skip until Essy murmured, *"Rien ne va plus,"* and a moment later she swept Iyere's losing chip away from the board.

"So, you're new?" Iyere asked. She had the sense that Essy barely managed to avoid an eye roll, surely having heard the question a thousand times over by now from various lecherous parties. Still, Iyere liked to think that there was a significant difference between being a lecherous party and an interested one.

"Not really," Essy said. "Was on days before. I asked to switch shifts because I prefer the night time crowd. They're more-"

"Desperate?" Iyere offered.

"If you like. Bets, please," Essy said, placing the tip of her right index finger on the polished chrome handle of the wheel as she waited. Iyere wasn't sure how old Essy was; she was one of those women whose skin was so dark and unlined that it was always hard to tell. Younger than her at least, despite the wrinkled skin of Essy's large hands, and Iyere was seized with the abrupt desire to lose herself in every single fold of them.

Iyere put a stack of chips on the table.

Essy nodded and then started the wheel with a brisk whisk of her wrist. They both stared in silence at the ball, Essy eventually making a soft sound of consolation in the back of her throat before sweeping Iyere's stack away. "Let me guess," she said, pausing for a moment to survey Iyere once more. "Teacher?"

Iyere gave a surprised smile and tipped her glass in acknowledgement.

"Working here gives you all types of party tricks," Essy said. "What do you teach?"

"Fairy tales," Iyere said. "The taxonomy of them. Did you know, for example, that pretty much every country has its own version of Little Red Riding Hood?"

Essy considered for a moment before shrugging. "Makes sense. Show me a country where girls aren't hunted by wolves. Bets, please."

Iyere lost another stack of chips.

"Desperate, you said? Earlier," Essy clarified, as she swept the chips away. "But you know what I think? I think 'desperate' gets a bad rap. Desperation gets people closer to being honest."

"Honest about what?"

"About what they're doing," Essy said. "Bets, please," she repeated, waiting for Iyere to place a short stack of chips on the table before continuing. "I mean, who isn't gambling, really? It's just that most of you like to pretend otherwise. The girl who fucks a fuckboy because she hopes that good sex might tempt him into being a better boyfriend has placed a bet, no? All of the components are there; consideration, chance and prize."

Iyere choked briefly on her drink, both somewhat thrilled and taken aback by the boldness of Essy's language. She wiped at her mouth with the back of her hand before meeting Essy's gaze. "Well, I wouldn't call a fuckboy a prize," she said.

"Ah, but the girl in our example doesn't know that yet – no one does, until she lays down the stakes. Schrödinger's Fuckboy if you will. Bets, please."

Iyere lost another two chips. "My sister thinks I have a problem," she said.

"Why?" Essy shot back. Because it's three a.m. on a Wednesday and you're at a casino, wearing pyjamas and your hair is still wrapped? Bets, please."

Iyere pushed the remainder of her chips onto a number, but her eyes were fixed on Essy's face instead of the wheel. There was something about her tugging at Iyere's memory but she couldn't quite place it, faint as it was and overwhelmed by the flutter in Iyere's chest whenever she allowed her gaze to rest on the curve of Essy's full lower lip or the gleam of skin at her collarbone.

Iyere lost again and Essy shrugged, sweeping the chips away with a flourish before folding her arms. "Well, it seems that you're out of –"

"I had a daughter," Iyere blurted out, unable to stand the idea of having to leave Essy's table now that her money had run out. She had never spoken of Ofure to strangers before, not like this and she wasn't even sure what drove her now. Something in Essy's gaze perhaps; it seemed soft but also demanding, as if her attention, once bestowed, required great things in exchange.

"I had a daughter and now I don't," she continued. "I was a mother, and now I'm not. What do you call that, I wonder? What's the word?"

Essy's eyes seemed to glow momentarily, and Iyere watched the pink flicker of her tongue dampen her lower lip. "I don't know the word in English," Essy said, her eyes fixed on Iyere, travelling over her face. "But then there have always been other tongues."

Iyere nodded, considering the idea of a grief translated, wondering if her heartbreak might taste differently in new words. She felt more speech rising in her, almost unbidden as she asked Essy if she could see her after her shift.

"Why?" Essy asked.

"Because you want to take me home with you and the house always wins?" Iyere said with borrowed confidence.

Essy laughed and Iyere realised it was the first time she had seen a genuine smile cross the other woman's face. Iyere wanted to know everything she could about that unknowable face, kiss everything she could from this stranger's lips and much else besides but she would be happy with whatever Essy might allow.

"Fraternising with patrons outside of the casino? We're not supposed to," Essy mused, making the pale marble of the roulette ball weave through a twist of her fingers as she thought. "But I'm open to persuasion."

"Hospitals. Police stations. Mortuaries. Strip clubs." Essy counted the words off her fingers as she listed other places she had worked. They were sat in her kitchen, drinking hot mugs of peppermint tea. "Always night shifts. It's just better. I prefer the places and times where you meet people at a crossroads, so to speak."

"Why?"

That's how I feed.

Or at least this is what Iyere thought she heard but when she looked up, Essy had her mug to her lips and appeared to still be pondering her question. "I guess you could call me a people person."

Iyere thought this was both true and untrue. She was not entirely sure that Essy *liked* people so much as she liked collecting their stories, and there was something undeniable about Essy that made people want to share them. Iyere had already exhausted her own sticky mess of secrets; the stolen money, the gambling, Ivie being sick, and what happened to Ofure.

"Grief," Iyere found herself saying, "has skinned me."

Essy nodded and leaned forward slightly, her elbows resting on the grubby Formica table top. "Go on," she murmured, and it took Iyere a few moments to recognise the look on her face; it was the same avidity, she realised, that Ivie would wear on the days that her lips were too cracked, her throat too sore to eat anything of substance. On those days, she liked to sit and watch Iyere eat, her eyes tracing the column of Iyere's throat as she swallowed, and though Iyere hated it, hated the feeling of being consumed by her sister's gaze, she allowed it each time.

"Grief has skinned me," Iyere repeated, "but I think that maybe you might change that." Iyere didn't know she meant to say it until she did, but she was struck by the rightness as she uttered the words.

"*I* think," Essy said, setting her mug down with a smirk, "that you might be overestimating the restorative powers of a one-night stand."

Then they went outside to Essy's back garden, the night lining their skins and their lungs smoky with petrichor. Iyere's idea; she had half remembered something about a meteor shower tonight and so she had suggested they go out and look.

"The Perseids." Essy sighed, her eyes scanning the skies as if she could see things that Iyere couldn't, her gaze somehow able to penetrate the light pollution and constant cloud that hugged this part of the Earth's atmosphere, to reach the stuttering trail of meteors shaking themselves free of comets.

Iyere knew fuck all about astronomy, but she had managed to watch half an episode of the *Sky at Night* once, and so she'd remembered that shooting stars weren't even stars at all, just bits of rock, debris and dust burning up as they tore through the atmosphere, blazing themselves into nothing, mostly gone before they could hit the ground.

Iyere took a deep breath so she could exhale her daughter's name. She sensed Essy shift as she listened. Iyere had noticed this about the woman; she liked to listen with her whole body as if words were vibrations that she needed to catch and recalibrate before she could issue the right speech in return.

"What's your favourite fairy tale?" Iyere whispered.

Essy shook her head, her eyes gleaming suddenly. "People don't remember my favourites the way they used to. Some do, but not like before. Maybe not even you, Professor," she said, her already raspy voice further thickened by a sudden emotion Iyere couldn't decipher.

Iyere watched the way Essy's right hand was working, as if she were still making that roulette ball dance through her fingers, and, without giving herself the chance to second guess, Iyere grabbed those fingers and entwined them with her own, before bringing their joined hands up to her mouth.

"Let's go back inside," Iyere said, the words damp against

Essy's skin.

"What now?" Essy said, her hint of a smile unfurling into another grin when she saw Iyere's sudden bashfulness. "What are you after? Something new for the scrapbook?"

"I've been with women before," Iyere replied, allowing a mild dart of irritation to colour her voice.

"No doubt," Essy nodded, her gaze pinning Iyere where she stood. "But you haven't been with me." She was silent for several long seconds, scanning Iyere's face while the latter held her breath, scared at the thought of being dismissed, but equally scared at the thought of getting what she was so clumsily asking for.

Essy shifted the hand that was still in Iyere's grasp so that she could trace a light finger across Iyere's cheekbone, leaving a tingling warmth in its wake. "You said grief had skinned you...I guess we'll see."

"How will we see?"

Essy shook her head slowly. "I'll need an offering."

"All right," Iyere said, Essy's hand cupping her face by now, her thumb resting at the corner of her mouth and so she turned her head slightly so she could lick it, kiss it, envelop its oddly nutty sweetness in the dark warmth of her mouth for just a second and Essy smiled, delighted and surprised at Iyere's fleeting boldness. "All right," she repeated, as Essy gently rubbed a stripe of wetness along Iyere's jaw.

Essy's bedroom was quiet, teased with traces of moonlight and time went elsewhere.

The bed was a mess of sheets and Iyere knew that Essy's skin was the warmest she had ever touched, heat radiating from its every inch.

Things were different in this kind of darkness; the gleam of her knees on either side of Essy's head like the curve of smooth rocks breaching the surface of a pond. The curl of Essy's back as she writhed above her was like the roll of a night ocean and when they kissed, it was sugar and salt on their tongues.

Essy liked to stop and watch whenever she made Iyere come, the look on her face unreadable as she scanned the other woman's. Iyere never knew what she was looking for but when she found it, there would be a half smile and then she would lower her head and give soft little licks, lapping at the beads of sweat on Iyere's stomach, or a tear collected in the curve of an ear, or the dampness between her legs, and this is what she had meant, Iyere realised in a half-dazed wonder, when she had said she required an offering.

Essy's attention was relentless, of a kind that didn't care if the recipient could bear it or not, and there were times Iyere was not sure she could bear it, the sensations so thick that they seemed to slow her breath and blood. Each time she gasped, it was half a show of delight and half a reminder for her lungs to keep working, and she would tear her eyes away from Essy's penetrating gaze to the window, searching for the night sky with its trails of bruised clouds making distant cathedrals.

Her blood was still thundering in her ears when Essy sat up, her gaze solemn as she wiped wetness from her mouth. She stroked Iyere's face with the back of her hand and then she placed a cool palm on the centre of her stomach and pressed down firmly. Iyere jolted immediately, her mind transported to a sunlit afternoon in a cemetery when she'd sat by Ofure's grave after all the mourners had gone, save for Ivie. Ivie who had stood and watched Iyere as she'd sat by the mound of freshly turned over earth and dug her hands, wrist deep, into its coolness as she cried. Iyere had made unintelligible sounds that came from a place within that she had never known of, that she in fact suspected had not even existed until Ofure's death had torn her open somewhere, concealed claw marks that remained deep and bleeding.

Essy removed her hand and Iyere drew an agonised gasp of

breath, sitting up and scrambling away until her back was pressed against the headboard. "What did you –?"

"You gave an offering, I accepted, so… you get another spin of the wheel," Essy said.

Iyere stared at her blankly. "What are –?"

"You know what," Essy said. "And you know how."

And as she said it, Iyere realised this was true. Maybe part of her had realised it from the moment Essy had spoken of crossroads, because Iyere had heard of Essy's kind in half remembered stories from her aunt. While the old woman had called her by a different name, a different gender, Iyere recalled a couple of salient facts: a bringer of mischief and chaos in the guise of teaching a lesson.

This is how I feed, Essy had said.

Iyere had fed her and now Essy would give thanks by giving her a choice.

"I'm sorry about just now," Essy said, gesturing to her stomach. "I had to see what it is that you really want. People tend to lie, even at times like these. *Especially* times like these. It's strange, the way your kind does that. Even if it means you fuck up your chances."

"A chance to…Ofure?" Iyere stammered. "Back here with me?"

"Ofure," Essy said. "Although you should know that death has a scent."

"I wouldn't care."

"Hmm," Essy smiled thinly. "That's what they all say. More importantly, death will not be denied, which means we'd have to make a trade. No such thing as something for nothing after all. If Ofure comes back, someone else has to take her place."

"Someone else would have to die?"

"And it can't be you," Essy said quickly. "Can't be some random either. Has to be your blood, or close to it. Hey," Essy continued, raising her hands in supplication. "I don't make the rules. But I get them. I mean, if there's no skin in the game, are you really even playing?"

"No one would make that choice," Iyere said, her gaze fixed on the knot she had made of her hands in her lap. She was dreaming, she decided. She was dreaming and any minute now she would wake up.

"You'd be surprised at what people would do," Essy replied, her voice suddenly flat, her gaze dull, and Iyere remembered the fevered nightmare of the days just after Ofure had died; all the bargains she had tried to make with indifferent gods for just a second of grace. Iyere would have traded anything and anyone, a whole world perhaps, for one moment of Ofure's breath against her face, or the press of her chubby arms around Iyere's leg.

But the only person she had to give up was Ivie.

And she's sick anyway.

Iyere winced, trying to dampen the sharp voice inside of her.

Ofure was meant to have had so much more time, and if Ivie herself could choose, wouldn't she want the same thing, in fact, hadn't she said (albeit when her tumour was still a blossoming secret, even to her) that if she could change places with Ofure, she would?

You're dreaming, she reminded herself, but her heart was weighing options all the same. If such a choice were even possible, she understood that one couldn't make it without being diminished, without being punished in some way. No doubt there was a further, final offering that Essy was eager to collect?

"Why me?" Iyere asked, understanding now that it had been Essy who had chosen her tonight.

"Because," Essy shrugged. "Because out of all the people there, I could tell that yours would taste the sweetest."

It would be easier at night, Iyere realised, for Essy to find what she needed; people were so much more vulnerable during these hours, hearts tilted so they could spill more easily, wounds so much more visible in the right kind of light.

What Iyere wanted was both of them; Ofure on her lap and

Ivie by her side with the years stretching out ahead for all three of them like open roads. But if she had to choose, how to choose? After all, her aunt would always end her stories with the words 'You can't out trick a trickster god'.

You could refuse the bet, Iyere reminded herself. *You could walk away from the table for once, before you lose what you can ill afford to.*

But Iyere knew that she had been maimed by her daughter's death, grief skinned as Essy now knew, and the existence Iyere had experienced since then was for the most part in a half light, in half measures, the half-life of her devotion to Ofure one of the few things that allowed her to stand.

And yet, that memory of the afternoon in the cemetery, which had stretched into the evening, then an all-night vigil, Ivie with her the whole time. The following morning had been fresh with dewdrops, making their funeral clothes damp. The spring of grass blades beneath her hands. Hearing the growing tangle of birdsong as her ears became re-accustomed to sound. The weight of Ivie as she shifted, placing her head in Iyere's lap. The last of the night's thin trails fading from the sky, taking with it the strange gravity that made hearts tilt. Iyere had felt her own heart quiver and shift as it tried to right itself, but she hadn't wanted to let it, had wanted it to remain forever tilted, always on the edge of spilling with tales of *we loved her, she loved us and the daylight can't take back what is ours.*

What was the lesson, Iyere wondered?

Was it to seize second chances no matter the cost, or was it that your life simply had to be lived, tragedies and all, to make it complete?

Iyere, you're just dreaming, she told herself again.

But what if I'm not?

"Would I remember any of this?" Iyere asked. "I mean, if I made a choice, how would it work? And would I know what I had done?"

Essy just stared at her, her gaze implacable, and so Iyere took a deep breath, and decided.

Demolition

Nick Adams

The last lights went off in the old shopping centre this evening, and the demolition team have immediately moved in. The doors were locked to the public for the last time, and the team were handed the keys, and it was not at all ceremonial. They pass reverently through the dark halls and hollowed-out spaces, placing their explosives like they are offerings to the husk of a deity that lingers here. They all came to the centre as children and they remember that you queued for the cinema here and the screens let out just over there. The video shop was here, and this concrete bowl full of steel tubes and old pennies was a fountain once. It holds just under sixteen pounds in assorted, partially outdated currency.

They are watched by maimed mannequins as they work, and they talk about taking one home, taking it as a souvenir because who would know? It seems wrong though – it seems as if they belong here.

The implosion is to be carried out tomorrow. Metal barriers have been erected a safe distance from the entrance in the square and a good turnout is expected. There is an area of temporary seating and a small platform where the mayor is to stand and talk about regeneration and renewal and progress. Young people who come from different towns, who never visited the shopping centre and who are paid by the hour, are due to be armed with plastic bazookas, and are expected to fire t-shirts into the crowd bearing the name and logo of the new mall on the outskirts of town.

Except none of these things will happen.

In the small and fallow hours of the morning, the residents of the houses overlooking the square on which the old shopping centre stands will wake up, some teased slowly and some tugged sharply from their dreams. They will later report hearing the moaning of great slabs of stone splitting gradually and irreconcilably in two and the sigh and wheeze of old bricks crumbling. They will reflect on how much the noise of the rusting bones of the structure pulling themselves apart sounded like popcorn kernels exploding one after another.

The police station will receive a dozen calls between two and three in the morning, and the picture they get will be confusing. A living mass, a mess of concrete, they'll hear. An urban behemoth, a commercial golem, the old jeweller's bobbing past the window. This shambling thing will be seen propelling itself forward on blunted pillar-legs. It'll set a course across the market square and out onto the high street, dragging its blind shopfronts with it in a tangled parade. It'll leave scars in the tarmac, will grind bus stops into safety-glass confetti, will raise a cacophony of out-of-sync car alarms and will obliterate the peace statue on the mini roundabout by Sainsbury's.

Out past the sports centre and through the civic gardens it'll tear and stagger, shaking free the colonies of pigeons nesting in its encrusted nooks. They will scatter into the sky, dark on dark, and it will seem as if they are pieces of the fabric of the building itself falling away in upended gravity. The remnants of the ice rink housed in its now-exposed basement will shear off against the edge of the public library and come to rest atop the floral clock. There will be faded hoardings advertising restaurants that no longer exist strewn amongst the freshly planted tulips.

At around four in the morning it will disappear, lurching into the woods behind the Red Lion, swallowed whole by the trees. With it being early spring, the bluebells are out, and it will be a surprise, in hindsight, how few of them are trampled. By now the police will be out on the roads, and so will the fire brigade and several ambulances, as if nobody knows what kind of emergency this is.

There will be noise and disturbance in the woods, and it will soon pass out of range of human eyes and ears. The not-creature forcing its way through the trees will shake roosting birds from their nests and will drive badgers and foxes from their dens as its awkward movements wrench tangles of roots from the soil and collapse tunnels in on themselves.

The old shopping centre will reappear shortly after dawn, spotted by a dog walker as it makes heavy progress across farmland past the ring road. It'll soon have attracted a convoy of gawkers and there will be cars pulled over all along the hard shoulder and people with binoculars and cameras and flasks of milky coffee. They'll agree, more or less, that it looks as if it's not just dumbly ploughing forwards until it expires; it looks very much like it's headed straight for the new Shopping Village and Retail Experience at Brooks Field, due to open on Saturday with thousands of exclusive discounts and a range of free activities for the kids.

There'll be a litter of children trailing behind the thing now, steadily gaining confidence as it becomes clear that it doesn't notice or is indifferent to their presence. They will slalom amongst its crude footprints and scoop up pieces of flint and clods of earth to lob at its tattered backside.

There'll be much less of it now. Great chunks of it will have been hewn off in the course of its missing hours. The photo booth will eventually be found broken and dented astride a stile near Longhill Lane, the curtain still pulled across.

Only a long and ragged strip of the subterranean car park will still be attached, dragging behind the main body of shops and food court like a lame limb. The further it goes the more the central mass will haemorrage facilities; the creche jettisoned by the Barney's Chicken roundabout, the forgotten contents of the Lost and Found dashed across both lanes of the dual carriageway.

It'll slow to a stuttering shuffle by half past eight, but won't come to a halt.

The demolitions team will have been roused from their sleep and will be on the scene now, holding a crisis meeting at the Little Chef that offers a panoramic view of the monstrosity's progress. There will be representatives from the police and the council, and an executive from the Brooks Field team who will swear that there'll be a whole new scale of shitstorm if that thing gets any closer to the Shopping Village, and who'll spill her coffee as she gestures out the window.

There will be objections that it's simply unsafe to carry out a demolition now, without the proper precautions, without a perimeter established. The decision will be made regardless.

The detonations will take place at noon once the old shopping centre has reached the stretch of open fields between the bypass and the new complex. The public will see the execution of the great old beast as it plays out in neat synchrony, and will not know that this is part luck, part chaos — it will not resemble the planned demolition in the slightest. A series of blasts will cascade along the spine of the building and it will buckle and stumble. Its repurposed limbs will crumble away in clouds of dust and debris and the whole structure will seem to kneel submissively before its collapse.

Its metal skeleton will be exposed now, like the bleached remains of a once-beached whale. The escalators that ran through its innards will be turned to the outside and will grind at the grass and mud for fruitless purchase. The thing will shudder and groan, and will then fall into its own rubble, inert.

The field will be cordoned off for several weeks while the debris is cleared. The new mall will not open late, and will not offer any indication of what happened or nearly happened. People will come and shop and eat at one of nine popular food franchises, and park for free in a car park that is on its own bigger than the whole of the old building. They will watch small birds darting about amongst the neat, glossy vegetation under the great glass ceiling, and they won't know if they are meant to be there or if they're trapped. Then they will walk the short distance to the site where the old shopping centre fell. They will sift through the grass for shards of concrete and they will take them home as souvenirs.

You will own one of these shards, and you will keep it on your windowsill alongside your cactus, where it will catch the early evening sun. It will be a once-brick, an almost brick with one shoulder shaved off. Its face – what you imagine to be its face – will be worn and contoured by time, while the other sides will be rougher and covered with small, jagged points and ridges.

You will have it nearly a month before you have need to try to move it, and discover that you can't.

It won't just be stuck – it will be fused to the windowsill in such a way that you can't see the join, and you won't remember if the sill looked like this before, or whether this layered, flaking patina is something new. You'll detach the shard eventually with a hammer and a screwdriver and it'll leave a hole that you'll mean to sort out but will become a part of your landscape and a piece of your apathy, and will be invisible to you soon enough.

You will toss the shard into the weeds beyond the end of the garden, and you will bind and tie it inside a dustbin bag even though this seems excessive, even though you're not sure what you're guarding against, just to be sure.

Seeing as you don't follow the local news, you won't find out until much later that the same kind of thing has been happening at the new mall. You won't know about the low wall that will have appeared overnight snaking across the soft play area, and you won't hear that it has been knocked down twice only to reappear in a new form, taking a new route. It will have reconstructed itself once, curling around the customer services desk like a concrete tentacle, waist-high now, and it will have grown back again, winding through the changing rooms in Zara.

You won't find out about this until it's already happened and all the reports have been written, and you'll notice as you read them how the language shifts – from *appeared* to *reconstructed* to *grown*.

You'll visit out of curiosity, just like everyone else, and you will be part of the wave that gives the owners of Brooks Field false confidence. *Look,* they'll say – *people keep coming, people are loyal, we can ride this out.* The newly grown walls will be screened off behind temporary barriers and children will be scooped up onto their parents' shoulders to peer over. *They're higher now,* the children will report, the ones that have been before and can compare. *They're nearly touching the ceiling. It's like a whole line of stalagmites stuck together. Or stalagtites.* There will be discussion about which is which.

The barriers will not be temporary. Nor will they contain the new architecture blossoming throughout the mall. More structures will rise all the time, some of them inside the retail spaces and some of them out. They will take the forms of towers and turrets and buttresses and staircases that end in abrupt chasms, and they will be made of the same recognisable materials but they will be contorted in wild and organic ways. They will be described as Dali-esque and Geiger-esque, but they will continue to reproduce the same underpinning structures – there will still be handrails and lift shafts and fire exits – as if these things are hard-coded into their genetic make-up.

Contractors will work through the night, through several nights, to hack away at this unbidden exoskeleton with an arsenal of power tools. Clouds of dust will rise illuminated by the glow of sodium lamps as the mall attempts to wrestle back control and assert normality without disruption, without reference to the mushrooming carapace consuming its western wings.

Retailers will be relocated.

Shoppers will be re-routed.

Samples will be taken and retaken and scrutinised, and will be found to be nothing more than brick and mortar. It will be noted that the new walls are full of conjoined air pockets and will resemble warped honeycomb when sliced open.

Nature will not be as easily overpowered as commerce. Over the course of a long and wet summer, the mall's new hide will be scaled by jasmine and honeysuckle and climbing weeds. It will be clad in an armour of heavy emerald leaves, and pipistrelle bats will make homes in its myriad crevices, emerging half-seen at dusk to flit about and skim over the heads of the last of the day's shoppers as they return to their cars. Atop the distorted towers storks will build nests and pigeons will insert themselves into the gaps left behind amongst the wandering stairways where they open into the sky.

Sounds will be heard from within the abandoned areas, and they will be metallic or industrial or animal depending on who hears them. The great glass dome will crack and eventually shatter as the new skin contracts and rearranges itself, and the trapped birds will fly away.

Further tests will be carried out.

Researchers will enter the changed half of the mall and will return unharmed. Daredevils will break into the site after dark and will live-stream their explorations of the subsumed sections.

It will be announced that the new growth is entirely harmless to human health, that the mall is investigating ways of reopening the west wing.

Shoppers will be unsettled and deterred regardless. Rumours of the mall's closure will become commonplace. Heavy losses will be incurred. It will be assumed that it is only a matter of time.

There will be a folly growing amongst the weeds in the no-man's land beyond the bottom of your garden. You won't notice it until winter comes and the greenery falls away, and there will be discussions amongst the neighbours and consultations with the council regarding the best course of action. Lessons will be learnt from the mall and it will be left alone.

Other such structures will appear across town. They will grow to various heights and their uncanny shapes will suggest various natures and purposes. The one in the town centre just off the market square will be the largest and will have bloomed into the form of something hollow and conch-like, the rows of bricks running vertically out of the ground and meeting to make a hood which will loom protectively over the Nigel and Mabel Surridge memorial bench. This may or may not mean something.

Tourists who come to see what the mall has become will have their photos taken in front of these follies and a map will be produced showing a suggested route around town. Keyrings will be available at Visitor Information and the bakery will produce limited-edition gingerbread edifices. There will be no more demolitions.

The Redemption of Billy Zane

Liz Jones

I saw a dead body earlier. It was the first I've ever seen. Well, it wasn't the whole body. Just the arm. It – he – was being pulled from the sea. A man in the water to his waist was heaving out the corpse. In fact, I saw the crowd of people staring first, and I think I knew what they were gawping at without having to look myself. But I looked anyway. I couldn't drag my eyes away. And then I walked back along the seafront to the café, sat down at my usual table and waited for coffee.

Louise has been working in the café fifteen years. She knows how all the regulars take their drinks. She knows if their eldest daughters take communion yet. She knows which table they prefer, and whether they will speak to her in English, or Greek, Italian, French or Bulgarian. She knows which of the waitresses the yacht skippers are sleeping with that year. And the café's looked almost the same that whole time. Last summer they had new white umbrellas out the front, put there by one of the beer companies to replace the faded yellow ones. But there's a screwed-up tea towel down the side of the coffee machine that no one can remember getting stuck there.

When Louise started in the café she didn't know how long she would stay. That year, she was twenty-five and beautiful and she was screwing the café owner (now her husband), the guy in the car rental place next door and one of the skippers on a rotational basis. The car rental guy, Andreas, knew about the other two and he was cool with it. The skipper, Giorgos, knew about Andreas only, and was not cool with it, but pretended to be most of the time when he was with Louise. The café owner, Ilias, didn't know about either of the other two and would have gone ballistic. Louise never told him.

Ilias can't keep still. He and Louise have a place in the hills overlooking the town, a block that was never finished, reinforcing wires twisting out of the top of the concrete. They live in one room and they keep their savings in the TV because Ilias doesn't trust the banks. All day he flits on his pistachio-coloured scooter between the apartment building and the café and a place where he goes to play draughts, never lingering in any of these locations for more than ten minutes. Sometimes he puts Louise on the back of the bike at short notice to take her places. He doesn't like her to walk anywhere. He starts a million conversations he never finishes. Probably that's why she's thin. Being around that much nervous energy can do that to a person.

In the winter, Louise and Ilias go and live part of the time in his dead mother's house in the mountains, and pick greens in the fields to eat. There's an old olive grove, and Ilias stops dashing about, and there are snatches of peace. That is the island Louise says she dreams of. Ilias is older than her and I know she imagines a day when he will be dead and she will be there on her own, her skin turning slowly to leather, chewing on olives and listening to the cicadas.

For now, she spends all day knocking back bad white wine from a Coke Zero can she keeps under the counter.

One day back in June, someone new came into the café. An actor Louise had had a crush on twenty years ago, maybe more. He had a beautiful face, full lips that curled like water over a rock in a stream, and he was wearing a flat white cap to cover his baldness. She knew him at once, would have known him anywhere. Billy, he was called. No one else saw him come in, and he was alone. There was no sign of Ilias, though her phone had been buzzing at her hip all morning. Louise went to the actor's table to take his order.

He hailed her in Greek from a distance, but she stopped him

with a 'Hello there', and he looked relieved. Despite having lost all his hair, he looked much younger than his age, which was around fifty. He could have passed for thirty-five, with his smooth skin and clear eyes, petulant attitude held just in check. He wasn't wearing a ring, but Louise was pretty sure he was married. He glanced up at her with those melancholy eyes in his spoilt, tanned face. He looked deep into her soul, but all he asked for was a frappé, and she went inside the dark of the café, trembling, to make it.

He'd had a long career but it had peaked in the late nineties, when he'd played the villain in the highest grossing film of all time, earning a reputation as a cad and a misanthrope, indistinguishable from the character he played. As she frothed his coffee, Louise wondered how it would feel to hit the heights so soon and for it all to be downhill after that. She wondered too if he was staying on the island, or if he was visiting from Antiparos, where the A-listers usually went with their helicopters. Why was he slumming it there, in her café? It was not the smartest café on the strip, and it was far from the smartest strip in the Cyclades.

When Louise took the coffee out to Billy, he told her to pull up a chair and join him.

'Oh,' she said, 'I'd love to, but I'm working.' He looked up and down her legs and then glanced around the café.

'There's no one here. You can sit down with me for a minute.'

He spoke just as he did on screen. Privileged, commanding. Yet she felt sorry for him.

'You know who I am,' he said.

'Sure,' she said. She thought about mentioning a different film, pretending to mistake him for someone else, just to wind him up.

'I know you do, I can always tell. Let's just forget it now, though, shall we?'

'I can if you can.' She didn't care if Ilias came and saw her and got jealous.

'You didn't intend to stay this long, did you?' he said. 'Was this the first island you came to? I bet it was. You came here first, put your backpack down and you stayed. Married a local. Told yourself you were living the dream. That was twenty years ago.'

'Seventeen, actually,' she said, and, 'We have an olive grove. It's a good life.'

'Then why can I smell booze on your breath at ten in the morning?'

She opened her mouth to say something and then closed it again.

'It's okay,' he said. 'I won't tell if you don't.' He patted the outline of a flask in his grey linen trousers.

At that moment, Ilias swung round the corner, just off the scooter and pushing his hands through his wild hair.

'*Kalimera, kalimera*. What is this, Louise, who is this?'

'Billy,' – she felt a thrill using his name when they hadn't introduced themselves to each other – 'this is Ilias, my husband.' Ilias didn't stop to shake Billy's hand, walked towards the café. As he headed inside he called back over his shoulder.

'There is a fire on the edge of town. Nothing to worry about, they are fighting it. It will not come here, you can be certain of that.' He was always telling Louise about things of which she could be certain.

Ilias went inside and Billy looked worried. 'These fires,' he said. 'They spread fast. How can he be so sure?'

'There's nothing here to burn,' Louise told him. Ilias had told her this too, repeatedly. The island has few trees, sparse pines and casuarinas, it is mainly scrub. But scrub can burn, she realised. It can burn through so quickly that a fire might cover a huge area in minutes, turn the island unrecognisable.

Ilias was off again, bending to drop a kiss on Louise's head as he went. He stared hard for a moment at Billy. 'I know you?' he said, jabbing a finger towards Billy's chest but stopping just short.

'Ha! I don't think so,' Billy said, but Ilias had already gone, bored.

Billy came back to the café the next day, again while Ilias was out. There was a stiff breeze coming off the sea, and the saxophone riff from *Careless Whisper* looping in the background.

'I'll have what you're having,' he said. Louise reached for a Coke Zero from the fridge at the end of the bar, but Billy stopped her.

'No,' he said. 'The wine.'

So she went to the other fridge, under the counter, and poured him a glass from the box on the bottom shelf.

'There was a fire close to my place last night,' he said. He cradled the wine glass in a delicate hand with clean nails. 'I'm staying on the edge of town, and we had to get out until they were sure it was safe.'

Louise knew where he was staying, she'd asked around. She could see the roof of his place, picked out in fairy lights, when she sat outside on the step with Ilias and watched the last ferry leave, the way they always did before bed.

'It's strange,' Billy said, 'that I should like to watch fire. The fires have been closing in on me for two decades. I'm not what they think I am. Do you know what it's like for people to think a thing about you, and for that to be the only way they see you, the only way they can ever see you? Like you're not real, you're just an idea.'

'I know what it means to be just an idea,' Louise said. 'I have a twin sister. She's coming to see me soon.'

'Yeah,' Billy went on, not really listening. 'You know. Look at you, here every day, turning on your smile. Go on, give me a real one.'

She smiled at him.

'Ha!' he said. 'You can't. It's buried so deep, and none of them are going to prise it out of you. Perhaps I will. I've got ten days. You know, I might watch fire, but I dream of water. So warm. Life-giving, amniotic, it can hide you. But its surface is a mirror. A boundary.' He put down the empty wine glass, and left without paying.

That night, Louise woke from a nightmare in which she was dying in a fire. She was covered in sweat, but Ilias was breathing peacefully beside her. She went to the open window and looked out towards the town, across the roof of the big house where Billy was staying. There was a smell on the air that was new. Smoke and burnt vegetation, dead meat. Singed oregano and thyme, fires coming closer, just as Billy had said. The cicadas had stilled, and there was only the sound of the tourists' air-conditioning units working through the night. Beyond, the black void of the sea.

The next day, all the fires around the town seemed to be out. The hills were dark blue, smouldering, but the flames had died down. In the morning, it was cooler than it had been. The café was busy, and Louise didn't have time to think about the fires, or Billy, or much of anything. She was rushed off her feet serving all the old men, with their newspapers and their unfiltered cigarettes and their syrupy coffee.

By the late afternoon, though, the heat was building again and everyone suspected there'd be a storm. The air was heavy, crackling, and Louise had a pounding head. She'd been drinking all day, her regular amount, but this was different. It didn't usually give her a headache, it just induced numbness, distancing her from the world like a greasy pane of glass. But today, waiting for the first clap of thunder, and release, was unbearable.

By seven, the café had emptied. Usually there would be people coming in to wait for sunset with cocktails. Happy hour, margaritas for six euros. The sound of the hand-operated ice crusher and shouts from the yachts moored nearby. But that day, there wasn't going to be any sunset. The sky was low and grey, slowly darkening. All the yachts had left, perhaps had sailed round the island to Naoussa, not as good for sunsets but with smarter nightlife.

It would take just one spark to light everything again, and then they'd have to pray the rain came soon. Louise had started a rain dance on the empty café forecourt – well, more of a rain shuffle, self-consciously with her Coke can – when Billy came in again. He wasn't wearing his cap. He looked older, running a hand across his bald head.

'I'll take a glass of wine,' he said. He wasn't looking at her; he was looking back over his shoulder. When she didn't move right away, he said it again.

'Yes, sir,' she said. She might have saluted. She smiled at him and he didn't reciprocate. He probably had a headache too.

When she came back out there was a flash so intense she dropped the glass and it shattered on the concrete step. Wine seeped between her toes. All the car alarms nearby went off, then were drowned out by the thunder: immediate, incredibly close, ripping the sky apart.

The rekindled flames spread quickly. They started at the top of the town and rushed down through the squares, tearing through the ornamental pines and releasing a resinous scent. Then people crowded on to the café forecourt. Locals, tourists. Men, women and children. Shepherded there by the fire, all the routes around blocked off.

Some of the children came close to her, the ones on their own. Perhaps she seemed safe. Billy was still standing beside her, and the children packed in between them. Louise asked the oldest where her parents were. Lost, the child said. They'd gone out shopping and not returned, then the flames had come and she'd run from the house with her brother and sister. The smallest one, the boy, was holding a stuffed dog with three legs and sucking his thumb.

The other people, adults of various ages, Greeks and tourists, came to speak to them. Some could barely walk. There was an old island woman so bent that she seemed to be kissing the ground in front of her and walking on her hands as much as her feet. They all deferred to Louise.

'Should we go to the sea?' they said. 'Perhaps one of the yachts will let us on board?'

'They've all sailed,' Louise said. 'But yes, let's go to the sea.' Where else could they go? The sky behind the café was dark red, with black debris flying around, carried aloft by the heat. Louise wondered if the building would burn. She felt she should stay, the captain of her ship destined to go down with it, but Billy pulled her away. It was the first time he'd touched her, and she shivered.

They all moved to the edge of the marina, the heat at their back. The sky was dark but the water glowed with a pale green light. The flat stones of the sea floor were close beneath the surface. The water was shallow enough right by the wall to stand up in, for all but the smallest children. They could lower themselves into the sea and wait there for help or for the fire to burn itself out, and hope the smoke didn't spread and overpower them.

Louise was thinking of the mainland, near Athens, and the way people there had been trapped above the sea with nowhere to go. They'd reached a dead end above a cliff and been burned alive. Mothers holding their children, their husbands holding them, like in Pompeii. That couldn't happen here. Billy was already in the water, helping people down. The old bent woman was passed from man to man, lowered into the water and held up between two younger women. Children bobbed between adults, who kept them high enough above the surface to breathe.

There was nothing to do but wait either for the fire to abate or help to come. Though they were surrounded by people in the sea, and chaos on the land, Louise felt in those few minutes with Billy that they were alone in the world. Their surroundings receded and they could have been anywhere, contextless.

Then she heard the old woman saying quietly over and over that she was cold. She wasn't complaining, but she said it again and again.

'We need to get her out of the water,' Louise said to Billy. Some of the children were also shivering, teeth chattering in ghostly faces, and the sea was swelling with the rising wind. Gusts fanned the flames and the whole sky behind the buildings on the seafront was dark purple now, smoke mixing with the falling night.

'I'll go,' Billy said. 'I'll swim for help.'

'But the sea,' Louise said. 'It's turning nasty.'

'I have to. No one knows we're here. Perhaps someone can bring a boat round. You stay here, keep them calm.'

Before Billy went, they kissed. Louise didn't know how it happened, quite, but when they did, everything stopped. For the first time in her life, the noise ceased, the churning movement, the inner screaming, the constant anxiety. All came to a halt. Her heart should have been pounding, but it slowed and the blood beat in her ears like great wings. She felt she could be pulled under by the water, and at the same time lifted up, buoyant, its surface a skin that could catapult her into the sky, far above the smoke and the dirt and the destruction and into the endless blue. And then he was gone.

Billy didn't come back, but a boat did, and they were plucked out of the water just before the rain came down. More rain than they'd seen in years. The café didn't burn. The rain put everything out. Louise doesn't know what happened to Billy after that, assumes he went back to his wife, back to his A-list life.

They returned the children to their parents. Ilias came back on his scooter and found Louise dripping on the tiles of the café. Miraculously, no one had died or even been seriously injured. Around the town, they rebuilt things quickly. The summer was young, the people needed the money, and they patched up the damaged buildings and left the worst ones where they stood like rotten teeth. The café was untouched but for a persistent stench of smoke. Wounds closed over, leaving scars. By next year you won't know anything happened.

Just now, I went back to the spot where the body had been, and there were children playing in the sea while their mothers watched from the beach. I wanted to tell them to go somewhere else, but I couldn't find the words. So I just sat on the sea wall and ate an ice cream and cried. I was sobbing into the cone; it was running all over my hands. I must have looked a total wreck.

I'll always remember the hands. The man holding hands with the dead man. That's what made me cry when I thought about it afterwards. That stiff arm, its cold blue fingers. Perhaps I'll never see anything as beautiful again. The tenderness of the living leading the dead out of the sea. Taking care. Resisting the downward pull.

Now Louise is drinking again, more than before. Ilias has his head somewhere else; he's off in the hills shopping on the internet. He's trying to buy a used Mercedes. I asked Louise about the drowned man. She said no one knew who he was yet, or even how long he'd been in the water. It could have been weeks. He might have been partying too hard. Fallen off a yacht. Perhaps just a swimmer, cramp or a stroke. Or a migrant, off a boat. They wash up all the time.

Louise thinks she witnessed the redemption of Billy Zane, but she's polishing off three litres of Retsina a day. She's not witnessing much. She can't stop now. I want to help her, I'm so sorry for her. But my being here is not helping. I should go home. It's too hot for me here, all I want is a cold beer, and that's the one thing I can't have. You know how hot places smell? That distinctive, indeterminate scent of baking. Kind of dusty. And everything smells of the sea, and ozone, and sun-dried herbs on the wind, and other people's cigarettes, and roasting meat. There's a deep smell of pines. But every morning it smells clean as a bone once more.

What It Sounds Like When You Fall

Natalia Theodoridou

It's Uncle Pete's funeral today, so he puts on his good brown suit with the brass buttons, and we all set out for the cemetery before the sun is up, because we don't want to get too hot in our good clothes on our way there. Uncle Pete and Pa walk in front, me and Ma follow. When we get there, Uncle Pete's grave is waiting, shallow and open, and the plaque has already been engraved with his name. Under it, there's his date of birth and today's date, even though we don't know how long it'll take him to really die.

A fall of angels is crowding around the grave, cooing softly at the hole in the ground. I try not to listen to what they're saying because I know Pa doesn't like it. He shoos them away, says, "Filthy bastards – if only I had my rifle," and spits.

Uncle Pete hugs each of us before he goes into his grave, but he hugs me the longest. "Remember me, okay?" he says. "And get a good job when you're grown, don't end up like your silly Pete." I want to say he's not silly, but I like that he's my Pete, and anyway there's something stuck in my throat and so I don't say a thing.

Back home, Pa grabs himself a beer from the fridge and curses when he finds it "warm as piss" because the fuse tripped again while we were gone and the fridge stopped working. He yells for Ma to go and fix it, but I tell him she's already left for work, so it's going to be warm beer for him until she gets back.

He slumps into his armchair with his beer. I make my body small small small and slide in the armchair next to him and take his arm and wrap it around my shoulder. I pretend he put it there himself and nestle my head against his chest and breathe in his Pa smell. He doesn't mind. I know that because he doesn't tell me to go away and he simply sips his beer over my head.

"Pa?" I ask, and he grunts. "Why did Uncle Pete have to die?"

He takes another sip. "Because his time was up, kid, and he couldn't buy any more."

"Can you buy more?"

He unwraps his arm from around my shoulders and the space between him and the armrest gets smaller. "Pete was older than me," he says, rubbing the stubble on his chin. "I still got time."

Uncle Pete didn't look much older than Pa to me. And if Uncle Pete couldn't buy any more time because he'd lost his job, how will Pa?

"How much older?"

Pa sinks deeper into the armchair, squeezing me out. There's no space left for me. "Go on now," he says, his eyes glassy. "Go on and play outside."

There's no point arguing, so I leave the house and go to the back yard and wait for the angels to gather. I never play with them in the front yard because Pa might come out and shoot them and then sell them to the government man down the road. It's only pennies for a dozen, he says, but they add up to beer money if you keep at it.

I take the piece of stale bread the priest handed out at the funeral and I scatter the crumbs around my feet, waiting for the angels to descend, and they do, two sets of wings to each, flapping mightily, raising a ruckus. There is a fine for feeding angels – the government man says it gives them more time to make angel-babies if they don't have to look for food all the time – but out here there's no one to catch me, so I don't care.

I save a few crumbs that I place on my palm and open it, a peace offering. "I'm sorry Pa kills your kind," I tell them so that they know I mean no harm. Two small ones come and sit on my arm, peck at the crumbs and look at me with their large, hungry eyes. "I'm so sorry," I say again, and they don't say it's all right, but they do speak to me of the sky, of heaven, and of the places people go when they die.

Pa and I go back to Uncle Pete's grave the next day. An angel with grey and brown wings is sitting on his tombstone, but it frowns and flies away when it sees Pa. I find a trinket left on the fresh soil we packed on top of Uncle Pete's coffin, a gleaming little thing. Angels are like magpies, thieves of the shiny. Pa picks it up and throws it away in disgust.

He taps his foot on the ground.

"Not dead yet, brother?" he asks of the grave.

"Not yet, brother, not yet," Uncle Pete replies. His voice comes out muffled from all the soil.

Pa pokes me in the ribs. "Talk to your uncle, kid, what are you waiting for?" Then he goes to the bar across the street for a quick drink.

I kneel on the grave and put my ear to the ground so I can hear my Pete better and he can hear me better as well, but I find that I don't know what to ask of someone who's dying.

"Is it dark in the grave?" I ask after a moment.

"Yes," he says.

"Are you scared?"

He doesn't reply, and I don't know if it's because I whispered too much but I don't want to ask again, so instead I say, "There are angels on your grave. They bring you gifts. They told me you'll go to heaven."

Uncle Pete takes a long time to speak and I think he won't say anything else but then he does. "That's nice of them, isn't it?" he says and then he goes silent again for a long time.

Then Pa comes back and sits on the grave next to me and talks to Uncle Pete about his bad back and the hard time Ma is giving him and then he tears up a little and talks about the time when they were children, hunting angels together with slings after they first fell, before the government issued rifles for everyone to get rid of the pests.

"You were always so much better at this than me, little brother," Uncle Pete says. His voice sounds more distant now, as if his coffin is sinking further and further into the earth. But I don't think that's what is happening.

"Okay, say goodbye to your uncle now, let him rest," Pa says, standing up, so I stand up too and dust off the soil from my bare knees and say, "Goodbye, Uncle Pete."

"Goodbye, sweetheart. Goodbye, brother. Don't get yourself in too much trouble, okay?"

At night, in bed, I imagine Uncle Pete in his dark grave. I imagine him lying on his back, his arms by his sides, but then I think he can't move much in there and my chest feels heavy and hot. He definitely can't sit up and he probably can't even turn on his side. I remember that time when he got a day off work – that was before Pa needed so much rescuing and Uncle Pete still had his job – and took me to the river in the woods and we swam and then sat at its silty bank and angels sang above us like trumpets.

I turn on my side, as if to prove I can, but I can't fall asleep, so I get out of bed and make my way to the kitchen.

The house smells like stale beer. Pa is passed out on the couch, snoring, so I walk out into the cold night. My feet are bare, but I don't mind. There's no moon in the sky, so everything is dark.

I think I see shapes moving in the trees above.

"Angels, are you there?" I whisper. But none answer.

In the morning, Pa goes out to hunt and Ma is getting ready for work. I linger near the kitchen door, trying to stay out of her way as she tidies. There are dirty dishes piled up in the sink. When she fills the tub to do the washing up, I say, "I can do it," and she turns around and looks at me, with surprise or something else, I can't tell. "All right," she says. "I'll be late today so you and your father are on your own for dinner, okay?" This means we'll have toast and tea for dinner again, but that's okay. I can save the crusts for the angels.

I do the dishes and let them dry on the tray and then change my wet top and go to the cemetery to visit Uncle Pete. The grey-brown angel is sitting on his tombstone again, but this time it doesn't fly away.

I stand on top of the grave and stomp on the soil the way Pa did.

"Are you there, Uncle Pete?" I ask. I know that's not really what I mean, but I can't bring myself to ask "Are you still alive?"

"Still here, sweetheart," he says. "I'm glad to hear your voice."

I notice a small brass bell at the bottom of the tombstone. I pick it up and shake it and it sounds like a door opening and closing.

"What is this sound?" Uncle Pete asks.

"The angels brought you another gift." I shake the bell again. The angel looks at me and says nothing. I think it has kind eyes, but I don't know if angels can be kind. "Why do they bring you gifts?"

"I saved one of them, once, when your Pa and I were out hunting. They can be good to you, if you're good to them."

"Good how?" I ask.

"I knew someone they liked when I was young. He broke his back saving a young one from a trap. The angels offered him a golden ring that bought him two whole years when he couldn't work."

"But they only bring you useless trinkets and shiny things."

"They can't tell the difference, sweetheart," Uncle Pete says, "but they do their best." He pauses and I think I hear him sigh, and I wonder how much air there is still left in his coffin. We packed the soil loosely on top of it and left a tiny gap between the shell of the coffin and the lid, but now I wonder if we should have nailed it tight, even though Pa said that might be murder and we would all go to prison and also to Hell.

"How's your father?" Uncle Pete asks.

I shrug, but then I realize he can't see me, so I say "He's out a lot. We don't see much of him."

"He's lonely too, you know," Uncle Pete says.

The angel coos, as if agreeing.

When I leave, it follows me all the way home. It perches on the tree outside our front door, and I have this feeling like a hole through my belly, where my navel is. "Is this what it felt like, when you fell?" I ask the angel, but it only looks at me with its large, human eyes, and it doesn't even speak of sky.

Pa is not yet home when Ma comes back from work. She spent all day cleaning gutters of feathers and angel droppings, and yet she sits in the armchair, waiting for Pa to come back, her head drooping forward every minute or so. There's still angel down caught in her hair.

He comes home hours later, carrying two bunches of dead angels hanging upside down, little talons tied together with string, wings limp, faces calm, eyes open. Pa reeks of alcohol, I can smell it all the way from the back of the kitchen.

Ma tears into him before he even has a chance to put down his prey. She says his brother is not even dead yet and he's already back to his old habits and the next time he finds himself in jail there will be no one left to bail him out. He screams at her to get off his back and that he's just lost his brother and she should respect his mourning, and she says it was his fault his brother is dead because he's the reason he lost his job and that he's "a leech that will sap the life out of all of us."

Then she turns to me and says my father is going to get himself a grave soon and that he doesn't even care enough for me to do anything about it and even the pennies he earns from shooting angels he wastes on drink. She goes to the bathroom and slams the door behind her and Pa throws down the angel corpses and walks out of the house and I know we won't see him again until morning.

I look at the angels crumpled on the floor, worried I'll see the grey-brown one among them, but I don't, even though they all look more alike when they're dead than when they're alive.

I lie on the floor and put my head next to them. They smell like baby powder mixed with dust. I run my fingers over their wings, the soft feathers of their bodies. I don't want to touch the skin on their faces, but I swallow hard and I do, I close all of their eyes, one by one, so that they look more asleep than dead. When I reach for the last one, its eyelids flutter and it looks at me, giving me a fright.

It's still alive.

"It's okay," I whisper, "you're okay."

I release it from the bunch and cradle it into my arms. Its body is shivering, its heart beating very very fast under the soft curve of its chest. There is blood under one of its top wings, but the pellet lodged there is easy to remove with some squeezing and a knife.

It looks stunned more than hurt. Pa must have forgotten to wring its neck after he shot it. I stand up and take it outside, its head draped over my arm, looking at its dead kin on the floor.

In the back yard, I kiss the wound until it heals. A fall of angels gathers in the trees, whispering, mourning. I release the angel and it flies up to join them.

"Can you give me something in return to save my Pete?" I ask them and they coo before they fly away.

I leave for the cemetery as soon as dawn breaks and I lie on Uncle Pete's grave. He's too tired to talk, so I just stay there listening to him breathe, waiting for the angels to deliver their gift.

I hear their wings flapping before I see them. They come one at a time or two, dropping trinkets on the grave – a piece of glass, a nest of wire, a pair of copper earrings. "No golden ring yet, Uncle Pete," I tell him every hour, "hang on," and one time I think he replies "It'll be all right, sweetheart, let me be," but hours pass and then it's night and there's a small heap of shiny useless things at my feet, but I cannot hear my uncle's breath any more, and he doesn't answer when I ask if he's still there.

Something hot climbs in my throat and I want to cry or yell or both and I look up at the trees, at the fall of angels that stare at the junk they've spent all day bringing me – the grey-brown one is there too, looking pleased, cooing stupidly at me.

When I get back home, the bunch of dead angels is no longer there, but there's a heap of copper pennies on the kitchen table. There's no one else in the house so I go out and sit on the steps at the front porch. The angel with the grey-brown wings descends and stands on the ground a few feet away. It looks at me with its stupid eyes.

Bile rises to my mouth. I don't want to be looked at by an angel tonight.

"Go away!" I yell, but it just sits there, silent.

I pick up a rock and throw it at the angel. I miss.

The angel takes an uncertain step away from me and blinks, and then it makes a noise like something breaking and it flies away.

It's not dark yet, but I go to bed anyway and fall asleep on my side and dream of black, black soil.

My Pa wakes me up, shaking my shoulder gently. It's still night outside.

"Come on," he says. "Time to go."

"Uncle Pete is dead," I tell him.

"I know," he says. "Let's go."

"Where are we going?"

"Hunting."

We walk to the woods and he holds my hand the entire way there. We arrive when the sun is rising over the mountain, its light splintering through the canopy. Then my Pa hands me a child-sized rifle and shows me how to prop it against my shoulder. He points at a thicket overhead and says there's a fall of angels there. He says I can keep all the pennies we earn today. He says I'll need to learn how to shoot them now that he'll be going out every day, looking for a job.

I hold my breath and listen to the rustling of leaves and the whispers of angels talking about the sound that feathers make when they fall.

Then I press my finger against the trigger, and I fire, and then I can hear nothing at all.

Competing Before the King

Leila Aboulela

Last summer he had seen Radia, kneeling on her praying rug, flying, the night around her static. Dia' was one of the lucky ones. 'She allowed you to see her', the other children said, those for whom Radia was an elderly woman, too infirm to do much but sit on her prayer rug. The children knew that Radia could fly, but they had never seen her flying.

'Radia died,' his mother said. She had just walked in and was taking off her cape. 'During the night, in her sleep.'

Dia' started to cry.

'You know what this means, don't you?' his mother said. 'The rug could be yours.'

His mother was intruding too soon, too sudden. He mumbled, 'She's not even buried yet.'

'Teacher put your name forward.' She could not hide the pride. The hope for her only child; some measure of pride for their small, charity-dependent family.

'Why did he do that?'

'Why did he do that?' His mother mimicked him, came close and kissed him.

'There'll be other competitors,' he said and walked out of the tent.

'Only one,' his mother shouted after him.

Dia' was weeping when he helped the men dig Radia's grave. They dug until the soil was moist and fragrant. Teacher lowered himself into the grave, smoothed with his hand the groove where Radia would lie. He was perspiring and his clothes were streaked with dust and grass. When he finished, he wiped his hands on his cloak and held up his arms as if he wanted Dia' to jump into them. Gently and slowly, the men gave him Radia, swathed in white cloth. She was light and he laid her down. He paused a little, then climbed out of the grave. The men started to scoop the soil back to fill the hole, their spades scratching and ringing in the silence. Before they finished, Teacher put his hand on Dia's shoulder and said, 'Look!'

Dia' stopped crying. He saw flowers start to grow around Radia: pink, white and orange, so that in a few minutes she was lying in a garden, not in a grave.

'I found out who the other competitor is,' his mother said.

'Who?'

'Taghreed.'

'Oh.'

'Oh,' his mother mimicked him.

'Maybe Radia's rug should go to a girl,' he blurted out. 'It would be fair – from one woman to another.'

His mother stuck out her chin in disapproval. 'It's for the king to decide.'

Dia' walked out of the tent. He wanted the sky. His mother's voice followed him, 'And she put her own name forward, Taghreed did. A tough girl...'

He lay flat on the grass and stared up at the sky. 'Take me, take me,' he whispered, and the clouds laughed back, teasing him.

So he would compete against Taghreed. He knew her well from school. She could not sit still; she always spoke out. He felt unsettled in her presence, her sharp eyes which missed nothing, her able quickness. But she had said to him once, in a grown-up way, 'You're mild, and this is a worthy quality'. She sounded as if she liked him and he had escaped her intensity, darting from the schoolroom to the sky outside.

He and Taghreed were to stand before the king and compete for Radia's flying rug. Why were he and Taghreed eligible? Because they had seen Radia fly; they were the only children who had seen Radia fly. And how had that happened? Taghreed had had the audacity to walk up to Radia one day and demand to see her in flight. And Dia'? He had done nothing, asked for nothing. On the day he lost his father, he had walked out of the house at night, lain down flat on the grass and instead of the usual solace it was as if the sky was crushing him, the grass burning his back. Maybe he screamed, maybe he said angry things, but then Radia revealed herself, a small shadow in the moonlight which got bigger as she drew close, close enough for him to see the wrinkles on her forehead and the tassels that fringed the rug. Following her movement under the clouds, he was soothed by wonder.

In the days before the audience with the king, Dia's mother cooked his favourite food. He ate, but dreaded her coming disappointment. The more she sparkled with hope, the more his heart sank. She looked very beautiful and confident these days, unsuited to the bareness of their tent. They could not afford a house of bricks, or even a straw hut like the one Taghreed lived in.

Dia' wished that his mother would remarry, and he would then have a stepfather and a brick house. He specifically wished that she would marry Teacher. That would strengthen the bond between them; Dia' would become more than just another pupil. But Teacher already had a wife, and she was in the best of health. She was lean and agile with boyish eyebrows. Dia' had watched her compete in the Women's Archery Championship and win. Her skill filled him with envy, the kind of envy that brought tears and bile and hatred of himself. An arrow could kill her, he had fantasised in class one day; one poisonous arrow would make room for his mother. Dia' would then move into Teacher's brick house and –

This deep dark wish for someone's death thickened inside him and emerged into a shape, the shape of a bat-like creature which flew around the class, stinking the air and making the girls (all except Taghreed) shriek. Teacher killed it with his dagger, pinned it yelping to the blackboard. Its blood dripped through a drawing of the position of the closer stars. It was Taghreed who washed the blackboard afterwards, while Dia' and Teacher went outside to bury the dead, heavy beast in the sunlit schoolyard. It relieved Dia' to put his dark wish under the ground. And Teacher did not demand to know the truth. Instead he talked to Dia' about his name; Dia' meaning glow. Teacher talked as if they were not in any hurry to go back to the class. He talked about radiance, about luminosity, the rays of the sun, the light of dying stars and how there were many, many many darknesses but only one source of light. Teacher talked and Dia' absorbed. It turned out to be one of the happiest hours of Dia's life, the badness buried like a turd and Teacher's voice telling him about light.

'Eat, eat,' his mother kept saying on the day before the audience with the king. She herself could eat nothing.

He was full of her food when he stood before the king. The king, seated on his floating throne, studied Dia' and Taghreed, his eyes deepening from blue to purple to black. The king's beard was like Teacher's, but his voice was more beautiful, his accent more refined. He said, 'There are seven flying rugs in the world. They remain with their owners till death, then they are passed on. It is understandable that your village wants to continue to possess the blessing of the rug. But if both of you fail today, I will have no choice but to give the children of another village the chance to compete for this rug. Now reflect before you speak.'

He began the questions. Thousands heard the questions, Dia's replies, Taghreed's replies; there was no privacy that day. The first questions were easy. Why was the Great War fought? What did it bring an end to? What took its place? How tall were the people of the past? What is the distance between Uranus and Montar? This Taghreed knew and Dia' didn't. How long did the father of humanity live? Dia' said, 'One thousand years'. But Taghreed knew the correct answer – nine hundred and sixty years.

When Dia' turned to look at Taghreed, he saw that she looked scrubbed and on her guard. The king's eyes changed colour to green, to indigo, to beige. A breeze blew through the court. Behind the king's throne was the sea, with sailing boats, the wail of gulls. Dia' must not get distracted, he must not look around. How small he was in this vast space! The questions rolled from the king, his eyes lightening from purple to azure.

'What is your ego?'
Dia answered, 'My ego is as big as the moon and just as familiar.'
Taghreed said, 'My ego is a statue, its curves moulded by my own hand.'

'What does the best teacher teach?'
'Rein in your ego, ride it, don't let it ride you.'
'Rein in your ego, ride it, don't let it ride you.'

'How should the pupil reply?'
'I do my best. Work very hard,' she said.
'I love you, Teacher.'

'Tell me something wrong you have done. None of us is blameless.'
She said, 'I was so angry once I couldn't see. I picked up a knife and dug it in a tree. When the tree winced from pain, I cried over it in regret. The background of sin is a blindness that is red.'
'I stole a bottle of bubbles,' Dia' said. 'At first my conscious pricked me, then I let the feeling of guilt subside. The background of sin is blur and smoke.'

'What does the devil say?'
Taghreed answered, 'He says, 'I am worthy of respect."

Dia' answered. 'He says, 'Eat from both the allowed and the forbidden. They are the same."

'Why do you deserve Radia's rug?' the king finally asked.
'I am a woman like Radia. I want to fly.'
'It will make my mother happy.'

When the decision was announced, Dia' felt Taghreed wince and wrap her strength around her to smooth over the disappointment. But the pain was in her eyes for all to see. A broken look that did not suit her. She had wanted the rug too much. Too much to be in awe of it. And the king only handed out power to those who didn't want it.

'Will you still like me?' Dia' asked in a whisper, his tongue loose from victory.

She did not reply.

He did not have time to question her uncharacteristic silence because his mother pounced on him and hugged him. Weeping, she threw herself at the king's feet, hugging his calves and kissing his shoes. This outburst restored Taghreed and Dia' to their normal selves. Taghreed firmly led his mother away and Dia' plunged back into silence and disgust.

Their homecoming was triumphant. His mother must clutch the precious rug, show it to everyone, laugh with the sheer delight of being, for once, envied rather than pitied. Teacher exaggerated by slaughtering a camel and feeding hundreds and boasting of his pupil. Even his serious wife sang a song about a new dress. The excitement lasted well into the night until exhaustion took over and everyone slept. Everyone except Dia'. The rug was blue and smooth under his feet. When he knelt, he breathed in a musk that went to his head. It took him by surprise how pliant the rug was, stirring under his fingers, moulding itself under his knees. How ready to give up itself to him, an intimacy that made him smile.

Dem Bones

Lavie Tidhar

1.

From the second floor window of the abandoned building, Ezra could see something he thought impossible. Behind the wall of the derelict structure that was once a textile factory, a sort of wild garden had sprouted. Ezra could see tomato bushes and dandelions, bluebells and blackberry bushes leaning to against the muddy pools that collected on the ground. And there, in a sort of enclosure of rusted barbed wire and crude sharpened sticks nailed to the ground, the impossible: a wild apple tree, sprouting with fruit.

It had taken him months of furtive searching through this part of the city, going by vague rumours that led to nothing but dead-ends. He had done a five-year stretch up north where he shared a cell with a guy who first told him about it. Said how, in this neighbourhood, long before, it was all apple orchards. How the houses came up and the trees came down and the factories were built for the workers to live around, but the damn apple trees came back, like thieves, growing here, there, in alleyways and places where you'd least expect them.

Well, Ezra thought the guy was full of shit, but he was desperate once they let him out. In prison they gave them a slice a day and that was just enough to ward off the worst of it, but not all, and the doctors prowled the prison corridors at night with their snicker-snacks, and the tread of their heavy boots on the concrete floor kept Ezra awake in the dark hours. The guy who told him all the stories didn't make it out, but Ezra did, and he'd been scouting the neighbourhood ever since.

Now he stared at the garden and at the tree.

It *looked* abandoned. But that didn't mean it was.

Ezra knew people lived here, still. Trying to stay out of sight, and getting very good at it. There used to be more, but many of them couldn't keep up the schedule and sooner or later the doctors took them away. Just like they did his cell mate up north.

So he watched, and he waited. But no one showed up. No one entered the garden and no one picked the fruit. The apples were just *sitting* there!

And he was running out of time.

He had to get some of the stuff. He had to.

He'd killed an old woman in a gas station for a grocery bag of old wizened apples and that was two weeks back.

He kept watching the old abandoned factory grounds but he could *swear* he couldn't see anything or anyone.

Maybe all the stories really *were* true.

2.

'They say God lives there,' Carmichael said. He looked at Ezra across the table and downed his shot. 'That's why no one ever gets in.'

'It's just an old factory building,' Ezra said.

'Yeah, well.'

Ezra knew Carmichael from a previous stint inside. That's how he got to know most people, to tell the truth. Carmichael was one of those people who could get into places other people wanted to keep people like Carmichael out of. There was this thing about him, too. He always had an apple on him.

'Old textile factory, I think.'

'Yeah, well.'

Ezra suspected Carmichael used to work for the syndicate back east that ran most of the apples down that way. He was either retired or fell out with the bosses, or something, but he still kept on getting a regular supply somehow. The doctors had nothing on him.

'So are you in, or are you out?'

'I'm in, I'm in,' Carmichael said. 'Hold your horses, will ya?'

Ezra signalled the waitress for two more shots and stared out of the window. The street light glowed and a dark shape moved underneath it with unhurried steps and he flinched. It was a doctor.

The doctor wasn't very easy to make out. He wore heavy studded boots, and an elongated gas mask for a face. Some people said they had snouts, others that it was just people underneath. The doctor stopped. He turned and stared through the window – stared straight at Ezra. Ezra stared back. He had as much right as anyone to be there, he thought.

The doctor went up to the door. His face under the flashing neon sign was vaguely demonic. Ezra wasn't the religious type. He'd given up on church eighty three psalms and nineteen years ago. The doctor stepped through the door and conversation ceased. The only sound was the damn boots as they slapped the floor.

He came and stood by Ezra's table.

'Here,' Ezra said, unwillingly. He reached in his coat pocket and came back with one of the two apples he had left from the old lady. The doctor stared at the offering in his hand. His eyes were hidden behind the big glass windows of the mask.

'What?' Ezra said. 'I'm good for it.'

The doctor nodded. He took the apple. Turned to Carmichael, who already had one in hand, just waiting. A nice, fresh, green apple. Plenty of juice. The doctor nodded in appreciation and took that apple too.

He turned his back on the two men.

'Another day, another apple,' Carmichael said.

The doctor's heavy footsteps echoed in the silent bar. He made almost to leave but then he turned abruptly. There was a man sitting slouched at the counter. He had a half-drank glass of beer in front of him. He had a face that's given up on everything other than that drink in front of him. The doctor tapped him on the shoulder and the man didn't stir. The doctor, with difficulty, spoke. He had a raspy, strained voice, as though forming words caused him pain.

The doctor said, 'Ah-pfelh.'

The man turned with his drink in his hand and bashed the glass in the doctor's face.

The doctor wiped broken glass from his gas mask face.

'*Ah-pfelh.*'

The man spat in the doctor's face.

The doctor said, '*No* ah-pfelh?'

'Go to h–' the man said, or started to.

Ezra didn't want to watch. The doctor's snicker-snacks snapped out and a fist equipped with impossible blade-claws wrapped around the man's neck and pulled.

The man fell from his stool and the stool crashed to the ground. The doctor dragged the man by the neck and along the floor and out of the door.

A doctor's car waited outside. The vehicles always came for the doctors. They were black and compact, more like weird beach balls than cars. The doctor dragged the patient into the car and it rolled down the street and was gone.

The waitress came and placed two new drinks on the table for Ezra and Carmichael.

Ezra only sipped this time. It was strong and he felt a little light headed. The door opened and a thin young man came in and plonked himself in their booth, beside Carmichael. He had a lean, hungry face. His name was Noah.

'Did I miss anything?' he said.

'You got the stuff?' Ezra said.

Noah nodded. 'Sure.'

'Then let's go,' Ezra said.

3.

They stood outside the walls of the garden but not for very long.

'Razor wire,' Carmichael said mournfully, looking up. 'You want it quiet or you want it loud?'

'I want it fast,' Ezra said.

'Then loud it is.'

The boy Noah nodded. 'No worries,' he said, and set to work. He attached a small block of C-4 to the wall, carefully stuck in the detonator, then unspooled the cord and the three men moved away.

'Go.'

The explosion tore the wall neatly inwards. The old bricks collapsed and with them came down the rusted razor wire. The explosion was loud and then it was quiet again. It was very quiet. The men waited for the dust to clear. When it did, they stepped over the breach.

Ezra move cautiously. The gardens were large, larger than they had seemed from the window across the street. It was quiet but now he thought he could hear birds calling in the distance, and the rustling of grass, and the slithering of a snake in some shrubberies. But he couldn't see the tree.

Noah came up to him. 'Look,' he said. He pointed up. Ezra looked at the sky. It was very black and clear and the stars shone in a multitude of bright lights, as though the three men weren't even in the city anymore, as though they were in the middle of a desert or on an island, somewhere where there was no light pollution at all.

'It's weird,' Noah said, 'but I can't see any of the constellations and the North Star should be –'

Then he stepped on what looked like an old soda can. A puzzled look came onto his face. There was a faint glow and a weird whooshing sound. Ezra ducked.

Noah didn't.

The thing came seemingly out of nowhere. It was like a sword of flame. It slashed clean through Noah and vanished. Noah dropped to the ground.

'What was that?'

'Some sort of trip wire, I think,' Carmichael said.

Noah's blood soaked into the earth. Tiny centipedes and fat black beetles came crawling onto the corpse. They swarmed over it. Ezra cursed and lifted his foot. He and Carmichael moved away.

'I don't see it,' Carmichael said.

'It's got to be here somewhere.'

Ezra realised he couldn't even see the hole in the wall anymore. They must have gone deeper into the garden than he'd realised. But the apples had to be there somewhere. He drew his gun and motioned for Carmichael to do the same.

'Watch your back,' he said.

4.

There were so many trees, everywhere he turned to look. Oranges and pomegranates, a grove of ancient olive trees, pear and avocado and almonds. And he could hear monkeys in the trees, and wild birds singing, and again that slithering sound. He could no longer see the garden's walls, or hear any sounds of the city, and all the stars overhead were unknown.

'Carmichael, don't –' he said. But Carmichael had reached for a peach and bit into it with relish. The juice ran down his lips and chin.

'It's good,' he said. 'It's real g –'

Something lunged at them from between the roots. Ezra fell back. He couldn't quite make out what it was. Some sort of scaly reptile, hissing. It struck Carmichael's calve and, for a moment, Ezra could make out a gaping mouth and long, sharp fangs. Two bright, lidless eyes stared at Ezra. Then the creature was gone.

'Carmichael?'

But the man never said another word. Ezra knelt beside him. He took Carmichael's wrist and felt for a pulse but there was none.

He let the man's hand drop.
Left him there to fertilise the garden.
Went back into the trees.

5.

How long he wandered there he did not know. There was night and then there was day.

Then he saw it. It was just an old apple tree. It was surrounded by crude sharpened sticks driven into the ground, and bits of barbed wire and broken glass shards. But he just kicked most of it away. Then he hesitated, standing there in the shadow of the tree.

At last he reached for the lowest apple and plucked it from the tree. He held it in his hand. It felt warm and smooth. He took a bite from the apple, and then another, and another, until he ate the whole damn thing. He laughed. He saw that really the garden was not that large at all. And there was the hole in the wall. He dropped the apple core on the ground to feed the garden. He left the tree where it was and then he went back into the world. It started to rain then, a light soft rain, and it smudged all the colours and made the street seem softer. Ezra began to walk. He walked until there were people on the streets again. He walked past the bar where he'd met the others. He walked until he was nearly on the highway. For a moment, he felt almost free.

Then he heard the tread of studded boots. He turned and the doctor was there, like he'd always been there, waiting. Ezra stared at those lidless eyes.

'Ah-pfelh?' the doctor said.

'No Ah-pfelh,' Ezra said, and for a moment he felt almost sorry.

It had stopped raining. The day felt very fresh and clear. There was a rainbow somewhere over the highway, with all the little cars going underneath it, blowing out fumes. A doctor's car came rolling to a stop and then another, and more doctors stepped out, their gas mask faces solemn. Ezra had known about good and evil but he had thought them different. Now he could see more clearly. He hesitated there, on the edge of the highway, as the tiny cars zoomed past, to and from, just before the doctors took him away.

Sin Eater

Chikodili Emelumadu

All my life I waited to get into university, but nothing could have prepared me for the experience.

I am the last of seven siblings, the unpaired amongst three sets of twins: two boys, a boy and a girl, and two girls. Then me, skewing the data and making it so that there are more girls than boys. Awkward. All the twins are kind and nice and all, but you can see why I've always wanted to get away, live my own life in my own place.

I choose Nnamdi Azikiwe in Awka, and move into to a hostel, even though my folks lived forty minutes away by bus in Fegge and don't want me, their 'tail child' to leave their house empty.

Of course, I get a weird roommate.

Her door in the flat stands closed all afternoon. At night, hunger pangs wake me. I click on my rechargeable lantern and make my way down the hallway to the small communal kitchen where I'd dumped my loaf of bread, a bunch of bananas and an old Seaman's schnapps bottle full of roasted groundnuts.

My flatmate stands naked at the end of the corridor.

"Hi," she says, rubbing her stomach. "I'm Nchedo. Hope I did not wake you?"

"Okay," I reply but she doesn't move. Only being in an all girls' boarding school makes her nudity sort of normal to me. But not the other thing.

Not the bit where she is covered in blood.

The crimson sheen to her thighs startles me. It glistens, fresh and wet. Her hands are broad swathes of yellowy-brown, mixed in with waves of dripping red.

"You mean this?" she asks, even though I haven't said anything. "It's just period blood. I am a heavy bleeder."

I nod. "Me too… but you know what? No matter how heavy my period gets, I never bleed from my mouth."

She cocks her head, a micro movement before comprehension. Nchedo wipes her face.

"It's still there," I say. She licks a thumb and works it on the corner of her mouth. "I think you need more than a thumb."

She drops the hand. "You're not afraid."

"Of what? All I need to do is wake up and I will be in my bed."

"You're not dreaming," she says. Her stomach gurgles loudly. She winces, clutching at it. "I need to ease myself, before I do it on the floor. Don't run, you hear?"

I freeze in the act of retreating. The fluorescent lantern in my hand dances jerkily, its beams cutting jagged lines across her body.

"We need to talk, okay?" She's staring into my eyes, waiting for me to agree.

"I'm not running," I say. "Take your time."

Nchedo finds me on Nnamdi Azikiwe expressway, trying to flag down a ride.

"I thought you said you weren't going to run?" She seems only mildly disappointed.

"I'm not running. I just… forgot something at home." She shakes her head, amused, as if I am a naughty puppy, takes my hand in her warm, dry one and we are back at the flat, in her room.

"I won't hurt you, I swear." Her eyes plead. The curtains are drawn. The single bulb in the ceiling burns low from the half-current that we've been supplied this night. There is a human head on the bed in a tangled, viscous mess. It doesn't look quite real, but the smell, heavy and saturated with metal, says otherwise. I back away. Something gives underneath my slippers. I throw up, long and hard and I have no control over my body, this opening and expelling that takes everything in me. I keep going even when nothing else comes out.

"See, you're supposed to help me clean this, not add you own." Nchedo sighs.

"Sin eater? Like in 'supernatural' or what?" My voice is muffled behind the headscarf I've tied around my nose and my own breath bounces back against my neck. I'm sweating. The meagre electricity gives the room a sickly glow.

My flatmate pauses. "That bread-dipping thing? How conveniently neat. Abegi," she rolls her eyes. *Please.* "As if there would ever be a male sin eater."

She tells me. School and freedom pale in comparison.

"It's my first time. I finally graduated, and this was my first assignment." She stares at the metal bucket full of sloppy human DNA. "I guess I bit off more than I could swallow."

Her stomach is flatter underneath the wrapper tied around her chest. I have on a pair of surgical gloves from the packet I stole from my father's pharmacy. Cutting out three of the fingers on each hand will give you a sleeve over an existing pair. It's not the first time I've had to clean something disgusting. In boarding school, I was a pounder – one of the girls whose job it was to pound the mounds of shit in the toilets with logs so that it could pass through the old, encrusted pipes. It takes a lot to make me vomit.

The room is near spotless when I'm done. Who said boarding school is useless?

"Fine, I'll help you," I say, even though she doesn't ask.

"Yay," she claps. Her teeth are whiter than sun-bleached bone and shimmer with their own light. She is gorgeous. I shudder to think of the mincemeat they made of the guy she'd eaten.

I raise my hand. "Under one condition: no more cleansing in the flat."

Cleansing. That's what she calls it when she takes a sin away. The man she ate had beaten his wife for the three years of their marriage. One day, he beat her too hard and she did not get up. We pour out his remains at the foot of a tree, in the bushes where his wife has been secretly and hastily buried.

"Should we get some suya?" she asks. "I'm a bit hungry."

I resolve never to eat meat again.

Our next mission is a houseboy who is poisoning his madam. A man of about twenty-two, he carries a metal bucket with a lid into the grinding quarters of the market. I watch. Nchedo just stands around attracting okada riders who pull up in their motorcycles and ask where we want to go. She waves them away, worrying at her cuticles with the strong, white nails of the other hand.

The industrial grinders are noisy, shrill. I cover my ears as they work grains, seeds, whatever, into a pulp. The boy comes out, lugging the lidded bucket.

"Maybe his madam is wicked," I say. "You never know, she could be a witch of a woman."

"You're justifying poisoning?" Nchedo snorts. "Anyway, this isn't the first madam he's killed," she says. "It's his second."

The boy drops the bucket near the base of the Worker's Union statue, three men with shovels and pickaxes on a plinth. He slides the lid off with the side of his leg and tips something in, sloshing the bucket to mix it. Nobody in the busy market pays attention to him.

"Rat poison. His Oga is away today. He's making mai-mai. His madam loves mai-mai. The kids don't. Really, it's the children he's after."

The boy picks up the lidded bucket. His steps are jaunty.

"The children?"

"Mm. He wants to sell them to traffickers and retire across the border. His madam suspects something is up with him but Oga thinks she is being hysterical. She's just had a baby, after all.

And she *is* sick." She shoves me. "Ngwa, go."

My skin crawls. I am small. I have almost no breasts. Sometimes, I wonder how far Nchedo's powers extend. Can she see the future? Did she choose me to be her roomie?

I tap the houseboy. "Excuse, can you tell me where Okwadike stadium is?" The stadium is old, run down and isolated. It's overgrown and nothing good happens there. Drug deals, quick-action prostitution in cars, rape, a few murders. It is a red flag to a bull.

He looks me up and down and points the way. "That way, then when you come to the junction you turn left, then pass one woman selling recharge, turn right and walk o… In fact, come let me escort you."

I refuse, thanking him. When I set off, he waits and then he follows.

It's easy to pretend that I am lost. I haven't been to the state capital since Children's Day in primary school, when the stadium bore the name of the then-governor. There's a new stadium now, bigger and everything. Things change each time there is a new person in power.

I sing, both to cover up my nerves and the fact that he is following. I'm aware of my jeans, the gap between the waistband and the top of my t-shirt. Who's afraid of a little girl? A wrong turn here, another there. I lead him down an alleyway. My voice is small and disappears as we pass behind the lumberyard. A wall. There is no through-way. He fills up the narrow passage, blocking my exit.

He is bigger than I am, strengthened by hard city living. The alleyway stinks of urine. Someone has wiped their shitty behind on the wall. A used condom lies in the corner, covered in soil and flies.

"Shift and let me pass!" I say.

The houseboy laughs and hate blooms in my chest like fungi, fertilised by all the times I have felt unsafe. I wonder how

Nchedo will do it, but I needn't have worried. She's behind him, footfalls muffled on the sawdust from the nearby lumberyard. He doesn't hear her but when I look behind him, he whirls around, eyes flashing, instantly aware that he has become prey. He relaxes a little when he sees Nchedo, his shoulders coming down from around his ears. She is only a woman.

"Pius, how now?" Nchedo says. He stares at her, surprised she knows his name. I turn away, gazing at the pylons, like so many cobwebs above the city. I don't see what she does, but there is a twisting and crunching.

"Finished." Nchedo is out of breath and looks about seven months pregnant. She yawns. "I need to lie down." Her strappy lycra dress has gone from calf-length to above her knee. When we emerge from the alley, the okada men draw lots as to who will take the pregnant woman, and if they recognise her from before, they don't say anything. That's Nigeria for you. We live side-by-side with the supernatural. The pastors take our money for deliverance sessions when things get malevolent; otherwise, it's Aluta Continua.

We end up on the lowest bike with the slowest rider, a portly man with wiry hair growing out of his ears. Nchedo has to pull her dress almost to her waist to get on.

When the houseboy comes out a few hours later, it is in a steady stream of black sludge. We finish all our buckets and jerry cans of water trying to flush him down.

"At least this is better than before, abi?" Her voice is hoarse from throwing up. The houseboy's remains go down, but the inside of the toilet is stained black no matter the amount of Jik bleach I pour inside it.

"What about the people he works with? He can't have planned trafficking those children alone. There must be a network."

"So, you want me to cleanse *all of them*? With which stomach? Not my job, abeg," she says. "Let's hit Diamond Pizza. I want the

218

biggest jollof with coleslaw and a half-chicken." She grins her usual grin, but it doesn't reach her eyes. I order a soft serve ice cream and eat it slowly. She's distracted, staring off into the distance. Her ears twitch as if she can hear something I can't.

Later that night, she climbs into my bed, waking me with the warmth of her body. A wind blows through the open windows of my room, setting the empty plastic hangers on my rack a-clanking. She curves around my back. Lightning streaks intermittently across the ceiling of my room, but neither thunder nor rain follow.

"What is it?" I ask, but she doesn't answer. She's already asleep, her breath heating up a spot on my back through my pyjamas.

Nchedo mentions her sisters a lot. It is obvious she misses them.

"My sister Makuo used to protect me when there was a storm. I have never liked them. Amadiora, the god of lightning, he can be one kain changeable."

I shake my head to dislodge this information sharpish. I can accept what Nchedo is, but talk of mythical Igbo gods and goddesses is a step too far.

The sisters then: there is Obegolu who loves to eat mangoes and Akabeze that sets fires because she is always cold and nearly burned down their mother's house. Stella is the crier of the family, everything brings tears. Beluchukwu, and Hapuluora her twin sister, Mgborie...

"Mgborie? Who still calls their child Mgborie? Your parents did not do well at all!" I'm laughing hard. "And how many sisters do you even have anyway?"

"I don't know." She shrugs. "My mother has them when it is time."

I stop laughing. A thought has occurred to me. "And the boys? Doesn't your mother have boys?"

Nchedo snorts. "What can boys do, except cause wahala and

then die?"

I don't ask her by whose hand. It is as if I already know. "I have brothers," I say.

She rolls her eyes. "Hashtag, not all men."

We mutually decide not to talk about her family again. That is to say, I don't ask and she doesn't volunteer.

Another assignment.

"How do you know if a person should be cleansed?"

"I just do."

"But how?"

Nchedo sighs. "How do you know when you need the toilet? Or when you're hungry?" She takes a glug of warm Star beer straight from the bottle.

I get the point. The girl we are following though, I'm not sure. Her name is Chimere, one of the most popular girls in school, with her light 'half-caste' skin and long, curly hair. Even though she is a fresher like we are, you'll never find her under the sun, queuing for a bus. Her boyfriend is a fraternity guy, a Buccaneer, one of the fine boys on campus. He picked her right out of secondary school in Enugu, before she'd even finished. The story is that he worked it for them to be at the same uni. A rotation of vehicles brings Chimere to school every day, that is when she deigns to attend lectures. She doesn't need to be in school to pass her classes. Who would mess with a capone's chick?

Looks like we will.

"What did she do?"

My flatmate makes a face. There are dark circles under her eyes. "I can show you," she says. She slides a hand through my sweat-tangled braids and lays it against my scalp. It heats up, and just when I think I am about to scream from the pain, it fades, and I am standing in a new place.

A dim room. There are curtains on the windows, a creamy

chiffon underneath heavy burgundy brocade. A sliver of light comes through the middle of the chiffon, where the heavier set of curtains does not quite meet. The air on my skin is cold from the air conditioner. A hotel room, with maroon carpeting overlaid with beige and brown squiggles, cream walls and a double bed. Chimere stands beside me, modelesque in her heels. Her hair smells of chemicals, hair spray or gel or something. She holds a phone pointed at a bed, around which three men…

It's as if my head is cracking open, the sound is so loud. I'm in the beer parlour again, sitting under an awning. My ears ring and I waggle my jaw to pop them. Nchedo is watching Chimere and her bodyguards picking up cartons of booze from the supermarket next door. Chimere hangs her wrist, as if she is too delicate to do anything. The same hands that held the camera phone. Every pore on my body opens and pours forth sweat.

Nchedo burps, speaks, without taking her eyes off Chimere and her serfs. "It's how they break them. The video just helps them stay broken. You say 'No' to the Buccaneers, and that's what they do. You say 'Yes', same thing."

I want to scream, shout, cry. The Buccaneers like to call themselves the gentlemen of cults. Whatever. A sword is just a fancy knife. And Chimere's hand is on the hilt.

The party is by invitation only, but that is just a gimmick to make it more appealing. Everybody wants something they can't have. The bass-heavy music pounds in my heart. It makes me anxious. It's one thing getting houseboys, but we have entered the lion's den. I'm just one small person.

"Relax," says Nchedo. "Drink something. I won't need you." But I can't. Everyone is drunk. There are drugs going, openly, everywhere. I'm afraid somebody will roofie me. I don't want to end up a girl on a bed in a hotel room.

Nchedo moves to the middle of the floor and dances as if she is alone in the place. I retreat further into the crowd. The

Buccaneers watch her: campus boys, men who've graduated and others like the Capone who should have left school ages ago but hasn't. They're all too handsome to sweat, so they stand by the walls. They stare from the cordoned-off balcony where the Very Important alumni point at girls and have them sent up.

Someone steps on my foot.

"Jesus!"

They don't say sorry. In the time it takes for me to look up again, Chimere is approaching her man on the balcony, climbing each stair like a baby antelope learning to walk. She curls a hand around his bicep, frowning, and whispers something in his ear. He doesn't turn towards her. Nchedo dances, fluid as water, and it is she that the Capone watches, biting his lips like he's a Nollywood leading man or something. His shirt is open and a gold pendant gleams in the forest of chest hair. I can see why he's the boss man.

Other girls join Nchedo on the floor. Two have blue-black Sudanese complexions and look identical. Many are bronzed and copper-coloured and ochre, all possible hues of black. I can see the similarity in the way they dance as if it's something they've learned together. They are dressed in skin-tight trousers, mini-skirts, batty riders and cut-out dresses, hips working, thighs strong and arms taut. I relax because it means we might not die today. Reinforcements. I'm sure these are Nchedo's sisters.

Chimere's capone gets a look in his eye. He nods at someone and immediately black t-shirts swoop in, smiles, such charming smiles, hands on waists, on bums, giving the girls drinks and leading them off. Nchedo doesn't look at me when she goes off but somehow, I hear her clearly in my head: Go home.

Does it still count as a massacre if there are no bodies? Seven boys are missing. And Chimere. The Black Axes claim responsibility.

The bags under Nchedo's eyes are bigger and she can't even finish a tuber of yam by herself anymore. At night, she burns with a fever and her breath stinks of abattoirs. I try to take her to the hospital but she refuses.

"You may muddy a river, but it will flow itself clean again."

"What the hell are you talking about?" The scarf is back across my nose. It frightens me, seeing her like this.

"I mean," a pause to cough, "Think about it. You jump into a river and muddy it up. When you leave, it clears itself. It can become vapour, or liquid or a solid, but water doesn't just disappear."

"And what does that have to do with the price of garri in the market?"

She laughs.

I snap at her. "If I drink the water, it disappears." My phone is in my hand. "I'm calling Drop to take you to Amaku." The nearest teaching hospital is ten minutes away by okada, but what if she falls off the motorcycle?

"If you drink water it becomes blood and urine and sweat," Nchedo says. "Water has no beginning and no end. People drive themselves mad looking for the source of this and that, but all water is the same water." She coughs again. Clears her nose and swallows it, laughing when I make a face.

"It's in the bible sef. 'Now the earth was formless and empty, darkness was over the surface of the deep, and the Spirit of God was hovering over the waters.' Water has always been here and so too, Idemili, the Mother of water, you know?"

I bring her a glass of water and she takes it, gratefully.

"They are burning her house. Our house. All over this state. You know, if they burn your mother's house, won't it make you sick?"

Burning water makes no sense but I don't say that.

"Are you dying?" I don't want to cry but it doesn't matter. A blink and I am crying anyway.

"Shut up, you big taata," she says. "Who told you I'm dying? You're worse than Stella, I swear." I watch her as she falls asleep.

By morning, I am on her bed alone. Her things are scattered all over the flat, but her phone is missing. She's gone. I spy a note near the shoe rack by the door.

'I am coming back,' it says. So Nigerian to be coming when one is going.

Despite wishing for space all my life, I am not good at being alone. Time stretches, folds in on itself. The nights are twice as long and I wake constantly, pulled from sleep by the silence.

How did I not notice that Nchedo didn't give me her mobile number? I have no other friends. My phone does not ring, and the only beeps come from my parents Whatsapping annoying forwarded messages. It adds to my restlessness and worry.

It is this worry that drives me to evening service a few days later. I go to pray that whatever is happening to Nchedo resolves itself. I pray that she is healthy, and her family is well. I pray for her to come back soon, right after I realise I cannot even go to find her because she hasn't told me where her family lives. All this prayer, and I no longer believe in the kind of God in whom I was taught to believe, the kind that lets bad things happen to people like me and does nothing, 'for his glory'. I like having my own personal avenging angel or demi-goddess or whatever Nchedo is. I pray anyway, because speaking my wishes aloud calms me somewhat.

As I cook dinner for one that night, I turn my small radio on so that it feels as if I am surrounded by lots of people. It's hard for me to cook for one.

The seven o'clock news comes on and the newsreader announces clashes in communities, people burning shrines and artefacts hundreds of years old. I eat my Indomie and egg, out of the pot, standing over the kitchen sink.

When I was a little girl, I knew things happened at night while I slept. My siblings would tell stories to scare me: witches who ate small children, monsters grabbing from under the bed, shadows that aren't shaped like their owners. They stopped telling them when they realised how much I loved the fear. It was like a loose tooth to me, salty and painful and I prodded it with my metaphorical tongue.

In the night, while they slept, I stayed awake and waited for things to happen as my bladder filled up. I wanted to *see*. But the night is tricky, and her children are cunning. Sleep would take me before long. Over the years, I trained myself not to flutter my eyelids as I lay there, waiting. I let my body go slack, breathing deeply and steadily, watching out of the corners of my eyes.

It's a smell that wakes me, thick and pungent, masculine. I wake up behind my eyelids as the intruder bends over my face, breathing staleness. This is no Night's child, playing in the shadows. This is real and present danger.

He seizes me by the throat and pulls me out of bed, dashing me to the floor. From below I can smell the greenery on his skin, as if he's been living in the bushes while campus war is being fought.

"Where is your friend, eh?" Capone delivers me a backhand when I am slow to answer, and I smash my face against the wall. I have never felt such pain before.

"I don't know," I reply, but he kicks me in the stomach. The Indomie is sour when it comes back up, and the pepper I'd added burns through my nostrils. He steps on my back, pushing my face into my vomit as if I am an errant puppy.

"I knew something was up... Those girls. Me! You people tried me! Who sent you? Where are my boys?" He's talking to himself. If he wanted me to respond he would let up on the pressure. My mouth is full of my own vomit. He presses and my teeth cut into the skin behind my lips. "Where is Chimere?" He drags me up by my hair and the braids around my temples snap and break. I cover my head so that I don't bang it anywhere. My wrists bear the brunt of his beating.

"Please..."

"You are begging? I know you people did something. My dibia does not lie. You see this?" He rips his shirt and the buttons fly. There are dark marks on the top of his stomach, made by razor blades and filled with something black. Juju. "This is why you could not get me. No Black Axe, no dirty bagga can get me. If you shout, I will kill you here."

I hadn't seen the knife before, but here it is now, drawing the eye.

"Open your mouth!" He slips the knife in. "Now talk or I will cut your tongue, I swear to God. If you no wound today, call me bastard! I will kill you and nothing will happen."

I'm glad Nchedo didn't tell me where she was going. I look Capone in the eye and see an animal. If I knew anything, I'd have told him. As it is, I don't. My head is a basket of agony and one of my eyes cannot open. He pushes the knife deeper into my mouth and my throat spasms, cutting itself in the process. Blood. He fumbles with his trousers in the other hand. He is pinning my body with all his weight and I can't breathe. I can't swallow with the knife in my throat. I'm choking. I am going to die.

There is a bang, and the pressure across my chest is off. I gulp air, coughing, retching, while chaos reigns around me. My roommate is here, clinging onto Capone's back and encircling him with her limbs. He reaches around, trying to hit her, but his trousers tangle his legs and they both go down. I want to say her name, but my throat is fire. I slip in my own vomit.

They roll about on the floor and there is a cracking sound, like many dry sticks breaking. Capone screams and brings down the hand holding the knife. It comes up and down again, red, but Nchedo holds on. She is strong. The veins in her neck are thick, pulsing, but Capone is strong too and Nchedo is weakening. His struggles are violent but targeted. Nchedo has not managed to seize that arm. It comes down again and I grab it, but my hands are slippery, so I bite down on his wrist hard. His skin is tough. My teeth hurt but he screams and drops the knife, hitting me away.

It is enough. Nchedo tightens her grip and there are more loud pops. He is still fighting. I crawl back to them and hang onto his ear with my teeth. It is bitter with wax.

Nchedo looks me in the face, but her eyes are different, yellow, glowing like the sun. I clasp them both from behind, digging my hands into his windpipe, trying to crush. Nchedo throws her head back, grimacing with effort.

We are in a death embrace. She opens her mouth and her neck elongates, widens. She brings her jaw down on the Capone's head and there is a sound of breaking coconuts. I clasp her arms as she forces him down like a ball of stubborn eba. It looks painful and I help her, taking off his clothes, flinging the belt away. I rub my roommate's arms as she swallows, cleanses our campus of sin.

I will never be alone again.

Thank God in the Acknowledgements
Jess Brough

34 hours down, 12 to go

I bought you a present!

Bec burst back through the door to the study room, wearing a face of triumph and carrying a pizza box in each hand. Maya, yanked out of her unblinking reverie, turned from the computer screen to see her best friend salsa dancing towards her, boxes balanced on open palms.

I thought you were only picking up some crisps?

Jesus Christ it's hot in here. Listen. We need a proper midnight snack. I was walking towards the shop and then it struck me that we haven't had a hot meal or any form of vegetable in two days. Two days! We might get scurvy as well as no Masters degree. Also, the shop was closed, looked a bit like it had a break-in. So, pizza!

Outside, a circus tent flew past the window by Maya's desk and off into the distance. She raised her eyebrows, looking at the Domino's boxes with admiration. It was true that they hadn't eaten properly in days; the two friends had been living off a diet of sausage rolls, breakfast tea and instant porridge. Bec's face had a slight grey tinge. Maya's bones ached.

I got us chicken tikka with red onions and peppers. Two vegetables! Plus protein, for energy.

There was no part of the desk unsmothered by study notes, so Bec set the sustenance down on an empty chair.

Isn't is carbs that give you energy?

She took a slice.

God I love you so much.
    Wait, me or God?
    You! Both? I haven't decided about God, think I'll see how I feel after we get our marks back. But then she's famously not fond of being tested. I guess we have that in common.
    I love you too.

They ate the rest of the pizza in silence, quickly. Fullness and comfort returned to their bodies, a kickstart of life.

36 hours down, 10 to go

Did the room get smaller? I feel like the room got smaller.
    I feel like everything is getting smaller. Is my dissertation getting smaller? I fucking hope not.

Bec looked over to Maya's screen.

That's definitely more words than you had a few hours ago. Well done! Jesus I'm sweating my life out. What are you on now?
    Zadie Smith. Just finished my bit on Andrea Levy – moving swiftly on from historical accounts of Black Britishness into the contemporary.
    Very cool.
    You?
    Tidying up the Results section. My graphs are hot but the tables are janky. This part's quite cathartic really.
    Formatting's the best part.

The fire alarm went off in the building next door and a tree broke from its trunk, piercing a window on the floor below the study room. A distant scream followed the noise of shattering glass.

When was the last time you slept, Maya?
    At least three years ago.
    Come on.
    I actually don't know. I guess Tuesday?

And don't forget your power hour nap.

God, that was a mistake. I actually felt worse when I woke up and my back's still aching from that tiny sofa. I don't know how Silent Amy does it. There's not much time left. I wonder how fucked she is.

Neither of them knew if Amy was actually the name of the girl who had come into the study room almost five hours ago and had immediately gone to sleep on one of the purple sofas. They could see her eyebrows poking over the top of a blanket.

How is there hardly anyone else here? We can't be the only people who don't have our shit together.

Bec, are we fucked? We're fucked, aren't we. How much have you got left to do?

Finishing and polishing the Discussion, writing the Conclusion, Abstract, References and Acknowledgements. Oh, and Contents Page. I'll probably just thank God in the Acknowledgements, to save time. You?

I've got about seven more papers to read and the last three chapters to write, plus referencing. And editing. My front page is good to go, though.

They looked at each other and sat in silence for a moment, holding real panic in the space between them.

Crêpe?

Fuck! Absolutely.

Outside 50 George Square, the busy central hub of the Edinburgh Fringe was waiting for them. People staggered around the streets looking drunk and lost, two men were crying in a corner near a theatre's box office and a police car had found itself jammed in a busking spot, surrounded by tourists singing *Don't Let the Sun Go Down on Me* with a local musician. Lines of abandoned, overpriced hot food trucks lit up the dark sky.

The friends approached the only truck still staffed and tried to focus their tired eyes on the expensive menu. Maya got lemon and sugar and Bec got cheese and ham, so they could swap halfway and enjoy both main and dessert. They went to sit on some nearby concrete steps.

I kind of feel like this crêpe van is the only thing worth living for at this point.

How do I inject the joy I feel eating this crêpe into the rest of my actual life after the crêpe is gone?

Maybe I don't need a Masters or a PhD. Maybe all I need is a crêpe van.

You could drive around universities during deadline season, inspiring and nourishing the last-minute renegades. It could be your life's purpose, a divine duty. You could call it Crêpe Cadet.

Crêpe Suffragette.

Crêpe Cold Sweat.

Crêpe Regret.

They rose, dropped the folded paper plates and greasy napkins into the nearest bin and headed back inside.

41 hours down, 5 to go

Get up, let's dance.

Bec stood.

What?

Let's dance. 30 seconds. I need to move, I know you do too. Put your headphones in, choose a song, let's dance. They used to do it on *Grey's Anatomy*, Meredith and Cristina, a thirty-second dance party. I think it motivated them. We might as well try.

I can't, it's too hot and I'm half-way through finishing this paragraph. I can't just stop and leave it. What if I forget what I was going to say and...

You won't. Now save it and get up.

After staring at the last sentence she'd written for eight blinks of the text cursor, Maya saved her work and stood up. Bec set a timer. Thirty seconds. They put their headphones in and clicked play to different songs and moved their bodies in different pathways, and they did it together. Their noise-cancelling earbuds and loud hip hop blocked out an evacuation announcement going on over the intercom. Silent Amy, now awake, stared at her phone screen. The timer rang. Thirty seconds. They went back to work.

43 hours down, 3 to go

Did you bring a lighter?

Yeah, wait. Oh fuck, no. Just light it off the flames in that bin.

I've got about 3 Vogues left, do you think that'll last us?

Probably? One each now and maybe a victory one to share at the end?

Still can't believe someone left half a packet lying around. If that isn't a sign from God that we needed to schedule breaks, I don't know what is.

That's the universe telling us we need to chill. Do you think you'll keep smoking after this?

Probably not. I don't think a day and a half is enough time to develop a habit.

They sat on the concrete steps, inhaling and exhaling. Elsewhere in George Square, festival workers were arriving to see their places of work ransacked, colleagues trapped behind flaming bars and show posters littering the pavements like blankets. A man hurried past carrying thirty headphones for a silent disco and fell into a sinkhole.

Your knee is shaking.

It's been doing that for a few hours now. My body has taken matters into its own hands by trying to physically exhaust me to sleep.

Bec rested a hand on Maya's knee.

Did you see that guy who just walked past?

The one in the suit?

Yeah that one. He fetishizes Black women.

How do you know?

He told me after we matched on Tinder.
Trash.
Trash.
Back in?
What if we go back in and the room is on fire?
Extenuating circumstances.

44 hours down, 2 to go

Fuck!
Fuck!
What the actual fuck, is that the real time?
What do you have left to do? I have all these pages, they're everywhere! How did I end up with so many pages printed out? Why did I do that?
Visual aids? Easier to proof-read? You definitely had a reason. Fuck, I've still got the Conclusion and the Abstract and, honestly, fuck the Acknowledgements. I acknowledge nothing but my mindless tenacity at this point. You?
I need to cut down two-thousand words and proof-read everything! Fuck it!
I'm not going to proof-read, no time. I speak basic enough English, the majority should make some sort of sense. As long as I haven't accidentally written "fuck" or "shit" in there it'll be fine.
Fuck it!
Okay fuck okay, let's go.

45 hours down, 1 to go

Nothing really matters, does it? I mean, in the grand scheme of things.
Humanity's wrecked so what does it matter?
Success is a social construct.

45 hours 15 minutes down, 45 minutes to go

Silent Amy answers a phone call and runs out of the study room, leaving behind her laptop, shoes and blanket. The back wall falls away from the building and crashes into the street below, allowing a severe draft to enter the room.

Thank god, a breeze.

I'm so delirious I can't read what I'm writing any more.

I'm just chopping up and cutting out whole sentences. Entire sentences!

Do I even need an Abstract? Just read the fucking paper! I feel like Abstracts are like spoilers.

Screams echo from beneath the mountain of rubble outside. A rattled pigeon flies into the study room and crashes into a filing cabinet.

If I don't get a distinction on this, I can't do my PhD.

45 hours 30 minutes down, 30 minutes to go

The computers near the back of the study room fall out of the building as the floor gives way. A siren goes off outside.

What are you doing?

Proof-reading! For peace of mind!

Fuck, I still haven't proof-read. Fuck proof-reading, I don't have a title yet!

Bec types something in Cambria Math font-size **22**.

Is this witty and punny but still gets the overall research point across?

I like it. I have no idea what your dissertation is about, but I like it.

45 hours 45 minutes down, 15 minutes to go

Maya is crying. A low humming can be heard from Bec.

45 hours 50 minutes down, 10 minutes to go

All right bitches! I'm uploading this shit! You can't polish a turd!

It's not a turd, you're brilliant and I have every faith your dissertations slaps. Stand up for a second, let's shake this off. Then we can use the last ten mins to make sure everything is where it needs to be.

Okay fuck, okay mm, my arms! Oh, I can feel my shoulders loosen!

Drink some water!

I love water!

Okay last check. Let's do this!

45 hours 58 minutes down, 2 minutes to go

The blinds on the windows in the study room catch fire and the sprinklers immediately turn on. The room tilts to one side as the foundations of 50 George Square melt into the ground.

I'm uploading!

I'm uploading!

We're brilliant! Two minutes early? Come see success!

Come see excellence!

I love you, you're amazing!

We fucking did it! We smashed the system!

Hold my hand while I click submit?

Hold my hand while we leave this hell hole behind?

They submit.

The clock hits noon and Maya falls asleep at her desk. Bec brings out a bottle of tequila from under the table and sips.

Outside, the festival disintegrated as the sinkhole swallowed George Square whole. Somewhere, two dissertations were uploaded to a plagiarism-checking system, and the Earth took one last trip around the Sun.

O Cul-de-Sac!

Tim Major

O neighbours! If only we might speak!

Do you feel as I feel? Do you think as I think? Here we are, all crouching in our circle, so close to one another. It is maddening.

I see your people come and go. I hear snippets of their conversations. They are happy, your people, are they not? It is healthy, all this coming and going. But we remain rooted, facing one another implacably.

We are so young: sixteen this coming year. How many people have we had between us?

Recently I have paid less attention to your people than to mine, I confess. But in those early days, in those first glimmerings of consciousness, I was empty and I watched you all with intense fascination. There seemed so much to learn, and the opportunities for my education so few. Your people hurried to and fro – on what errands I had no way of imagining – and when they returned they appeared so grateful to see you. I came to distinguish between adults – more direct in their routes across our cul-de-sac, bustling into the cars on your driveways – and children, who dallied and bickered, whose movements were a joy to me. The children belonged to the adults and the adults belonged to you. When your people were nestled within you I gazed at the sky and the fields. I tested the radius of my attention, peering as far beyond my walls as possible. I perceived the disturbances of animals in the long grasses and swooping above me, I saw trees bending with the force of an unseen hand. I saw the rust-coloured roofs of the village that is tied to our cul-de-sac by an umbilical lane. I called out to you. I beckoned to your people. I was alone.

I was unoccupied.

My first people came a year later, following a smattering of visitors who declared me too large or too expensive or characterless. Their names were Anton and Beverly Grieg. They joked about show homes and the plastic fruit that still filled the wooden bowl beside the sink in my kitchen, but they were happy to have arrived and I was happy to receive them. More than happy! I embraced them from the moment they removed their shoes and padded inside me. Perhaps you remember the too-large white lorry with its rear end awkwardly jutting into our cul-de-sac, blocking three of your five driveways. Anton and Beverly Grieg set to filling my rooms with their furniture, their friends, their conversation. How they talked! Beverly was a lecturer at the university in York. Anton had once been her student and was, if anything, more passionate about learning than his wife. They talked of books and Francis Bacon and the governance of Britain and jazz music and the preparation of food and desire. These were the elements of their world, but they taught me about mine, too. They described the stars in the night sky, patterns hitherto unnoticed by me but suddenly, spectacularly, clear. They named the plants that encircle the lawn of my garden; they defined the willow, ash and pine trees. They lifted tiny creatures in their cupped hands so that I might better see them.

It wasn't only their teachings that provided my education. Two radios – one in my sitting room, one tickling and buzzing in my kitchen – were rarely turned off. Anton and Beverly Grieg watched documentary films and news reports. Through them I was given the ability to see far beyond our cul-de-sac and I came to appreciate the enormity of the world.

Anton and Beverly Grieg occupied me for four years, four happy years. When they announced their intention to leave I struggled to hide my disappointment, my window frames creaking with the ache of mourning. However, I allowed myself to dream. I watched your people come and go, the great numbers of them within each one of you. I dreamed of a family of my own.

I was disappointed. Evie Rattle was a solitary figure, content to spend her time alone. That might not have been a disaster, I told myself at the time. Mightn't we become all the closer, she and I, for the lack of other company? But she confided in me no more than in any human. She was absent for long hours each day, returning only in darkness and retiring quickly to bed. Worse still, she rarely watched television or listened to the radio, so my absorption of information was dramatically curtailed. Her work was as a laboratory technician – of what nature I still do not know, though the spines of the books on my shelves spoke of chemicals and pharmaceuticals. For a time, with my youthful lack of context that might allow me to distinguish between real and make-believe, I suspected her a witch.

Evie Rattle stayed with me for only a little over a year, thank goodness. Did you hear me when she left, o neighbours? It was with only the merest trace of guilt that I called out to you, hooting with triumph.

Then there were the many years spent with my most recent occupants, Piotr Brzezicki and Tom Grace. Though you may have thought me unchanged, judging solely from my exterior, inside I became a riot of colour, filled with mismatching furniture, colourful artworks and plastic trophies of their favourite television programmes. How I loved Piotr Brzezicki and Tom Grace! And I know that you loved them too, all of you – how could it be otherwise? Their joy in the pursuits they loved and in having found one another was infectious. Every day I awoke with renewed delight in seeing them happy. And they spent so much of their time with me, both pursuing their careers whilst burrowed inside me; Tom playing recordings of music as he tapped at his computer keyboard, Piotr listening to radio news broadcasts as he illustrated children's books, bent forward over a tilted board. I spent the days lazily shifting my attention from one of my bedroom offices to the other and back again, constantly unearthing new details to be savoured. At night I watched them sleep until I myself slumbered.

And yet your people felt differently, did they not? I noticed it from the start. Your people watched from their windows, the adults ushering the young indoors when my people appeared together at my doorway. For so long I understood nothing about sexuality and the limitations and rules that your people perceived about it, and when I did I wished I did not. I only knew that Piotr Brzezicki and Tom Grace were happy – so happy! – when they were safe together within my embrace.

I was despondent when they began discussing their plans to leave me. When they yanked their trinkets and trophies from my shelves, their banners and posters from my walls, I felt myself sag. I felt myself no longer a youth. I felt myself settle into my foundations and, worse, beginning to show my age. I watched from each window in turn, trying to keep my people in sight as the two lorries backed noisily from the cul-de-sac, followed by the tiny car containing my Piotr Brzezicki and my Tom Grace.

I sat alone for months.

I cried out, but none of you paid me attention, full as you all were with life of your own.

It is wrong to be presumptuous. One does not need to be human to understand that wonderful things will never occur to those who expect wonder. I learned this not from the television or the radio or the spines and tiny print of books; I learned this from my experiences with those that I have loved.

I did not presume, and yet they came.

Carly and Marie and Oliver Scaife.

A family.

Marie Scaife is the oldest. Her hair is white at the crown and that white will creep inexorably down, I am certain. There are lines on her face that converge into arrowheads that point to her eyes, which are full of sadness and pride.

Carly Scaife celebrated her twenty-eighth birthday the day the family arrived. Marie – her mother, though Carly has never referred to her as such – set a cake on a plate on a pile of packing cases that first evening, and Carly struggled to blow out candles embedded in it, and it was all I could do to stop myself from flinging open my windows to let in the wind to help her and to demonstrate my delight at having them within me.

Oliver Scaife is an infant.

He is all I have ever wanted.

He is small and incapable of much. He arrived strapped to Carly's chest and wailed. I whistled through my chimney in conversation. He is hairless and rarely opens his eyes. Marie says he is three months old.

Have you seen them, o neighbours? Have you seen them? I would send them to be witnessed by you, if I were not so reluctant to let them out from within me. Send your people instead and they will provide their reports. There has never been anything so wonderful in our cul-de-sac as Oliver Scaife and his mother and her mother.

I am watching you. For now I am content to let my people stroke at my insides and murmur at one another. I am hesitant of intruding upon them in these early days.

A change within oneself prompts other ways of seeing the world, does it not?

O neighbours, are your people as happy as I thought? They come and go often, but my ability to scrutinise, from my position here at the mouth of our cul-de-sac, is limited. They squint at the sky as they emerge from you. Their cars and bicycles buzz noisily from your driveways. When they return they hurry in.

Number four, your people have attracted my attention for so

long. Five people, including three children! And yet the eldest only scowls as she stares around at our cul-de-sac, her hands upon her hips. The other two squabble and hit each other as they are pushed into their car seats by one or another of your adults. They are all tired.

Number two, are you as alone as I was with Evie Rattle? You have only one person. He wears a black suit and walks briskly out of our cul-de-sac and briskly back in. There are so many long hours in between.

Number five, I know there are people within you; I have seen your lights turn on and off and I have seen black shapes at your windows. But who they are is unknown to me. They do not look out at our cul-de-sac. Do they speak? Is it wonderful having your people with you constantly? Or is it agony?

Number three, I see that you have new people too, a man and a woman. Their overalls are spotted with paint. It must be a delight to receive so much attention. I am certain that your hopes are high of their loving you. Send them to meet my people, won't you? Perhaps, vicariously, we may be friends. From the little I can see of your rear garden, it requires their attention.

Number six, have your people remained with you too long? That infant who was once so adorable is now almost an adult. His parents are wrong to leave him alone with you for such long periods. He has the face of somebody one should not trust.

Carly Scaife is learning, just as I am learning. She is not yet confident with Oliver Scaife. She struggles to feed him from her breasts and he struggles to get what he wants out of them. She listens to broadcasts on a mobile telephone wired up to a speaker in my master bedroom; the broadcasts instruct her to sleep when the baby sleeps. She tries but she does not sleep when Oliver Scaife sleeps; when he sleeps she kneels in her bed, leaning over the wall of his adjoining crib to watch him breathe. He is content when he is like that, but the only time I have seen Carly close to contentment is when her child is sleeping upon her chest while she sits on the wide sofa in my sitting room and she is watching comedies on the television and never once laughing.

The family have been with me for over a week and yet it is only now that I realise that we are alike, she and I. Carly Scaife is a mother and so am I. The infant began life within her, just as this family are within me. She holds him tight.

Carly's hair is cut short. Marie remarks on it often; it seems that the hair was longer until very recently. To Marie this is significant. Carly wears floral print dresses and black leggings. She says she can no longer wear contact lenses, which means she must wear glasses in order to see. I sympathise. My attention sometimes wavers and often I wish I had more clarity of vision. Within my walls it is often dark and, while I do not yearn for my days spent with Evie Rattle, it is difficult to focus on more than one person in more than one room at a time. When Oliver is asleep I feel compelled to watch him.

O neighbours! I know what I said, but they are drawing me into myself. I have barely looked beyond my walls these last few days. You might all have disappeared and I would not know it.

Carly sometimes cries herself to sleep. Marie does not seem to understand her fully. She offers to help placate the infant, but Carly rebuffs her and keeps the bedroom door tight shut. What Carly needs is an embrace. If her real mother will not provide it, then I will.

Oliver Scaife likes to look at patterns on the wall. I angle my windows just so, to catch the sunlight and make shadow patterns of leaves above his crib. He thanks me for it, I am certain he does.

Marie Scaife is also a mother. But she cannot remember what it is to hold somebody within oneself.

One week after they arrived, Marie left the house on foot and was absent for an entire day. Carly and Oliver crept downstairs.

Carly shifted the coffee table aside and stood in its space and whirled Oliver around and around above her head. Oliver did not laugh or smile, but he stared at her and then he twisted his body as she held him. It was difficult at first to know whether the contortion spelled delight or disgust, but then he looked up and around him – at *me* – and he spread his arms as if to say, "Is this not magnificent?"

When Marie returned she was driving a car. She parked it on my driveway, crunching its handbrake to prevent it from sliding back down the incline and into the turning circle of our cul-de-sac. She entered me and then backtracked, coaxing Carly to stand beneath the overhang of my porch. Carly held the infant and gazed at the car.

"I'm not getting into that," she said. "Oliver's not getting into that."

"I've had it checked over," Marie replied.

Carly glared at Marie until she closed the door, hiding the car from her. I shifted my attention outside: was the vehicle so bad? I glanced at the cars belonging to your people, the cars perched on your driveways, humming and cooling in the evening air. They all look alike to me.

"We might need it if we want to get away," Marie said as they ate pasta at the kitchen table, hours later.

Carly glanced at my door, at the invisible car beyond.

"We need money," Marie said. "I'll get a job."

Carly bent to fuss over Oliver in the basket on the floor beside the table. Then she rose, ate a mouthful of food, and nodded.

I do not know what employment Marie has found for herself, and I find that I do not care. Only occasionally does she take the car from the driveway. She is gone for long parts of each day and I am better able to relish spending time with Carly and Oliver.

My doorbell rings. It startles me – I have been watching Oliver in his crib and so has Carly. She is humming a melody that I find very beautiful.

I struggle to tear myself away, but then I shift my attention downstairs and outside before Carly's feet have touched the carpet of my master bedroom.

I watch the boy standing on the doorstep warily. It take several moments before I recognise him; people look altogether different up close. Number six, he is yours, is he not? His wild, long hair pushed under his cap is unmistakable. On the front of the cap is written in blue text *SO WHAT?*, which is a reference to a composition by the jazz musician Miles Davis.

He scowls and pushes my doorbell again. I try to stifle the sound. There is a child in here, asleep.

Carly edges toward the door slowly, slowly. She glances several times at the staircase and the trailing, invisible rope that connects her to Oliver in his crib. I am capable of metaphor, o neighbours.

I consider jamming the door, holding it fast.

Carly is quicker than me. Even as it appears she is having second thoughts, she yanks at the lock and pulls open the door. It stings like a wound.

"Yes?" she says in a voice that is not quite level.

The boy pushes back the peak of his cap. When I last paid him any attention he suffered from acne; now I see that it has cleared. He reeks of confidence.

"Kieran," he says. That is his name. "From across the way."

He gestures over his shoulder with his thumb. Carly tilts to see past him and so do I. I was right: number six. Number six, you sent him and I will hold you accountable.

"What do you want?" Carly says. She sounds very tired.

"My dad said we should say hi sometime."

"Where's your dad?"

"Work. Summer holidays, but not for him."

"Your mother?"

"Same."

"You're on your own?"

"I'm sixteen."

"All right then."

"Yeah."

Carly and I are so close that my anxiety transfers to her.

"So you've done it," she says. "You've said hi. And hi back at you."

"So do you know anyone round here?"

"No." Abruptly, Carly shudders. I see it and Kieran does too.

"If you want I could –"

"No."

Kieran stares at her and Carly reaches out a hand. She holds the brass knocker that is fixed to the centre of my door. Her grip is tighter than I would expect; it hurts.

"Want me to wash your car?" Kieran says.

Carly looks at the car as if she has never seen it before. "No."

"I wash everyone's car. Everyone in the cul-de-sac, I mean."

"It's new. It doesn't need a wash."

"It's grubby. There's sand in the air came from the Middle East on the wind."

"In Yorkshire?"

Kieran shrugs. "That's what my dad said. Middle Eastern sand. Gets your windscreen proper filthy."

"Seriously. Kieran, was that your name? I don't want my car washed." I see something in Carly I have never seen before. A hardness inside.

"Twenty quid."

Carly splutters. "For a car wash? You've got to be kidding."

"It's what everyone pays." He waves an arm to gesture at you all, o neighbours, as if it proves something.

"No. Off you go now."

Kieran grins and I do not know what it means. His eyes leave Carly's face. He is looking at her body and now I know what the grin means.

Carly presses my door closed and Kieran's head tilts, trying to keep her in sight through the narrowing gap.

Carly stands looking at the door. She shakes her head and then pads upstairs, following the rope back to Oliver, bundling it in her fists as she climbs.

I see her safely up, then I turn my attention back to the boy outside. He slinks back to you, number six, but within moments he returns. He is carrying a bucket and a sponge.

I raise myself from the sag of my foundations to see as far from my walls as possible.

That village at the end of the lane. How many roofs can I see – twenty? Thirty? The sunlight multiplies the number of surfaces that are visible to me. How many people do they shelter in total? A dizzying amount.

The people of our cul-de-sac so rarely encounter one another, but I understand now that this is not usual. People are not relegated to their family units. Any of them might speak to any other. Once free of their wombs, they are capable of travelling anywhere, and perhaps they do, every day. I look at you all; I consider the six of us sitting in our tight circle. We are so close and yet we do not speak. Perhaps our indifference has affected our people.

Beyond the village there is more life and movement, more and more. An aeroplane is a distant speck.

On the mantelpiece in my sitting room is a painted wooden doll. Carly shows it to her infant and then pulls its upper half free of its lower half. Inside is another doll, and inside that another and another.

I dream of a life free from my lumpenness and my rootedness. But I am a mother. I understand my responsibilities.

The boy was right about the sand on the car. Now that he has dragged his dirty sponge across its bonnet the copper-coloured streaks are clear to see. But the dust has been disturbed and nothing more. The car looks far worse than it did before.

Even after finishing with the car Kieran must have been watching and waiting. The moment that Marie appears at the mouth of the cul-de-sac he emerges from you, number six. He follows Marie along my driveway. She notices him only as she is struggling to locate her keys whilst grappling with a holdall that threatens to slip from her forearm.

"Is your daughter in?" Kieran says.

"I hope so." I think Marie is trying to hide her being startled by him.

Kieran moistens his lips with his tongue; a grotesque action. He opens his mouth to speak, then closes it. After a pause he says, "She owes me twenty pounds."

Marie turns to face him fully. She folds her arms and her holdall knocks heavily against my doorframe. "Don't be so silly. What for?"

"Is she all right?" Kieran says, quickly, as though he has spoken before he is ready. He tries to look past Marie.

"She just needs peace and quiet. She's a mother now. We don't want visitors."

Kieran gives up. He nods at the car. "I'm all finished. Twenty quid. We agreed."

Marie's expression is unchanging as she surveys the mess on the windscreen and bonnet. "Wait there."

She plods inside and groans as she deposits the bag in my hallway. She calls out for Carly, who I know is upstairs in the nursery that Oliver uses only for play and not for sleep. I do not follow her. Instead I wait, watching Kieran, making sure that he does not step over my threshold. Number six, what have you inflicted upon us?

I sense raised voices – o neighbours, do you suffer from these same uncomfortable vibrations, even when your attention is elsewhere? – and then Marie is clopping down my stairs again. She strides to the door brandishing a twenty pound note.

"We both know it's extortion," she says.

Number six, you should be ashamed. Kieran smiles and takes the money. He demonstrates no remorse. He tries again to see inside. He is looking for Carly.

"Go home now," Marie says. She closes the door and I sigh at the healed wound. My attention rises to my upper floor. Carly is standing in the nursery at my window. She is gazing down at Kieran as he lollops away. Oliver rolls ineffectively on a playmat behind her, unable to turn himself onto his front. Carly lifts both her hands and her fingertips graze my glass.

Oliver Scaife keeps us all awake. He squeals and snorts and rattles the bars of his crib. Even when he sleeps his breathing is as loud and abrasive as the pipes that lead from my boiler, which have been maintained inexpertly and shudder when anybody showers.

Carly's attention to the task of placating Oliver wavers. Sometimes she hushes and soothes him, leaning over his crib in her nightdress or, more often, hefting him to lie like a sack upon her while she is cradled by pillows in an awkward half-sitting position. Sometimes she remains lying in her bed and pulls one of the pillows over her head. I understand this impulse. We all love Oliver, but why won't he quieten? When will this stop?

At this moment she is walking up and down in the darkness of her bedroom, bouncing Oliver Scaife in her arms. She tells him that she will do anything for him, but he grumbles whenever she pauses and then his grumbles swell into splutters and then piercing howls. It is too dark to determine whether his eyes are closed, or whether hers are.

I think Carly may be weeping. The holdall that Marie was carrying is now in the bedroom. It bulges with its contents and I fear that Carly may be intending to slip away from me. My wish that there were some way for me to help reminds me that there is somebody else in the house, after all. Where is Marie right at this moment? I shift my attention across to her bedroom and peer at the bed. The covers have been thrown off. There is nobody here or in my bathroom.

It is with a sense of excitement rather than anxiety that I scour my other rooms. She is not upstairs. A thought occurs to me and I am not ashamed of it: perhaps I am more a mother to Carly than Marie is.

I find Marie in the dark at the foot of my stairs, an area that some of my previous occupants designated an entrance hall but which the Scaifes have made a dining area by means of putting a mahogany table here. They seldom use it; they almost always eat sitting at the pine table in my kitchen, almost always one at a time, one of them washing dishes or cradling Oliver while the other chews food.

Marie is walking slowly alongside the dining table, up and down its length and then up and down again. She is wearing a dressing gown but I can see her day clothes underneath. Occasionally she glances at my staircase. She can hear Oliver's shrieks, I am positive. Can she also hear Carly's sobbing?

O neighbours, I do not want to say that I hate Marie.

Something happens. It is Marie's sudden spasm that alerts me, rather than the sound itself. She freezes and cocks her head.

I am upstairs in an instant.

Carly shouts, "Stop!" And again: "Stop!"

She means Oliver and his howling, but Oliver does not stop it. Even in the dark I can see the black O of his mouth, a hole wider than his head ought to allow. The sound he emits is more than mere sound. I am blinded by it.

Marie clatters upstairs. She pauses outside the door to Carly's bedroom.

"I'm here," she says, so quiet that I wonder whether she really wants Carly to hear.

I am inside watching Carly. In the darkness I see her head snap up. She faces the door but does not speak.

Oliver continues his shrieking.

"Can I do anything?" Marie says outside the room, shifting her weight from foot to foot, an itch upon my floor.

Carly's head drops again. She speaks to Oliver in a softer, kinder voice: "Stop, now."

Oliver stops, now.

After that squall of sound the silence seems like deafness. Carly comes to a halt at the foot of her bed, beside the holdall. I cannot see her expression, whether there is triumph or only relief.

Outside, Marie watches the door. Her face, I can see. Her eyes gleam with wetness. She rubs her cheek again and again, as if she has been slapped. She turns and creeps away to her bedroom. She leaves the door ajar and climbs into bed. As soon as I see that she has fallen asleep, I swing the door closed slowly and she flinches only slightly at its click.

It is after ten o'clock when I rouse myself. Do you wake early, o neighbours? Do you even sleep? When I am unoccupied I am capable of sustaining myself with infrequent naps or a constant doze. But a family of three is exhausting and I find more and more that when they are sleeping I must sleep also.

Marie must already have left for work and Oliver is snoring in his cot. For a moment I panic at not finding Carly close by. She is not in my bathroom or my sitting room or my kitchen. I spread my attention wider. I peer into my garden that, so far, the Scaifes have not explored, then, in desperation, beyond. Then Carly shuffles somewhere and I find her.

She is in my smallest bedroom. There has been a desk and a chair and nothing more in here since the day the family arrived. Now there is a computer with a folding screen upon the desk and Carly is sitting before it, circling her index finger on its black surface. Her feet are tucked beneath her on the chair, which rotates slightly with each of her movements. She is humming that same song as before. I think of Tom Grace and his joy at hearing music. Perhaps later I will send a surge of electrical power to the rarely-used stereo in my sitting room, and perhaps that will operate it, and perhaps Carly will take to listening to music too. There is little that I desire nowadays, but I desire music.

I look at the computer screen and see images of bright-coloured things. These are pictures of toys, like the ones that litter Oliver's playmat in his nursery. He shows little interest in them. He prefers clutching at Carly's necklaces or watching the play of light on the grey bars of my radiators. On the computer screen I see dolls and animals and cubes and twisted wires strung with beads. Carly is deliberating over these pictures, clicking on one and then another as she hums her song.

When Oliver wakes, Carly goes to him. She lifts him and then holds him under his armpits and pretends that he is walking downstairs, tickling me as she scuffs his feet on each of my steps.

She feeds him at her breast while she sits on the sofa and – joy! – she turns on the television and together we three watch a documentary programme about ceramic artists. Then she assembles a lunch for herself; it occurs to me only now that it is rare for her to eat during the daytime, when Marie is absent. She eats a little of the salad leaves and tomatoes, but afterwards she retches into the sink.

Then she carries Oliver to my back door and she throws it open and it is not so much like a wound as a cleansing. I pull the breeze inside, tousling the hair of the two of them, tugging the air along my walls and ceiling and floors. I gasp at first and then I sigh in contentment.

They leave. It is not so terrible; I can see all parts of the garden. Although I cannot feel any sensations it is almost a part of me, in the same way that Carly's short hair is part of her – do you feel the same, o neighbours? The discomfort is only in my mind, a fear that having gone this far they might stray further.

But Carly deposits Oliver on his back under the shade of the willow at the garden's eastern edge, and then she lies upon the grass herself. I watch from my windows, first at ground level, then above.

I think of Carly watching Oliver asleep in his crib and I am terribly tired and I feel that if I could I would cry.

In my swoon it is difficult to tell how much time has passed. Carly and Oliver reenter and I welcome them back with all the warmth I can muster. When Marie returns I snarl at her, but she does not react. Her attention is fixated on Carly, who descends my staircase dressed entirely in black.

"Are you okay to watch him?" Carly says. She means Oliver.

Marie watches Carly with her eyes narrowed.

Carly laughs. "You look like you're going to say, 'You can't go out looking like that'."

She goes to the utility room beside my porch and fumbles until she produces a pair of shoes. She has not worn shoes since she arrived, and these are not the pair she was wearing that day. They are bright orange, sickeningly vivid against the black of her leggings and her long-sleeved top.

"Where are you going?" Marie says.

Carly stands and looks down at her outfit. "To the opera, obviously." I clench with anxiety before I recognise that it is a joke. "I'll be twenty minutes. Thirty, tops."

She pushes her way past Marie and through my front door and she sets off at a sprint.

Carly is absent for forty-seven minutes. Marie frets as much as I do. She moves from window to window, watching as the sun drops behind you, o neighbours, and then when Oliver wakes she is occupied with pushing toys towards him where he lies on the playmat and pleads with him not to cry. He squeals each time she tries to come close. Who can blame him?

She and I both rush downstairs the second my front door

slams.

Carly is soaking wet. I did not realise that it has been raining. She is panting heavily and she is grinning. When Marie stumbles into the dining room carrying Oliver, I notice her expression of revulsion. Is she so old that she cannot remember the delight in physicality? For an awful flash of a moment I feel that Marie and I are alike – static – but I push the thought away.

Carly wipes a hand across her mouth. There is a sheen of sweat on her face. She is unimaginably beautiful.

She reaches out for Oliver. Marie seems reluctant, but Carly tugs the infant free. He settles upon her neatly like a sheet upon a bed.

When Marie speaks her voice cracks. "Were you safe?"

"Of course."

"Did anybody see you?"

"Nobody."

Carly hefts Oliver onto her shoulder and carries him back upstairs. He is asleep even before she lays him in his crib. She tiptoes to the bathroom, a mere shadow in those clothes. She hums as she peels the outfit from her body. I hum the same melody to myself as she showers and I watch her, wondering what it must be like to be so alive.

Oliver Scaife cries throughout the night.

I edge my window open to let the breeze stroke Carly's cheek. I miss her terribly when she is asleep. O neighbours, do you feel the same about your people, your favourites among them? Perhaps mothers are only ever complete when they are with their children.

All the pleasure of yesterday has gone. Oliver's nighttime mewling has left Carly desolate again. Is it any wonder that when he wakes – my breeze has inadvertently roused him too – she scurries out of the bedroom and downstairs?

"You go to him," she snaps at Marie. Marie has the sense to obey.

Later, after breakfast, Carly says to Marie, "Don't go out."

"I have to work."

"Don't leave me here with him."

"You're his mother."

Carly leans upon the kitchen table. She gazes down at Oliver in his wicker basket. "I would never hurt him," she says.

Marie hesitates, then rises and stands before her. Carly tries to look past her at my garden.

"Why did you say that?" Marie says.

Carly doesn't answer.

"Carly."

"Go to work. We'll be fine."

"First tell me why you said that. Why you said, 'I would never hurt him'."

Carly scoops up the basket from my linoleum floor. "I'm just tired. Go on. Go."

Marie checks all of my doors and windows before she leaves the house.

An hour later my doorbell rings. Oliver is strapped to Carly's chest and for thirty minutes she has been walking in circles in the front room. At first she told Oliver again and again that she loved him but her voice lowered and lowered in volume until it became only a shush. I have been trying to distract myself by watching documentary footage of an auction on the television, but Carly's circles have been drawing my attention and I do not know what to do. I am happy about my doorbell ringing because it rouses Carly from what almost seems like sleep. She goes quickly to my front door. Perhaps she is grateful too.

"Who is it?" Carly whispers, without opening the door.

"Delivery for Mrs Scaife?"

Carly scowls. "Miss. Or mizz."

"Sorry. Miss."

They wait, Carly inside and – I check – an obese man in dungarees outside.

"I'll need a signature, miss."

Oliver shifts on Carly's chest. He is asleep. "I'm feeding my child. Put the signature thing through the letterbox?"

The delivery man lifts the letterbox. He is holding a bulky electronic device. "It won't fit, miss."

Carly's jaw clenches. She yanks the door open and I wince. She holds out a hand for the device. The delivery man glances at Oliver, who is beginning to stir, and then relinquishes it. Carly scribbles upon the screen of the device with a pen attached to it with a cord, then hands it back so quickly the man almost drops it.

"Right," he says. "Back in two shakes, then I'll pop them wherever you want them. There's a whole lot of them, isn't there?"

Carly looks the obese delivery man up and down. Then she moistens her lips, which makes me think of you and your odious Kieran, number six.

"Just leave them outside," she says.

"Can't, miss. Not with the value of them. I have to show they're in their right place and take a photo."

"You're not coming inside," she says, and I could not love her more.

Oliver emits a tiny cry. The delivery man looks at the infant and then at Carly and he takes a step backwards. "All right, miss. All right."

Carly presses the door closed and takes a deep, ragged breath while the man returns to his absurd red lorry parked on the kerb of our cul-de-sac. I watch as he heaves each bulky box from the tailgate and into the lee of my porch.

Across our turning circle I see you, number six, and I see Kieran at your kitchen window. He watches me with undisguised interest, but I am watching him right back.

I had not even noticed that I had a phone. When it rings I scratch around, trying to locate the itch.

Carly answers it. The phone is in the cubbyhole beneath my staircase, where Anton and Beverly Grieg placed a drinks cabinet they opened only when entertaining guests which contained only bottles of gin.

She listens attentively. I strain to decipher the hum in the telephone wire: nothing. I watch Carly's face.

"Come," she says. "Please come."

Marie is making her way downstairs, showered and dressed after her day at work. I force each step to emit a loud creak as she descends.

Carly replaces the handset carefully and turns to face Marie.

The suspicion comes upon me slowly.

I am a mother. I care for all of my children. But one of them in particular requires my careful supervision. Carly is at risk. From what, I do not know.

But what I do know is this: Marie is not capable of protecting her.

Carly is protecting Oliver and I am protecting Carly. Marie is protecting nobody. Marie does not belong here.

I have another suspicion. A question.

Is Marie really Carly's mother?

They share the same surname, but that could be a ruse. It is only visitors to the house – removal and delivery men, an obnoxious estate agent – that have spoken the name Scaife. I spend many hours examining one woman's face and then the other. They share no physical characteristics that I can see. Marie's face is a lattice of creases; in another context I might describe it as kindly. Those arrowhead lines that point to the corners of her eyes suggest a life of laughter, but she has never laughed that I have seen. It is another ruse.

Carly's face is a wide, pale circle. She has no creases despite the torture that Oliver puts her through each night. She might never grow old. Her front teeth are bent inwards slightly, as though she has bumped them on something hard.

Take him away, number six. We have no time for your people.

Kieran knocks again, louder.

Upstairs, Carly crosses my landing to look out of the window and down at my porch.

She covers her mouth with a hand. She watches your Kieran, number six, as unflinchingly as I watch him. Then, hurriedly, she turns away and goes to my bathroom and vomits into the toilet bowl.

Kieran finally stops his knocking. He turns and runs a finger across the bonnet of the car.

After dinner Carly excuses herself. Marie coos at Oliver in the sitting room but he is happier without her intervention, stretching his little arms toward my fireplace where the painted wooden doll sits on its mantelpiece. Perhaps he is imagining himself free of her. I watch Marie intently, ready to shriek if she tries anything untoward.

When Carly returns she is wearing her black clothes again. She has already put on her shoes, which are an even more nauseating colour than they were yesterday. They are filthy with mud as red as copper.

"No," Marie says.

"I need to," Carly replies. She grips my doorframe at the entrance to the sitting room. She rolls her neck and it clicks.

"You mustn't. Please. There must be something else."

Marie has risen to her haunches. Oliver rolls onto his side but I will not let him injure himself on the hearth. Carly glances at the infant but she does not move from the doorway.

"If you cared, you wouldn't stand in my way," Carly says.

Marie presses both her palms to her face. I imagine touching that crenellated surface and it is all I can do not to shudder.

"I care," she says in a voice full of fatigue.

"I'll be quick, I promise. I know where I'm going."

Marie scoops up the infant, ignoring his squeals. She holds him before her, presenting him to his mother. But it is only to allow Carly to kiss the boy on his forehead.

Slowly, Marie shakes her head. "No. Don't be quick. Take your time, do it properly. Go as far away as you need to and be careful."

Marie sleeps downstairs in a wing-backed armchair that she shifted from my sitting room and into my dining room.

When Carly returned Marie and I scrutinised her: was her mood improved? She was exhausted and covered with copper-coloured mud and bark. I followed her upstairs and watched her undress and shower and feed Oliver and slip into bed, cooing at her infant asleep in his crib. When I turned my attention back to Marie she was already in the dining room with the lights so dim and her body so slight that the large chair might as well have been empty.

Piotr Brzezicki loved to watch fiction on television. Before that time I had been accustomed to documentary films and at first I was startled by these visions of the world outside, of outlandish creatures, dizzying animated illustrations and arguments upon arguments. Tom Grace did not enjoy crime fiction, so Piotr and I watched these types of television programmes together when Tom was busy working or sleeping. In these television programmes everybody has a secret and one can only look away once the most important secret has been revealed.

Television has taught me one thing: the ways in which humans can create obstacles to other humans' happiness are too numerous to count.

I have dwelt upon the themes of these crime stories. I believe I have an idea about what may be happening here, within me, right at this moment.

I believe that I am a sanctuary. That Carly is here to hide from something outside, something from which only I can protect her, and of which Marie is aware and afraid. I have seen stories on television about people who hide away from their enemies or even their lovers. They change their names and they hide for days or months or years.

Here is my reason for believing this: even in the dark of the dining room I can see the thin black pole that is propped against Marie's chair. I am convinced that it is a rifle.

I watch Carly pick her way carefully past Marie sleeping in her chair.

Upstairs, Oliver stirs softly.

It is just before dawn and it is raining outside, heavier than it has rained in weeks. The water slops against my roof and it is funnelled through my guttering, an almost unbearable prickling.

Carly searches the room beside my porch and retrieves an indigo waterproof coat and waterproof trousers that crinkle as she pulls them on. Marie turns her head toward the sound but does not wake. Carly hops from foot to foot as she squeezes into lime-green Wellington boots.

Oliver splutters. Carly looks to my staircase but does not approach it.

She pulls open my back door and she is in the garden.

I beg her not to go any further. There is something out there and she must not go out alone, not without warning Marie, much as I dislike the old woman.

She cannot leave me with Marie and Oliver.

It is difficult to make Carly out through my windows smeared with rain. Her silhouette twists unnaturally as she makes her way away from me across my lawn. She stops at the picket fence that marks my boundary. I sigh with relief: surely she will turn back.

With some difficulty, she clambers onto the fence and then drops down onto the other side.

The wind grows stronger, tossing rain at me, and I howl through my chimney.

I watch as the spindly speck that is Carly crosses the lane and pushes through a hedgerow, beginning to plod through the cornfield opposite. I watch until she passes the point where the trees obscure my view.

I have two contradictory thoughts. One is that she must be kept safe. The other is that she must not escape.

I know it is the rain, but I feel that I am weeping.

Perhaps Oliver hears me. He bellows and rattles his crib.

Marie – stupid, careless Marie – finally wakes. She looks at my window, at the rising sun and the rain, and she grabs for the gun. She blinks and finally recognises the sounds that Oliver is making and she staggers upstairs. She bursts into the bedroom still holding the rifle and I hammer my windows against the frames – *watch what you're doing, you oaf!* Then she runs from room to room, searching for Carly, but Carly is gone and perhaps she will never come back and it is all Marie's fault.

When Marie has finally convinced herself that we are alone, she returns to the infant. She hovers with uncertainty, looking from Oliver to the rifle and back. Finally she props the weapon against the bars of his crib. She carries Oliver downstairs – he kicks and shouts – and attempts to warm a bottle of milk in the microwave whilst holding him, then attempts to feed him. He yells and casts around and looks up at me, pleading for my help.

An hour passes before Oliver falls into sullen silence. In my sitting room Marie wrestles him into a hammock chair made of cushioned fabric and wire. She presses the chair down to set it bouncing and then she joins me in looking out of my window into the garden.

We watch, both worried mothers. At this moment I do not

hate her at all.

We are so absorbed we do not hear my front door opening. When I hear a sniffling sound from outside the sitting room, I hurtle away to find Carly bent on the doormat, waterfalls streaming from the shell of her coat. She picks something up from the mat. It is a piece of notepaper, folded once. She unfolds it and reads it – I strain to see past her, but her coat makes her bulky and obscures my view – and then folds it again.

She glances out of the window at our cul-de-sac.

Marie catches up with me. She comes to a stop in the dining room, horrified at the vision of Carly in her gleaming wet shroud.

"I don't want to talk about it," Carly says. Then, "I need your help."

Marie tries to speak, fails, then clears her throat. "Anything."

Carly points at my front door, which hangs slightly ajar. Outside, barely protected by the porch overhang, the boxes that the delivery man put there are disintegrating in the rain. Some of the cardboard has ripped and fallen away entirely.

"Help me bring these inside," Carly says.

The boxes contain toys and books and clothes. The largest cardboard box, the one that was ripped even when it was outside, is the size of a coffin and contains another box that is so heavy that Marie and Carly struggle to bump it up my stairs. It is a toy chest with a heavy, padded seat that is also a hinged lid. Its sides are decorated with colourful illustrations of dinosaurs and trees.

For most of the night Oliver is inconsolable. Carly sings to him and pleads with him and strokes his bald head and his back and his stomach.

"I'm doing all this for you," she says softly, again and again.

For the rest of the night, for hours until just before the sun is due to peep above your rooftops, o neighbours, Carly is in my third bedroom, the nursery. It is black dark. There is a cot in here, larger than the bedside crib, but Oliver has never slept in it. In the darkness Carly kneels before the toy box. I cannot see her face but I can hear her stop-start sobbing and I can make out her hands wiping at her face again and again. I do not know why, but I find it revolting.

Before she returns to my master bedroom she carefully places all of the new toys into the toy chest.

"Perhaps it would be best for all of us if he were dead," Carly says at breakfast.

She is gazing down at Oliver in his basket.

Marie stares at her and Carly says nothing more.

In the silence I replay Carly's enunciation of the phrase as best I can. Her tone was almost neutral, but was there a slight emphasis on 'he'?

I wake in a panic.

Carly reaches my staircase in the dark before I have collected myself and before I am ready to help. One of the steps halfway down has long caused me problems and I fear that without attention it will only get worse. Its loud creak echoes from my walls and I curse my age.

In my dining room Marie springs up from her chair.

Carly continues her descent.

"Stop," Marie says hoarsely.

"Or what?" Carly replies. Her voice sounds slurred. She is dressed in her black clothes again, which have not been cleaned since yesterday. I notice that her face is already smeared and dirty. How has that happened? The last I saw her before I fell asleep, she was kneeling again before the toy box.

Slowly, uncertainly, Marie raises the rifle to point at Carly. I am transfixed and unable to do anything to intervene.

"You've got to be kidding."

Marie shakes her head. "I'm not kidding. You can't do it this way."

"Because?"

"Because you'll be found out."

"There is no other way. You don't understand."

Marie shifts the arm holding the rifle to wipe at her eye with a dressing-gowned shoulder. Like me, she is half asleep. Perhaps this is only a nightmare.

Both women turn their heads. They are looking upstairs.

"He'll grow up," Marie says. "And then he'll be able to look after himself. It won't be as long as you think. You'll see."

"I hate him."

"No, you don't."

"No."

After a few moments of silence Marie says, "I do understand, though."

Until now Carly's attention has been only on the weapon, as though she has been judging her moment to escape. Now she looks at Marie's face.

"I was just the same as you," Marie says in a weary tone that makes her sound even older than she is. "I guess it's a family thing."

In the morning Marie says, "I won't go to work today."

"You don't need to hang around here."

Marie is thinking what I am thinking. Carly wants Marie gone so that she can leave the house again, and when she does she will leave Oliver alone. I am afraid. I cannot care for Oliver on my own.

Marie shakes her head. "I'll go out. I'll get more for the toy box."

Carly's foot stops its rocking of Oliver's chair. She and Marie watch each other and I do not know what to make of it. Is it a secret, Carly's nighttime crying at the toy box? After their encounter last night Carly went directly to my unused nursery. Marie remained in her chair downstairs, the rifle on her lap. If she went into the nursery it must have been when I finally fell asleep myself.

"You will?" Carly says. Her eyes shine.

"If that's what you need."

Abruptly, Carly is crying.

When Marie returns in the afternoon she goes directly upstairs and places two orange plastic carrier bags beside the toy box. They remain there until night when Carly enters the nursery in darkness. I cannot see into the bags, but Carly coughs and cries and swallows noisily as she rifles through their contents. She does not open the toy box until just before she leaves, an hour later.

Marie does not dress for work. She stays downstairs in her dressing gown and casts glances at my staircase.

The phone rings and she answers it. She waits only a moment – barely enough time for the caller to make an introduction – before she speaks.

"Don't you *fucking* dare," she says.

Carly is singing to Oliver. I recognise the song, which was one of Anton Grieg's favourites: 'Doctor, Lawyer, Indian Chief' by Hoagy Carmichael.

I prefer Carly's rendition. Her voice is very beautiful.

I sway to her singing and I let my attention spread beyond myself. Today it is wonderfully sunny outside. O neighbours, you look like palaces sparkling golden! The village at the end of the lane is an island in its cornfield sea, its spires the tallest trees. It is possible to be content with so very little.

I am enjoying looking directly upwards at the sky. At first it appears steel-coloured, but the more I look the more I am able to see the speckles of stars and even the pale apparition of the moon. Every so often I shift my attention back to Carly, to her lips forming the words, to Oliver pressed tight against her chest as she dances. She is holding him too tight.

She is pressing Oliver tighter and tighter to herself as she spins towards my window. Oliver lets out a muffled cry.

She will harm him like this.

I remember Carly's words. Was that yesterday, or longer ago? *Perhaps it would be best for all of us if he were dead.*

The threat is not out there in the golden sunlight.

O cul-de-sac! Send help!

We all wait nervously for the day to end. We all fear the night.

Marie and Carly speak only to arrange their meal and to soothe Oliver.

Carly goes to bed early. She kneels in her bed, watching Oliver in his crib. I beg her to be kind.

Downstairs, Marie does not sleep or even sit in her chair. She holds the rifle in both hands and paces up and down the length of my dining room. She looks out of my front window, peering into the blackness, and then my window that faces the void of the garden.

I do not understand why she is looking outside. Is Marie wrong about the nature of the threat, or am I? Whose maternal instincts are the stronger?

Marie checks her gun and presses her nose to the glass.

She sees something out there, before I sense it myself. O neighbours, what is it?

I pray that it is an animal, a fox. But it is not.

It is a human. It is standing at the picket fence in my garden.

Marie turns from the window to look up at my staircase, but she does not move from her position at the window. If she will not warn Carly then I will. In a flurry I race upstairs.

Carly's bed is empty.

I search for any sign of her. She is not in the nursery. The toy box is open and toys are strewn on the playmat and spilling under the wooden cot. Inside the toy box I see a collection of long struts that gleam white in the moonlight. They are bones.

Hanging from them are ragged scraps of meat that are copper-coloured like the soil on Carly's clothes. I realise now that it is not soil but dry blood.

Carly must be here somewhere.

I dart from room to room, struggling and failing to turn on my lights.

All I can think about are bones and flesh and blood.

Carly brought in that toy box. She filled it with something unspeakable and she forced Marie to help her carry it inside me.

Back downstairs Marie moves from window to window, watching and clutching the rifle.

I cast my attention outside. Whoever is out there has moved closer and has almost reached my walls.

"Carly!" Marie cries suddenly. She spins and clatters upstairs. She and I scour my rooms.

Where is Carly?

I push downstairs into my kitchen, my sitting room. I am certain Carly is here somewhere. She is moving somewhere, her bare feet tapping at my carpeted floors. But if she is here she is a shadow among shadows.

I realise that Marie has stopped moving and I fear for Oliver. But Marie is not standing beside his crib; she is at the other side of Carly's bed. She is reaching for a piece of paper that sits upon Carly's pillow.

It is not folded now.

If we peer closely Marie and I can make out the words handwritten upon it.

I know it's crazy, the note says, *but I think you're in trouble and I want to help.*

And: *I'll come after dark on Sunday night.*

And strangest of all: *Kieran*

It is Sunday night and Kieran is in the garden.

With a start I realise that Oliver's crib is empty.

Marie and I move in synchronicity. We career downstairs, my

boards creaking to match Marie's strangled cries.

There is another sound: something snapping.

And another: that same stop-start sobbing I heard when Carly knelt before the toy box. Or perhaps it is not sobbing but something wet and awful.

I think of those times that she left me and I realise now that she was not seeking escape.

I roar with the horror of it.

Marie hears me. She jerks and the rotten middle step of my staircase cracks and gives way and she slips. I try to catch her but she bounces and then her neck twists and her head strikes my bannister and then she bumps down my stairs, turning and turning and coming to a halt in a heap on my carpet.

I was wrong.

My rear door, the door to my garden, is closed, but a chill tells me that it has been recently open. Outside I can see nothing.

I try to push my awareness beyond my walls, twisting, like Marie's neck twisted, to see back towards myself. It is agony.

But I do see something.

It is crumpled on the paved area outside my rear door. At first I perceive it as a heap of fabric. But there are limbs, too. Bones and flesh and blood. I see a forearm and the meat has been picked clean off. I see your Kieran's face, number six, and he is never coming home.

Carly is a hunter.

She must be here somewhere.

With a jolt I realise that I am empty for the first time in weeks.

I flail around and find Carly at the foot of my driveway.

Even from behind her I can see, from the way her arms are angled, that she is carrying Oliver strapped to her chest. I hear his faint gurgle and I know that he is unharmed.

"I'm doing all this for you," I hear her say.

He is under no threat.

And neither is Carly.

I was wrong.

I tell myself that this is not my doing. Carly and I are both mothers and we are responsible only for ourselves.

But I also know this: while we have our children, we will protect them as best we can.

Barefoot, Carly strides away from me without looking back. Her head swings from side to side as she looks around our cul-de-sac, gazing at each of you in turn.

O neighbours!

Additional Recommended Reading

Sadly, not every story can be included in *The Best of British Fantasy*. Here are fifty additional stories that didn't make it into the book. These are this year's 'honourable mentions' – all by British or UK resident authors and first published in 2019:

- Sandra Alland – "Smudged" (*We Were Always Here: A Queer Words Anthology* [404 Ink])
- L. R. Ambrose – "Long Enough" (*NevermorEarth*)
- G.V. Anderson – "The Harvest of a Half-Known Life" (*Lightspeed*)
- Tiffani Angus – "What Cannot Be Described" (*The Book of Flowering* [Egaeus])
- R. J. Barker – "Riggers" (*Three Crows*)
- Chris Barnum – "Sigmund Seventeen" (*Electric Spec*)
- Rose Biggin – "The Ghost of Cock Lane" (*Soot and Steel* [NewCon])
- Die Booth – "Of Water" (*Unfading Daydream*)
- Justine Bothwick – "Petrified" (*Confingo*)
- Sarah Brooks – "Everything Rising, Everything Starting Again" (*Interzone*)
- Daniel Carpenter – "Hunting by the River" (*Black Static*)
- Eliza Chan – "Knowing Your Type" (*Three Crows*)
- David Cleden – "Seven Stops Along the Graffiti Road" (*Interzone*)
- Jeremy Darlington – "Scent" (*Scent* [Comma])
- K. T. Davies – "Chosen of the Slain" (*Legends III* [NewCon])
- Malcolm Devlin – "A Dreamer Arrives in the Occupied City" (*Interzone*)
- Camilla Grudova – "Through Ceilings and Walls" (*Extra Teeth*)
- Olivia Hannah – "Peter's Ghost" (*Litro*)
- Joanne Harris – "Storytime"(Self-published)
- Cat Hellisen – "Oh Baby Teeth Johnny and Your Radiant Grin, Let's Unroll on Moonlight and Gin" (*Shoreline of Infinity*)
- Liam Hogan – "A Dragon, Sat" (*Daily Science Fiction*)
- Jonathan Howard – "O Have you Seen the Devle With His Mikerscope and Scalpul" (*Apex*)

- Rhys Hughes – "The Siege" (*Arms Against a Sea (and Other Troubles)*)
- Timothy Jarvis – "Brother Burgholt's Charm" (*An Invite to Eternity* [Calque])
- Tom Jenks – "Saccharine" (*Spelk*)
- Michelle Ann King – "In the Fog, There's Nothing But Grey" (*Black Static*)
- Kirsty Logan – "Between Sea and Sky" (*Hag* [Amazon])
- Vesna Main – "My Sinister Side" (*Litro*)
- Tim Major – "The Forge" (*And the House Lights Dim* [Luna])
- Ali Maloney – "Scan Lines" (*Haunted Voices* [Haunt])
- Conner McAleese – "I Live Alone" (*Haunted Voices* [Haunt])
- Maura McHugh – "The Mechanical Marionette Mob" (*Scarlet Traces* [Abaddon])
- Lisa McInerney – "Nowhere Now" (*Extra Teeth*)
- Amy McNee – "Sibling Rivalry" (*BFS Horizons*)
- Leah Moore – "One Gram" (*The Outcast Hours* [Solaris])
- Jon Oliver – "Turner's Apprentice" (*1816: The Year Without Summer* [Kickstarter])
- Heather Palmer – "Projector" (*We Were Always Here: A Queer Words Anthology* [404 Ink])
- Angela Readman – "Peasant Woman Number Four" (*Unthology 11* [Unthank])
- Jane Roberts – "The Salt Marsh Lambs" (*Tales from the Shadow Booth, v4*)
- Robert Shearman – "I Say, I Say" (*Tales from the Shadow Booth, v3*)
- Polina Simakova – "Hear Me Out" (*The Worlds of Science Fiction, Fantasy and Horror, Volume V*)
- Gareth Spark – "The Bear" (*PunkNoir*)
- M. Suddain – "Midnight Marauders" (*The Outcast Hours* [Solaris])
- Piotr Sweitlik – "Blood Thicker Than Water" (*Tales from the Graveyard* [Far Horizons])
- Heather Valentine – "Greenwoman" (*BFS Horizons*)
- James Warner – "Shots of Water are Free" (*Santa Monica Review*)
- Richard Webb – "Thought Surgery" (*Teleport Magazine*)
- Jack Westlake – "Pomegranate Pomegranate" (*Black Static*)
- Neil Williamson – "The Raveller's Tale" (*Once Upon a Parsec* [NewCon])
- Marian Womack – "One, Two, Three" (*Tales from the Shadow Booth, v4*)

About the Authors

Leila Aboulela was born in Cairo, grew up in Khartoum and moved in her mid-twenties to Aberdeen. She is the author of five novels – most recently *Bird Summons*. Leila was the first winner of the Caine Prize and her story collection *Elsewhere, Home* won the Saltire Fiction Book of the Year Award.

Nick Adams is based in the north of Spain and writes short, frequently weird, fiction. His stories have recently appeared in *The Shadow Booth* and *Shallow Creek*. He can be found on Twitter @_nickadams

Jess Brough is a PhD student at the University of Edinburgh, researching language biases. Jess has written for gal-dem and *The Skinny*, and has been published with an essay in *The Bi-Bible: New Testimonials* and a short story in Scottish literary magazine *Extra Teeth*. In 2018 Jess founded Fringe of Colour, a promotional platform and support network for Black and Brown people at the Edinburgh Fringe.

Christopher Caldwell is a queer Black American living in Glasgow, Scotland with his partner Alice. He was the 2007 recipient of the Octavia E. Butler Memorial Scholarship to Clarion West. His work has appeared in *FIYAH, Uncanny Magazine*, and *Strange Horizons*. He is @seraph76 on Twitter.

Eliza Chan writes about East Asian mythology, British folklore and madwomen in the attic, but preferably all three at once. Her work has been published in *The Dark, Podcastle* and British Fantasy Award nominated *Asian Monsters*. She is currently working on a contemporary fantasy novel about waterdragons in a flooded world. Find her on twitter @elizawchan or www.elizachan.co.uk

Matt Dovey is very tall, very British, and probably drinking a cup of tea right now. His surname rhymes with "Dopey", but any other similarities to the dwarf are coincidence. He has short science fiction and fantasy stories all over the place: find out more at mattdovey.com, or follow him on Twitter: @mattdoveywriter.

Chikọdili Emelumadu was born in Worksop, Nottinghamshire and raised in Nigeria. Her work has been shortlisted for the Shirley Jackson Awards (2015), a Nommo Award (2020) and the Caine Prize for African Literature (2017 & 2020). In 2019, she emerged winner of the inaugural Curtis Brown First Novel prize. She tweets as @chemelumadu

Melanie Harding-Shaw is a speculative fiction writer, policy geek, and mother-of-three who was born in the UK and calls Wellington, New Zealand home. Her short fiction has appeared in a range of publications, including *Daily Science Fiction* and *The Arcanist*. You can find her on Twitter as @melhardingshaw and at https://www.melaniehardingshaw.com/

Liz Jones writes fiction mainly for love, and edits non-fiction for money. She likes dark stories and dreamlike places, and tales of tangled memories. She lives in Somerset with her family. Find her on Twitter at @ljedit

Kirsty Logan is a professional daydreamer. She is the author of two novels, *The Gloaming* and The *Gracekeepers*, and three story collections, *Things We Say in the Dark, A Portable Shelter* and *The Rental Heart & Other Fairytales*. She lives in Glasgow with her wife and their rescue dog. She has tattooed toes.

Tim Major's books include *Hope Island, Snakeskins* and *Machineries of Mercy*, short story collection *And the House Lights Dim* and a non-fiction book about the silent crime film, *Les Vampires*. His stories have appeared in *Best of British Science Fiction* and *The Best Horror of the Year*. Find out more at cosycatastrophes.com

Helen McClory is the author of *On the Edges of Vision, Flesh of the Peach, Mayhem & Death*, and *The Goldblum Variations*. A new novel, *Bitterhall*, is forthcoming in 2021. There is a moor and a cold sea in her heart.

Maura McHugh lives in the West of Ireland and has written three collections, including *The Boughs Withered (When I Told Them My Dreams)*. She's written comic books for Dark Horse and 2000 AD, and is also a playwright, screenwriter and critic. Her web site is http://splinister.com and she tweets as @splinister.

Dafydd McKimm is a speculative fiction writer producing mostly short and flash-length stories. His work has appeared in *Deep Magic, Daily Science Fiction, Flash Fiction Online*, and elsewhere. For more information visit www.dafyddmckimm.com.

Tom Offland is a UK-born writer living in San Francisco, his short fiction has appeared in *Visions, Litro, The Junket, Vol. 1 Brooklyn* and elsewhere

Karen Onojaife is a short story writer and novelist. Her work has appeared in publications such as the *Callaloo Literary Journal* and *Closure: Contemporary Black British Short Stories*. She is a VONA/Voices fellow and has participated in the Hedgebrook Writers in Residence program.

Heather Parry is a Glasgow-based writer and editor. She won the 2016 Bridge Award for an Emerging Writer, the Cove Park Emerging Writer Residency in 2017 and was a prizewinner in the 2019 Mslexia Short Story Competition. Heather's work explores self-deception, transformation and identity. She is the co-founder and editor of *Extra Teeth* magazine.

Gareth E. Rees is author of *Car Park Life* (Influx Press, 2019), *The Stone Tide* (Influx Press, 2018) and *Marshland* (Influx Press 2013). He has written weird fiction and horror for anthologies including *This Dreaming Isle*, *The Shadow Booth II*, *Unthology 10*, *Mount London* and *An Invite to Eternity*. He is the founder of Unofficial Britain http://www.unofficialbritain.com.

Sara Saab lives in North London, where she long ago perfected her Resting London Face. Sara's a 2015 graduate of the Clarion Writers' Workshop. Her stories have recently appeared in *Shimmer*, *Clarkesworld*, and *The Dark*. You can find more of her on Twitter as @fortnightlysara. For a full list of her fiction and poetry, head to fortnightlysara.com.

E. Saxey is a queer Londoner, working in universities. Their short fiction has appeared in magazines and anthologies including *Apex Magazine*, *Escape Pod*, *The Fantasist*, and Lightspeed's *Queers Destroy Science Fiction*.

Natalia Theodoridou is the winner of the 2018 World Fantasy Award for Short Fiction, a Nebula Award finalist (Game Writing 2018), and a Clarion West graduate. Natalia's stories have appeared in *Clarkesworld*, *Strange Horizons*, *Uncanny*, *Beneath Ceaseless Skies*, *Nightmare*, and elsewhere. For more, visit www.natalia-theodoridou.com or follow @natalia_theodor on Twitter.

Lavie Tidhar's most recent novels are *By Force Alone* and *The Escapement*, both out in 2020. He is the author of the World Fantasy Award winning *Osama* (2011), the Jerwood Fiction Uncovered Prize winning *A Man Lies Dreaming* (2014), the Campbell and Neukom awards winning *Central Station* (2016), and many others, including the children's book *The Candy Mafia* and comics mini-series *Adler*.

Eleanor R. Wood's stories have appeared in *Flash Fiction Online, Deep Magic, Daily Science Fiction, Galaxy's Edge,* and various anthologies, among other places. She writes and eats liquorice from southwest England, where she lives with her husband, two marvellous dogs, and enough tropical fish tanks to charge an entry fee.

NEW FROM NEWCON PRESS

Nick Wood – Water Must Fall

In 2048, climate change has brought catastrophe and water companies play god with the lives of millions. In Africa, Graham Mason struggles to save his marriage to Lizette, who is torn between loyalty to their relationship and to her people. In California, Arthur Green battles to find ways of rooting out corruption, even when his family are threatened by those he seeks to expose. As the planet continues to thirst and slowly perish, will water ever fall?

Liz Williams – Comet Weather

Practical Magic meets *The Witches of Eastwick*. A tale of four fey sisters set in contemporary London, rural Somerset, and beyond. The Fallow sisters: scattered like the four winds but now drawn back together, united in their desire to find their mother, Alys, who disappeared a year ago. They have help, of course, from the star spirits and the no-longer-living, but such advice tends to be cryptic and is hardly the most dependable of guides.

Ken MacLeod – Selkie Summer

Set on the Isle of Skye, Ken MacLeod's *Selkie Summer* is a rich contemporary fantasy steeped in Celtic lore, nuclear submarines and secrets. Seeking to escape Glasgow, student Siobhan Ross takes a holiday job on Skye, only to find herself the focus of unwanted attention, unwittingly embroiled in political intrigue and the shifting landscape of international alliances. At its heart, *Selkie Summer* is a love story: passionate, unconventional, and enchanting.

Best of British Science Fiction 2019

Editor Donna Scott has scoured anthologies, magazines, and forgotten nooks and crannies to unearth the very best science fiction stories written by British and British-based authors in 2019. A feast of fine fiction from award-winning writers and masters of the short story such as Chris Beckett, Ken MacLeod, GV Anderson, Lavie Tidhar, Tim Major, and Una McCormack.